Valhalla Won

Valhalla Won

mike whicker

Valhalla Won

a novel

by
mike whicker

a Walküre imprint

This is a work of historical fiction

ISBN: 978-0-9995582-3-2

printed in the United States of America

mike whicker

For

Louis and Betty Minton

mike whicker

Important Historical Note

The Western Allies intelligence communities displayed no qualms about bringing Nazis into their clandestine societies after WW II.

During the Cold War, both the CIA and British MI6 made use of Nazis (some who were boldly unrepentant). Records show both organizations went out of their way to recruit Nazi agents if the Germans could offer experience or expertise in working against the Russians. The CIA not only maintained a close working relationship with Reinhard Gehlen, they helped him set up shop. During the war, Gehlen served as the German Army's intelligence chief for the Eastern Front. With protection from the United States after the war, Gehlen assembled a large intelligence organization staffed with numerous ex-Nazis and known war criminals—at least 100 of Gehlen's operatives were former SS/SD officers or Gestapo agents. Gehlen's organization eventually became the official West German intelligence agency—the BND.

Records from the National Security Archive of George Washington University show that at least five associates of the notorious Nazi Adolf Eichmann worked for the CIA and 23 other Nazis were approached by the CIA for recruitment.

The roll call of former Nazis who worked for the British during the Cold War is also long. Just one name is Horst Kopkow, an SS officer who during the war ordered the executions of approximately 300 spies (many were British and most were tortured before execution). After the war, Kopkow was arrested as a war criminal but ended up being recruited into the British intelligence fold in 1948. The British even faked Kopkow's death to deceive a war crimes tribunal.

The Soviets weren't ones to be left behind. The East German Secret Police they established after the war was filled with former Gestapo, SS, and SD agents.

Part 1

"One should learn even from one's enemies."

— *Ovid, Metamorphoses*

Chapter 1

Terrible is the likeness of her face to Immortal Goddesses.
— Homer, (ca. 700 B.C.)

Wales—March 1942

Opening a champagne bottle with one hand while steering a car with the other was a skill Henry Wiltshire had mastered of late. This talent could be performed even while driving at night with war-dimmed headlights. Keeping his eyes focused on the small portion of the rural Welsh road that the weak headlamps illuminated, he slowed before the approaching curve. Leaning the bottle against the side of his leg, he quickly downshifted, then deftly guided the huge, black Bentley around the narrow turn. After shifting back into a higher gear, Wiltshire grabbed the bottle and, with his right hand on the wheel, used his left hand to expertly nurse the cork free.

With a loud pop the cork rocketed from the bottle and ricocheted off the windshield. It landed somewhere in the back seat. The champagne, volatile from the bouncing car ride, geysered out onto the blouse of the young blonde woman in the passenger seat to his left. The shock of the cold liquid against her chest evoked a loud squeal. Wiltshire only halfheartedly tried to cover a laugh.

"Sorry, love," Wiltshire said with total insincerity.

"You did that on purpose, you wretch!" The blonde tried to sound upset, but she had already helped Wiltshire finish off a previous bottle since they left London an hour ago so her admonishment came forth more as a giggle.

"You can't mean it," Wiltshire replied. "Would I do a thing like that?"

"Bloody right you would," the woman answered while pulling the front of the wet blouse away from her skin. "I'll catch my death because of you." With that she unbuttoned and removed the blouse and the wet brassiere underneath. Wiltshire was thankful for the moon ahead that supplied sufficient light for an acceptable view of the young woman's exposed breasts.

"I suppose you're happy now, aren't you?" the woman joked.

"Are you sure none of it got on your skirt?"

The young woman ignored the quip and retrieved a blanket from the back. As she turned to lean over the seat, her breasts brushed against Wiltshire's arm. Momentarily distracted, the middle-aged man let the car's right fender brush against a hedge bordering the road. He jerked the car back to the left which made the girl slide hard against him. She shrieked again, then sat back down.

After using the blanket to dry off and cover herself, the young woman slid over and sat next to Wiltshire. She ran her fingers through his hair then patted the noticeable paunch above his belt. Her hand then went seductively lower, but only to take the champagne bottle from between his legs. She laughed, then took a long drink.

"What a tease you are, you little scamp," Wiltshire muttered.

"You'll see what kind of tease I am, love, when we get to St. David's Head." The young blonde said it with the wicked look that always raised the man's blood pressure.

◊ ◊ ◊

The young woman had been right about this place, Wiltshire thought as he leaned against a crooked fir tree on a hill high above the Irish Sea. It had been years since he had been to Wales. Wiltshire always considered it a place with nothing to offer unless your tastes were geared toward bogs and moors, but she had promised him St. David's Head was a beautiful place. On the extreme western coast of Wales, St. David's Head would be a welcome respite from the rat race in London.

Without being conscious of doing it, Wiltshire drew on his unlit pipe as he gazed out at St. George's Channel. He was far enough above the water that the breaking shore waves were barely audible. Behind the breakers, countless phalanxes of waves, their moonlit tips asparkle, marched relentlessly toward the shore like an invading army. To Wiltshire's left, the moon and an owl sat side by side in the naked branches of a tall birch. To his right and behind was the cottage he had rented for the weekend. Inside, he knew Margaret Harrison was bathing, primping, and waiting for his return. Yes, Wiltshire thought, this would definitely be worth the drive from London.

A cold March breeze ruthlessly hunted any exposed flesh, and Wiltshire pulled down his trilby hat and squeezed the collar of his greatcoat tight around his neck. He glanced again at the small, ivy-covered stone cottage standing half hidden within a stand of trees and tall hedges. A thin ribbon of yellow light escaped from the edges of the blackout shades covering the windows. Wiltshire knew even that much light was not allowed; you couldn't be too careful nowadays. Stationed in London during the worst of the Blitz last year, Wiltshire took the blackout seriously. He promised himself he would fix the shade when he returned to the cottage.

He lit his pipe with his back to the sea both for the sake of the blackout and to shield the fire's life against the wind. Henry Wiltshire was careful even when it came to the small light generated by the burning tobacco in his pipe. Wiltshire cupped his hand around the pipe's bowl to block the orange glow. He took several long draws to stoke the tobacco as he contemplated his good fortune.

With all considered, this war, which now raged over a large portion of the planet, was a personal boon to him. The war had transformed Wiltshire from a struggling university French professor with no tenure and a bad marriage to one of the top cryptographers of the British intelligence machine. Wiltshire handled communications with French resistance. He was proud of his work for his country's war effort, and proud also of the immense responsibility entrusted to him. Splitting his time between offices of MI-9 in London and the top-secret cryptanalysis section of military intelligence at Bletchley Park, Wiltshire was privy to almost all information concerning modus operandi and French resistance efforts involving the escape lines. These escape lines specialized in guiding downed British airmen trapped behind enemy lines and "escapers," prisoners of war who had escaped from camps or resistance personnel whose cover had been blown, to freedom.

Wiltshire's concentration broke when he heard an automobile engine start somewhere in the distance. He turned toward the faint sound. Carried by the wind, the noise came from the next cottage a couple of hundred meters down the coast. Wiltshire watched as the car, barely visible even in the full moon because of the distance, foliage, and diminished headlamps, pulled out onto the coast road and headed in the direction of the local village five kilometers inland. Probably a journey to the pub, Wiltshire concluded.

Several cottages perched as humble sentinels atop the rocky cliffs up and down the coastline of St. David's Head. The cottages were owned and rented out by a local farmer. When the blitz started a little over a year ago, business picked up. Places like this in Wales and other remote parts of England distanced from Luftwaffe targets became popular with people like Henry Wiltshire and the girl. People who, for a night or two, wished to get away from air raid sirens (and the apprehension that accompanied them). The girl found out about this place and she had taken care of renting a cottage for the weekend.

Ah, yes, the girl—more of Wiltshire's great good fortune. Amid the great human suffering this war inflicted upon millions, how could his life get any better? How else but within the great drama of a world war would a situation arise that would bring him Maggie?

He met Margaret Harrison at a cocktail party the previous fall. It was a particularly dreary affair as he remembered, hosted by some mid-level bureaucrat in Sussex. Dreary, that is, until *she* arrived. At the time, she was working as a secretary/quasi-reporter at a small circulation weekly newspaper in Greenwich. During the course of her work covering war stories, she met and occasionally dated a few British officers. One had asked her to accompany him to this cocktail party.

At the party, Margaret Harrison stunned the men with her charm and beauty and embittered the women who constantly kept discovering their men glancing in her direction. Here Wiltshire's recent luck stepped in again. Amid all the young, handsome officers it was he, Henry Wiltshire, the middle-aged, slightly overweight professor, who ended up occupying most of the young beauty's time and attention. Wiltshire had stepped out onto a balcony for some fresh air shortly before she did the same (he could understand her need for a break from the gaggle of admirers). A pleasant conversation ensued. When he discovered she spoke fluent French and some German (and wasn't particularly happy with her job in Greenwich) he suggested she contact the personnel people at MI. He told her whom to contact and promised her he would put in a good word.

Three weeks later she was working as a low-security translator in Room 840 of MI-9. Wiltshire's office, Room 900, handled the high-security translations. The relationship between the two grew until one night in December, after one of several Christmas parties, he found himself in bed with this fascinating creature. They had been practically inseparable for the three months since that night, a turn of events almost unbelievable to Wiltshire. Indeed, Margaret Harrison was someone special. The beautiful young woman ignored the office jokes about the "beauty and the beast" and the curious stares from strangers when the two of them were out and about.

Gazing out at the cold, foreboding Irish Sea, Wiltshire's thoughts returned to the war. Will Hitler invade by sea? If so, when and where? Surely never here, on this part of the western shore where cliffs rose steeply from rocky beaches. True, this western coast was much less guarded than the eastern, but Wiltshire still thought it made much more sense for the Nazis to come across the short distance of the English Channel than to swing the massive amount of men and invasion matériel around the whole of England to these western shores.

Another cold blast of air convinced Wiltshire it was time to suspend his sightseeing and ruminations on life in 1942 England. He pounded the burnt tobacco from his pipe, turned his back on the Irish

Sea, and walked briskly toward the cottage and the warmth of Margaret Harrison.

Inside the cottage a small fire danced weakly in the stone hearth, lighting the room with the help of two oil lamps. One lamp sat on a table, the other on a shelf. The cottage had no electricity. Wiltshire retrieved a poker from a bucket beside the fireplace and pushed around in the embers. From a small stack of wood next to the hearth he grabbed two small logs and placed them over the hottest coals.

The cottage was small, just one room with a kitchenette and bath. A small brown couch, two sturdy-looking wood chairs, and a small table were the room's only furniture except for a bookshelf that held no books. The bedroom was not one really, just a separate cubicle curtained off from the main room by a sliding portiere. A fireplace and a cook stove were expected to supply sufficient heat even during the coldest weather and Wiltshire imagined that they did a fit job of it. The room was warm and cozy at the present with just the small fire.

He heard occasional sounds from the bath.

"What's doing in there, Maggie? Making progress?"

"Soaking, love," Wiltshire heard her say from behind the door. "And since you finally decided to stop mucking about outside, would you mind bringing in the hot water on the stove?"

Wiltshire walked to the nook that served as the kitchen. On the stove sat a large kettle of water that was already steaming. He had not noticed the stove being fired when he entered the cottage. No wonder it was so warm inside. The water was hot enough to require Wiltshire to locate a couple of dish towels in order to hold on to the kettle's steel handles.

Inside the bathroom, Margaret Harrison sat soaking in the small, claw-footed tub. She reclined to a point which brought the water to her chin. The soapy water prevented any view of the female form within. Wiltshire poured the hot water into the tub at the end where Margaret's feet rested out of the water on the tub's rim.

"Thanks, Henry. You're a dear. Did you find anything interesting out there?"

"You were right, Maggie. Nice place. I bet it's even more beautiful in the summer."

"I told you," the young woman replied. "And you said Wales had only cows and cockneys. Such a closed mind for a professor."

Wiltshire laughed.

The young woman grabbed his hand which still had not warmed completely.

"Why you're chilled to the bone." She looked him in the eyes and added with the wicked look, "Why don't you get in here with me? The water will warm you,—not that there aren't other ways to accomplish that."

"I don't think we would both fit, Maggie. Why don't you finish up? I have a nice blaze going."

"Well, if you're afraid of a little water—." Margaret splashed a small amount of water on his pants. She then pointed to a towel that lay atop a small hamper. "At least you can dry my back."

As she rose from the obscurity of the water, she knew Wiltshire would blush. It was something he always did (quite to his embarrassment) when the lights were on and she was undressed. She looked for this customary sign of his innate shyness and smiled when it appeared on his face. She turned her back to him and waited. Wiltshire gently patted her back with the towel.

Wiltshire's reaction to all of this was, of course, male. What man, Wiltshire mused, would not experience a quickening of the blood when called upon to do his present chore? Here was Aphrodite, he thought, or Shamhat, the seductive temple girl, from Gilgamesh. Her arms were above her head, her hands against the wall for support as she leaned slightly over. This accentuated her curves. Her skin was clear but not pale—more like a delicate, golden hue. Her body had an athletic look, very much feminine, but strong. (She had told him that she was quite the tumbler during her teenage years and even worked out for a while with the boys' gymnastics team at school.)

When he finished, she turned and took the towel from his hand, placed it against his chest to shield him from her still-wet front, put her arms around his neck and drew him to her. They kissed, then he picked her up and carried her from the bath.

◊ ◊ ◊

A few hours later, an exhausted Henry Wiltshire awoke to the sound of the wind rattling a loose window pane directly above the bed. The fire had died so the room was cold and dark. Wiltshire pulled the covers tight. Through the rattling window came the only light in the room, furnished by the gypsy moon that had left the branches of the tree and the owl behind. The moon had tracked the Englishman and now stared down at him through the glass. Margaret was not beside him, but he heard her footsteps approaching from the direction of the bathroom.

"Ah, you're awake!" she said with glee as she jumped on the bed astraddle him. She was wearing one of his undershirts.

"Aren't you cold?" he asked incredulously.

"Never."

"I'm consorting with a madwoman," Wiltshire mumbled as he again tried to pull up the covers. She would have none of it, wrestling him and pulling away the sheets.

"Get up, Henry. I want to go down to the beach."

"What? Now? You *are* daft," he told her as he tried unsuccessfully to retrieve the covers. "What time is it?"

"It's around half past three, but who cares? Don't be such a fuddy-duddy. We're on holiday." She leaned over him and whispered in his ear: "I'll give you special attention on the beach."

"Come to bed, Maggie," Wiltshire replied as he finally managed to retrieve a cover. "We'll go in the morning when it's light."

"Well, be like that then. I'm going down to the beach, with or without you." She then goaded, "Who knows, while down there I might meet another gentleman who's not so worried about a little cool weather."

"I don't think your chances are very good to meet someone at this hour."

She rose, lit an oil lamp that she had moved to a small dressing table beside the bed, and began gathering her clothes.

"You're actually serious," Wiltshire said with exasperation. Maggie did not answer verbally but proved her intent when she began dressing.

Wiltshire sighed. He was dog tired; her energetic lovemaking usually lasted for hours and it always wore him out. But he could never be irate with this gorgeous female who had brought so much vigor into his life. He sat up on the edge of the bed and looked for his clothes.

◊ ◊ ◊

The drive was a short distance back up the coast road to a point where a narrow walk path led down to the shore. Margaret said she had seen the path when they drove in earlier that evening.

"It was dark when we arrived. You must be part owl to have spotted it," Wiltshire joked.

Following Margaret's directions, Wiltshire turned off the main route onto a bumpy road that led to the cliff's edge. He turned off the headlights before the car reached the end of the trail and let the Bentley roll slowly to a stop. He shut off the motor and engaged the emergency brake. After getting out of the car, Margaret grabbed Wiltshire's hand and led him, half pulling him along, down the steep, narrow path to the beach. Wiltshire was again thankful for the moon, but still the path was dark and it was hard to see where they stepped.

"Slow down, Maggie, we'll break our necks."

"Not to worry, I'll catch you," Margaret said happily.

As they drew nearer to the water, the crashing sounds of the breakers grew louder. Once on the beach, Wiltshire immediately noticed it was easier to see. The water and the pale sand reflected the moonlight. It was a rocky shore, and not much of a beach to speak of, but there was a small, flat area of dry sand at the base of the cliff that ran to the water's edge. Huge, dark boulders rose from the water on either side of this secluded mini-beach. These rocks produced large, vertical sprays when the incoming breakers slapped their slick faces.

"How about a dip?" Margaret looked at him and laughed.

"How about a straight jacket?" Wiltshire answered.

She sat in the sand and he joined her.

"The mountains or an ocean shore . . . I can never decide which I love better," Margaret said. "They are both so beautiful and serene."

"Yes, they are."

"I could stay here forever," she muttered dreamily.

They chatted for a few minutes, then she leaned her head against his shoulder. He put his arm around her. They sat without talking for several minutes, just listening to the symphony of water meeting land, one of nature's operas. She looked up at him and smiled.

"Cold?" Margaret asked.

"I'm okay."

"Well, I could stand a blanket," she said.

"You? The superwoman who never gets cold? I can't believe it."

She jabbed him playfully in his ribs and stood up. "There are a couple of blankets in the trunk. I'll get them."

"I'll go," Wiltshire said and started to stand.

"You stay here, love," Margaret insisted. "Let me have the keys. There is something else—a surprise."

Wiltshire looked at her and she grinned. He handed over the keys. She ascended the path almost effortlessly (he knew it would have taken him twice the time and he likely would have made a fool of himself by falling and rolling back down to the beach). When she safely reached the top, Wiltshire turned around and gazed back out to sea. One thing was sure, he thought, the Nazis would never land around here. The beaches were inadequate, and then there were the cliffs. He leaned back on an elbow and waited for Margaret Harrison.

"Close your eyes, Henry."

He sat up quickly. He had not heard her return because of the ocean noise and her voice startled him slightly.

"Oh, did I unnerve you, pet? I'm sorry. Here now, close your eyes like a good boy."

Henry grinned and obeyed. What in the world was she up to now? He felt cold glass against his lips and the smell of brandy. He opened his eyes and saw her kneeling beside him with the bottle. The brandy was her surprise. He heard the familiar, wicked little giggle.

"My intentions are to get you drunk and take advantage of you—again," she declared. She handed him the bottle. He took another drink then offered her one.

"Not just yet," she said. "You drink up. I have a promise to keep." She patted his stomach, then moved her hand lower.

Wiltshire took another drink of the brandy then sat the bottle in the sand. Suddenly he felt a hot sensation in his neck and scalp. He felt dizzy and faint. He tried to ignore it, but then an overwhelming fatigue came upon him. He struggled to remain lucid.

"What's wrong, love?"

Wiltshire heard Maggie's voice but it seemed a mile away.

"I don't know . . . something . . . wrong . . ." He never finished.

Wiltshire tried unsuccessfully to struggle to his feet. Turning, he knocked over the bottle of brandy, pouring it into the sand. He tried to make it to his feet but kneeling was as far as he got. As he faced the cliff, the last thing Wiltshire saw before he passed out was the unusually bright headlights of the Bentley, turned-on with the dimming shrouds removed, shining out to sea.

◊ ◊ ◊

Some nightmare! That was Henry Wiltshire's first thought. *I have to wake up.* He was lying on his back. Wiltshire struggled to turn, to move his legs, anything to force himself awake. Something was holding him! He struggled to open his eyes. He could not see! A panic waved over him and he heard himself yell out.

"Help!" Wiltshire shouted. Then he thought he heard something. What was that? Voices?

He heard it again. It was voices! Again Wiltshire hollered out.

"Help! For God's sake, help me!"

The voices seemed to come nearer. Wiltshire heard what sounded like a curtain being opened beside him.

"Halt's Maul, Engländer!"

It was a man's gruff voice. It was telling him to shut up in German!

"Where am I? Who are you?" Wiltshire demanded. He was now lucid enough to realize he was blindfolded and tied up.

"Halt's Maul!" The voice barked again. Wiltshire heard the curtain close.

He could now tell he was lying on some sort of bed or cot but it felt like the whole room was tipping back and forth. *It must be a boat. What the hell has happened?* Wiltshire tried to remember. *I was on the beach with Maggie . . . Maggie! What has happened to her? Is she okay?* The panic returned. He managed to lift his legs, which were bound. As he raised his legs, he kicked what felt like another cot above him. He kicked and yelled again.

Soon he heard the voices again approaching—all speaking German. One sounded female! *It is a female;* he heard it plainly now. *A female speaking German!* Again Wiltshire shouted and made noise by kicking whatever it was over him. He heard the curtain beside him open again. Wiltshire felt someone take off his blindfold. With the blindfold off, Wiltshire tried to focus on the form standing beside him. Eyes unaccustomed to the brightness and a red ceiling light behind the person's head made it impossible to see the face, but Wiltshire could tell it was a female form. The woman turned and said something in German to a man behind her. The man stood on the other side of the light so Wiltshire could see him better. Wiltshire recognized the German *Kriegsmarine* uniform of an *Unterseebootman*—a German U-boat crewman!

"Where am I?" Wiltshire screamed the words. "And where is the girl who was with me? Damn you!" He was sweating profusely and he felt he would retch. The shadowy female form standing over him spoke.

"Henry, please, you're making such a fuss."

It was the voice of Margaret Harrison.

"Maggie! Is that you?"

"Yes, Henry. But my name is not Maggie, it's Erika Lehmann and you're on your way to Germany, my dear."

Henry Wiltshire turned his head and vomited.

Chapter 2

Chicken and Dumplings

New York City—6 years later
Friday, 24 September 1948

The 835 from Washington arrived at 1:05 p.m., only five minutes late at New York's Grand Central Station. Very good for train companies who still had not yet fully recovered from government regulated transport of trainloads of soldiers from place to place during the war. Even now, three years after the war ended, the people placed in charge of the train timetables still struggled to readjust to peacetime civilian commutes.

Erika Lehmann and Zhanna Rogova grabbed their luggage and waited patiently to disembark. Once inside the terminal, they walked under the giant clock suspended from the high, arched ceiling and found a bench. Both women wore slacks.

Erika knew Leroy Carr had given them an opportunity to escape; otherwise, he would not have put them up in a hotel and allowed them to keep their handguns. This is why riding a train from Washington to New York City didn't concern her. If Carr was on their trail, the train would have been a bad decision.

They traveled light, each woman with just one medium-sized suitcase. Besides a change of clothes and a few personal items, in the bags were their handguns and sound suppressors. Erika's handgun of choice was the Beretta Brevetatta. The Russian, Zhanna, preferred revolvers over semi-automatics and she carried the Nagant M1895 developed by the Belgian industrialist Léon Nagant for the Russian military and the only revolver that worked efficiently with a sound suppressor.

The women took a taxi to LaGuardia Airfield. Here again the fact that Leroy Carr surreptitiously let them go was a great bonus. Instead of being forced to sneak out of the country on a slow-moving freighter, taking an airplane would cut their journey by days. Erika stepped up to the Pan Am counter and purchased two tickets on a Lockheed Constellation to London.

[that evening—Annapolis]

Al Hodge sat at the dinner table in Leroy and Kay Carr's home. Outside, a strong wind and rain from the Atlantic had made up its mind to sightsee Annapolis. Leroy Carr was the Deputy Director of the recently formed CIA and Hodge his long-time side kick and top lieutenant.

Hodge, a widower, often ate with the Carr's. Hodge's wife had died from cancer in 1937. They had been married only two years. Since then, Hodge had occasionally dated but none of the relationships progressed. He seemed reluctant.

Leroy opened the Schlitz beers and asked his old friend, "When did Erika and Zhanna disappear from the Mayflower Hotel?"

"Sometime between 2:00 a.m. and 4:00 a.m.," Hodge answered before he took a swig.

Carr nodded.

"Dinner's ready, boys!" they heard Kay shout from the kitchen. The men could smell the gratifying aroma of a homecooked meal. They rose and went to the kitchen to carry the food to the table. Tonight, Kay had cooked her husband and Al's favorite of her dinners: chicken and dumplings with a broccoli salad.

During the meal, Kay noticed that her husband kept glancing at her as if he were deep in thought. She had already apologized to him for getting arrested for the Chesapeake Bay joy ride she took with the Shield Maidens.

"Is there something wrong, Leroy?" she asked. Kay was an attractive brunette, several years younger than her CIA Deputy Director husband.

Al Hodge looked up from stuffing his mouth with drop dumplings, not knowing what was going on.

Leroy Carr knew Kay developed a bit of a bond with Erika Lehmann during a mission to South American last year when Kay was sent along as the group's Spanish interpreter—this, after years of hostility toward Erika by Kay dating back to the latter years of the war. Carr didn't realize how deep that bond was until this week. When Kay was arrested with the Shield Maidens last weekend, his wife had initially refused to leave the jail unless the other women were freed with her. Kay had to be forced to leave the Coast Guard brig.

"Nothing's wrong, Kay," said Leroy who was very protective of his wife. "But I might have to ask you to take a trip in a few days."

Chapter 3

Long Lost Cousin

London, England
Saturday, 25 September 1948

The tires of the Lockheed Constellation squealed and smoked as they kissed the dry concrete runway at London Airport located just southeast of the small hamlet of Heathrow outside England's capital.

Erika Lehmann was among the first passengers to descend the hatch stairs that had been rolled to the plane after the propellers stopped their frantic whirling. Zhanna Rogova followed her out.

The trans-Atlantic trip from the United States had progressed without weather skirmishes other than a brief bout with crosswinds over the west coast of Ireland late in the journey. Those attacks hadn't lasted long so all in all it was a serene flight.

After the two women descended the metal stairs to the tarmac, they walked toward the tail area of the airplane and waited for their luggage to be brought down. Once they had retrieved their bags they walked into the terminal, passed through customs, then walked outside and hailed a taxi.

When the cab reached Louis and Marie Minton's flat in Kensington (an upscale London neighborhood on the west end), Erika and Zhanna collected their bags and paid the driver. A moment later Erika used the door knocker.

Marie Minton, Erika's maternal grandmother, opened the door. Adelaide, Erika's seven-year-old daughter, stood just behind her grandmother, peeking out from behind Marie's dress.

Erika's grandmother told the little girl, "Ada, your mum is here."

The child didn't react.

◊ ◊ ◊

[Six hours later]

Dinner was on the table and everyone seated when another knock came on the door. The elderly Marie again answered and in walked a rugged-looking man who looked to be late-20s.

"Ian!" Louis exclaimed. "You're just in time for dinner." Louis Minton was Marie's husband and Erika's maternal grandfather. He then addressed both Erika and the young man. "Erika and Ian, I don't know if you two have ever met, but you must remember seeing photographs of each other from the family albums when you were children. Erika, this is Ian, my late brother's grandson—your second cousin."

Before Erika could say hello, Ada jumped out of her seat and ran to the young man, who snatched her up in his arms. "Adelaide," the man smiled. "Have you missed your uncle? I was just here a few days ago." Ada put her arms around his neck. Ian then looked at Erika. "So, you're Adelaide's mother? My long-lost German cousin? Hello, Erika."

Ian then locked eyes with Zhanna.

[same time—Washington, D.C.]

"Lehmann and Rogova landed in London six hours ago, Leroy," Al Hodge said. Carr and Hodge were in Carr's office in the E Street headquarters of the CIA. With the five-hour time difference, it was just now two o'clock in the afternoon in Washington.

"Your men didn't follow them from the airport, right, Al? Erika would have spotted a tail in a second."

"No. They laid off, but I had a couple men monitoring Lehmann's grandparent's flat in Kensington where Lehmann's daughter lives. A taxi dropped off both women there as we expected."

"Okay, tell your guys 'good work,'" Carr said, "and take them off surveillance. I'll talk to Kay tonight."

◊ ◊ ◊

[same time—the Kensington neighborhood of London, 7:00 p.m. London time]

To Erika, her cousin looked like a rugby player or a pug boxer. It was the granite jaw, mashed nose and cauliflower ear. Turns out she was right, at least concerning the latter.

"Ian is a bricklayer by day and quite an accomplished pugilist by night," Louis Minton said between dips into his soup.

"Is that so, you're a boxer?" Erika asked her cousin.

"Yes, I train at the Druid's Gym on the East End."

Ada had insisted on sitting next to her "Uncle" Ian. He was not technically her uncle, of course, rather a second cousin once removed. Nonetheless, Erika was happy that Ada was close to this family member and at the same time a bit hurt that Ada wasn't sitting next to her. Erika knew she had no one to blame for that other than herself. She had been separated from her daughter for the vast majority of the child's young life. Ada remembered her mother, but only in vague, fleeting memories of an occasional, brief visit now and then.

"I'm surprised, Ian, that I never ran into you until now," Erika commented. "I visit here as often as I can."

"My family moved to Cheltenham when I was ten. I didn't find enough work there and the town had no boxing gym. I moved back to London just a year ago."

"So you . . . we, have more family in Cheltenham?" Erika asked.

"Yes."

Louis Minton interjected, "Ian's grandmother, my brother's widow, and other family members on her side live there."

Dinner proceeded with more chit-chat, until it was Ian's turn to ask questions. "Erika, what is it that has kept you away for so long?"

"I speak German and French and work for the United States Department of State as an interpreter for dignitaries who travel to countries where those languages are prevalent." This was Erika's CIA cover job when asked. "I live in America now."

Ian nodded. "I see . . . it is your many travels that keeps you from taking Adelaide to America with you?"

"That's right." Erika couldn't tell him the real reason. She still had not been granted American citizenship because of criminal charges still looming against her from the war when she worked for Abwehr—German military intelligence. She might be in prison this time next year. Erika simply didn't know and couldn't take Ada with her until things were resolved.

Ian looked at Zhanna. Erika had noticed him glancing at her during the meal. "And Zhanna, what is it you do?"

Zhanna took a moment to swallow her food and answered, "I speak Russian. I also work for the Americans as an interpreter."

When dinner was finished, Louis Minton poured the adults a brandy and offered his nephew a cigar. He was surprised when both Erika and Zhanna told him they would also enjoy one.

As they drank the brandy and puffed on the cigars, Erika continued to notice Ian glancing at the beautiful Russian wearing a scarf around her neck.

Chapter 4

Beppe's

Baltimore, Maryland—that evening

Leroy and Kay Carr's favorite Italian restaurant was Beppe's located in Baltimore's Little Italy neighborhood. It was only a 45-minute drive from their home in Annapolis, yet they weren't what you would call regulars because Leroy's job required quite a lot of travel. Still, the Carrs usually made the trek to Beppe's two or three times a year.

Beppe and his wife both emigrated from Naples and the eatery was a true Italian mom and pop restaurant. Beppe, his wife, and their two daughters worked in the kitchen. Two of their sons and a son-in-law served as waiters. There was no hostess. Leroy picked a small table in a corner. There, the Deputy Director of the CIA could talk privately with his wife over the red and white checkered tablecloth.

Kay ordered lasagna and Leroy the Chicken Marsala and a bottle of Chianti for the table.

Beppe's was not a place for those in a hurry. The only thing made ahead of time was the marinara sauce, made fresh each morning. For nearly any menu order, a wait of an hour or even longer was not uncommon. This gave the Carrs plenty of time to sip wine and talk as they waited.

"Kay, tell me what you think of Erika and Zhanna."

"What do I think of Erika and Zhanna? Why do you ask, darling?" Kay Carr was not a CIA employee, but she had Level 4 CIA clearance (a mid-level clearance). Kay was fluent in Spanish, and last year she accompanied Erika Lehmann and Zhanna Rogova to South America on a mission where she served as their interpreter. Before that, Kay had had a very rocky relationship with Erika, the former Nazi spy, but Leroy had sensed that after the South America mission the two had developed some sort of bond.

"I need to know," Leroy said.

Kay took a sip of the red wine. "Leroy, it's no secret to you that I hated Erika after she helped Otto Skorzeny capture you during the war.

With that said, I grew to respect her, and I think she grew to respect me in South America last year. As far as Zhanna, I don't know what to say other than I think she's a psychopath who can kill people without giving it any thought. Erika has killed people. I don't have to tell you that, but she does so only as a soldier would. In my opinion, Zhanna does it aimlessly. She's as likely to stick a knife in a drunk guy at a bar who pinches her butt as she is to do the same to a bad guy on a mission."

Leroy didn't respond. His thoughts about the German and the Russian were the same.

Finally, Kay asked, "What's on your mind, Leroy?

Leroy put down his wine glass. "I need you to go to London, Kay. Erika trusts you more than she trusts me or Al. The reason I let her escape is I knew she would go to London to see her daughter and take Zhanna with her. We have a sensitive mission in London I need you to talk to both of them about."

Chapter 5

A Swiss Bank Account

Annapolis, Maryland
Next day—Sunday, 26 September 1948

It was Sunday, so instead of meeting at E Street, Al Hodge had driven to Annapolis from his apartment in D.C. He now sat in the Carr's living room sipping coffee with Leroy and Kay. It was two o'clock in the afternoon.

When Hodge arrived, he already knew the mission particulars and that Leroy needed Kay's help.

"Al, I've explained the mission to Kay," Carr said. "She's up to date."

Hodge didn't ask Kay if she accepted the assignment. He knew he wouldn't be here if she hadn't.

Carr continued. "Kay needs paperwork identifying her with the State Department and we can't get that until tomorrow."

"When are we leaving?" Hodge asked. Leroy had already told him he would accompany Kay if she accepted the task.

"Tuesday morning. An Air Force DC-3 will be ready and waiting on the tarmac at Andrews by 0900 hours. This will be a simple, and safe, low-risk job on Kay's part."

Kay smiled. "That's what you said about South America, darling."

Hodge was Leroy Carr's subordinate, but also a friend from their old OSS days during the war. He always spoke his mind. "Kay's right there, Leroy. When we're dealing with Lehmann, things can get fucked up in a hurry. Sorry, Kay. Pardon my French."

Leroy nodded. "That's why you're going with Kay this time, Al. It's your job to make sure it stays simple and low-risk for Kay. You know that we have men in London who you can call to duty on a moment's notice if needed. Your only task is to safeguard Kay. If the mission fails, so be it. I don't want a repeat of South America."

◊ ◊ ◊

[that evening—London]

Erika Lehmann had money, and a considerable amount of it not even her current employer, Leroy Carr and the CIA, knew about. Hidden away in a Swiss bank in Zürich was gold amounting to 140,000 American dollars her deceased German father left her. Because she was on the run from the CIA, she would be using her own funds.

Her grandparent's flat could not accommodate both herself and Zhanna. Erika stayed with her grandparents and slept with Ada in her room. She booked a room at the Savoy for Zhanna.

Erika had made up her mind. She would never again leave her daughter. She would give up the spy world and disappear with Ada to a foreign country. She had enough money to live on for years—at least until Ada was twenty or twenty-one years old and her daughter could make her own life. After that, Erika didn't care what happened to herself.

Across town, Zhanna and Erika's cousin were on a first date. Ian had asked her out after dinner at Erika's grandparents' home the previous evening. They had just entered the Hippodrome theatre where played the new and very popular Hollywood film, *The Three Musketeers.*

The lights had not yet dimmed when the usher led them to seats in the crowded theatre.

As soon as they were seated, Zhanna asked Ian, "Do theatres here have popcorn like they do in America?"

"Yes," Ian replied. "Would you like some?"

"That would be nice, indeed." Zhanna loved popcorn.

Ian rose from his seat. With his pug boxer's mashed nose and swollen, cauliflower ear, he was not attractive to most women and he had been surprised, and felt himself very lucky, that a woman like Zhanna had said yes to the date. His previous few dates over the past year in London had been with rather rough and bawdy East End girls. Certainly, he had never been out with a woman like Zhanna Rogova, who at dinner last night had impressed him as a gentle and fragile flower.

After the movie, Ian took Zhanna to an East End pub he occasionally frequented called the Last Leap, which wasn't far from the boxing gym. At the bar, Ian ordered a Newcastle Brown Ale and Zhanna asked for a straight vodka. Ian paid for the drinks before they took a seat at a small table.

"Erika mentioned at dinner last night that you are Russian," Ian said. "I thought as much because of your accent. Did you spend the war in Russia?"

"Yes."

"Was it hard for you?"

The Russian sniper and assassin credited with nearly 300 kills lied. "I helped the Red Army nurses with the wounded."

"That must have been hard. I know your country suffered much more than any other country at the hands of the Nazis."

"Yes. How did you spend the war, Ian?"

"I served with the 22nd Dragoons. I fought in Sicily and later in the campaign through France."

Zhanna nodded and turned up her vodka and downed it in one swallow.

"Thank you for going out with me, Zhanna. You're a beautiful woman." She was wearing a neck scarf, as she had done last night at dinner when he met her.

Zhanna didn't comment on the compliment. "May I have another vodka?"

They had spent almost an hour drinking and chit-chatting when a man who had been sitting at the bar stagger over to their table.

"Ian, who's the bird?" he asked with slurred speech. Obviously, the man had already lifted several pints.

"Go away, Cyrus, before I knock you on your arse."

The man ignored him. He was obviously no match for the large, hard-muscled boxer, but the alcohol had emboldened him. "She doesn't look like an East End bird. Is she a Piccadilly tart?" He then addressed Zhanna. "How much for a quick shag, love?"

Ian rose from his seat, grabbed the man by the scruff of his neck and dragged him back to his barstool. "Stay on your stool, Cyrus. It's either that or prepare yourself for a ride in the hospital lorry."

When Ian returned to Zhanna she could tell he was obviously chagrined.

"I apologize, Zhanna. I should have never brought you here. Let's go."

They rose from their seats. Ian dropped a one-pound note on the table which more than covered their drinks, and they left the pub.

Ian owned an auto—a ten-year-old Rosengart. He was the third or fourth owner of the car which required constant maintenance, but it got him around town. He wanted to take Zhanna to another place—a better place.

"I've had a grand evening, Ian. Thank you for the movie. But I think it's time for me to retire."

Disappointed, he nodded. *I should have never taken her to that East End dive. What was I thinking? Taking a genteel woman like Zhanna to a place like that!*

When he pulled up in front of the Savoy, he hoped for a kiss but Zhanna simply touched his hand, thanked him again for the movie, and quickly exited the car. A doorman held the hotel's entry door for her, and he watched her disappear into the lobby.

Ian Minton drove away cursing himself for his stupidity. She would never want to see him again.

After Zhanna had made sure Ian had drove off, she asked the doorman to hail her a taxi. This took only seconds, as many taxis orbited the streets around London's finest hotel.

After a twenty-minute drive, the cabbie dropped her off in front of Last Leap pub Ian had taken her to. She paid the driver and got out.

The deadly Red Army sniper who near the end of the war had served outstandingly and without any qualms as a cold-blooded assassin for the Soviet counterintelligence agency SMERSH, walked into the pub.

Cyrus was still there.

Chapter 6

Bayette a la Bordelaise

London
Wednesday, 29 September 1948

Kay Carr and Al Hodge finally arrived in London. It had been a long and at times harrowing flight. While landing in Newfoundland to refuel, a tire blew out. Fortunately, it happened after the plane had slowed considerably so there was not great danger, yet it ensured a long delay. Later during the journey, a radio transmission warning them of a severe lightning storm over Ireland forced the pilot to detour to Iceland and wait on a tarmac in Reykjavik for four hours waiting for skies to clear.

They had taken off from Andrews Air Force Base at nine o'clock yesterday morning. Normally a 20-hour flight, the trip had taken 32 hours. Add to that the time change, and it was well past dinnertime when the plane sat down in London.

They had been the only ones onboard the Air Force DC-3 other than the crew, so they could stretch out and catnap now and then. Still, both Kay and Al were exhausted. They would spend tonight at the American embassy.

[a bit earlier that same evening]

Ian Minton had not planned on asking Zhanna out on another date. He thought he had no chance after making the mistake of taking her to the rowdy Last Leap pub Sunday evening. Yet he summoned his courage and called her last night at her hotel and asked her to dinner. To his surprise, she accepted.

He was determined to not mess up this time. He took her to a fine French restaurant in the West End. Now, the only problem before him was he didn't understand anything on the menu and didn't want her to think he was just another stereotypical dumb, pug boxer. The prices also shocked him, but he had expected high prices and had brought everything he had earned from his last fight. He had enough money.

Ian cleared his throat and looked up from the menu. The menu items came with no English translations, so he had no clue what was being offered. He said to Zhanna, "It looks like there are a lot of good choices. What are you having, Zhanna?"

That told Zhanna he was at a loss as to what to order. She avoided the most expensive entrees, thinking he might be concerned with prices. She also assumed a boxer would be a lover of red meat.

"I think I'll have the Bayette a la Bordelaise (a skirt steak) with the L'Oignon Gratinee (traditional French onion soup)." It was the cheapest entrée on the menu.

"That sounds grand. I'll have the same," Ian said immediately, not knowing what would eventually end up on the table in front of him.

The French waiter appeared. Thankfully, the man spoke English and Ian ordered the meals by pointing to them on the menu. Besides knowing nothing about French cuisine, he was ignorant on the subject of wine.

"What wine would you recommend?" he asked the waiter.

"Of course, a Bordeaux would complement your steaks. We just received from France several bottles of Chateau Margaux—1938 vintage.

Zhanna gave the waiter a grim look that Ian did not see. She knew the Margaux was ridiculously expensive. "If you don't mind, Ian, I would prefer the Chateau de Ribebon. It is also a Bordeaux." Zhanna had never tasted the Ribebon, but it was a fraction of the price of the Margaux.

Ian nodded to the waiter, who bowed slightly and left with their orders.

Tonight was one of the rare occasions Zhanna Rogova was in a dress. This one was a blue evening gown she had bought at Harrod's that morning. Erika, with Ada along, had taken her to the famous department store. Her ever present neck scarf was silk and a matching blue. She disliked wearing dresses but knew a fine French restaurant would not welcome a female customer wearing slacks. Ian wore suit and tie.

Zhanna was not quite sure what Erika thought of her dating her cousin other than she seemed to get some amusement from teasing

Zhanna about it. Nevertheless, Erika had taken her to Harrod's and paid for the dress and scarf for tonight's dinner.

Ian was not one to put on airs. "Thank you, Zhanna. You knew I was at a loss about the food and wine."

She didn't want to embarrass him by admitting it. She was also honest. "I am certainly no connoisseur, Ian. I don't speak French but I've dined at enough French restaurants I'm familiar with some of the entrees. I'm also not a wine expert, but I know waiters recommend the most expensive wines because the restaurant owners give them a percentage of the bottle sold. It's only if you're a regular customer will you get an honest recommendation."

He changed the subject. "I want to apologize for taking you to that East End pub Sunday night. I thought after that you'd never want to see me again."

"Why did you think that?"

"I can tell you are a classy and gracious woman, and not accustomed to such places."

The Russian assassin looked at him and said nothing. The waiter delivered the bottle of wine, popped the cork, and poured a sip for Ian to sample.

Even though he didn't know good wine from bad, Ian said, "Good."

The waiter poured two glasses, sat the bottle on the table, and departed.

"The next time I see, Cyrus," Ian added, "it won't be pleasant for him." He thought again about what he had just said. "I don't mean I'll hurt him, but he'll get the straight skinny."

Zhanna again didn't reply. She had already ensured that Cyrus regretted embarrassing the man who had asked her out on a date.

After several minutes of conversation, the meals were delivered. After the plates and bowls had been set on the table, Ian said, "I have a bout Friday night, would you like to come and wish me luck?"

The Russian was not familiar with the English word *bout.* "What is 'bout?'

"I'm sorry. That's a fight—a boxing match. I have one Friday at the Druid's gym where I train. Seats will be set up around the ring."

Zhanna paused and looked at him before she cut into her steak. She answered in her sometimes still cracked English, “I will go to there to your wish.”

Chapter 7

Ghost from the Past

London
Next day—Thursday, 30 September 1948

Henry Wiltshire didn't get the memo to report to White Hall until after lunchtime and it was now nearly three o'clock in the afternoon. He was at a complete loss as to why he had been summoned from his office at MI-6. Finally, after over an hour's wait in an anteroom, a female Royal Army sergeant came to fetch him. She led him down a long corridor to the office of Sir James Ashworth, one of several top-level coordinators of international affairs for the government of His Majesty King George VI. Ashworth was the chief liaison between White Hall and MI-6. Wiltshire and Ashworth had had many dealings together since the war's end and were on a first name basis. Nevertheless, the call to report to White Hall was a surprise and Wiltshire was impatient to find out what this was all about.

When Wiltshire walked in Ashworth's office, two other people were there, a man and a woman.

From behind his desk, Ashworth said, "Thank you for coming, Henry. I apologize for the short notice. I know how busy you are."

Wiltshire, who spoke fluent French, was in charge of the MI-6 intelligence analysis department for any matters concerning France, whether it be political, social, or military. He supervised a staff of twenty-three men and four women analysts devoted to all matters French, in addition to secretaries, typists, and file clerks. Overall, he oversaw a staff of fifty-eight people. The only MI-6 foreign sections larger than his French section were the Russian and the section that analyzed the Americans.

"Henry, I want to introduce you to two of our American friends," Ashworth continued (Hodge stood), and with proper British etiquette, he first introduced the lady among them. "This is Kay Carr, and with her is Al Hodge. Mr. Hodge is with the CIA." Ashworth then turned to the

Americans. "Kay and Al, this is Henry Wiltshire, head of the French section for MI-6."

"How do you do?" Wiltshire asked. "It's always nice to meet our Yank colleagues from across the pond."

Kay said, "It's my pleasure, Mr. Wiltshire."

Handshakes were exchanged and Hodge sat down.

"Have a seat, Henry," Ashworth said.

Wiltshire took the seat that was already in place next to the Americans.

Ashworth started the briefing. "Henry, as you know, both we and the Americans are concerned about the current situation in France and the considerable communist influence there. De Gaulle has retired to write his memoirs, and the current Prime Minister, Henri Queuille, is a radical. Add to that the many members of the French Resistance during the war who were communist sympathizers makes the current climate in France a bit dicey. Of course, I don't have to tell you that."

Wiltshire nodded. "Yes, I am aware of the situation in France, Sir James. That's my job." More than anyone, Wiltshire was well aware of the growing communist influence in that country.

"With that said," Ashworth continued, "I'll turn this briefing over to Mr. Hodge."

"Thank you, Sir James," Hodge said. "Mr. Wiltshire, both of our governments have agreed that action needs to be taken to counteract communist manipulation currently affecting politics in France. With mutual agreement and input from your country and mine, we have devised a strategy. It will require you to go to Paris with Mrs. Carr."

Henry Wiltshire had never been sent on a field mission. He looked back and forth from Hodge to Ashworth.

Hodge picked up again. "Kay will go with you and you both will be protected by two of our best agents." Hodge handed Wiltshire a photo of Erika Lehmann and Zhanna Rogova.

When Henry Wiltshire looked at the photo of Erika, he turned pale. "I knew this woman as Maggie Harrison when I worked for MI-9 during the early years of the war, but she was in reality a German Abwehr agent. Because of her I spent over three years in a German Stalag!"

"We are aware of that history, Mr. Wiltshire," Hodge said quickly. "Still, we need you to put that aside. Her real name is Erika Lehmann and she works on our side now. I know you are aware that she is fluent in French. That's how she got her foot in the door at your office at MI-9 in 1942. The other woman is Russian and can be of service in that regard."

"Absolutely not!" Wiltshire exclaimed. He felt light-headed, as if his blood had started to boil. The 50-year-old analyst threw the photographs back at Hodge then turned to Ashworth. "Sir James, I relieve myself from duty. I'll fill out my resignation forms and send them to you by courier."

Henry Wiltshire stormed out of the room.

Chapter 8

Sandman

London
Next day—Friday, 01 October 1948

Inside the locker room of the Druid's gym, Ian Minton listened to last minute instructions from his trainer. His hands had already been taped and his boxing gloves strapped on tight. Tonight, he was fighting Stanley "Bonecrusher" McGrew. McGrew also trained at Druid's. Ian and Bonecrusher were both heavyweights and had sparred on occasion but tonight would be the first time they met in an official fight. Even though Bonecrusher outweighed him and had a two-inch reach advantage, Ian was determined to not lose tonight. Zhanna would be in the crowd.

"You have to stay in close, Sandman," his trainer for tonight, Lefty Gurk, told Ian. "That will counter his reach. The bum has a granite jaw; go for the body. If you kill the body the head will die. His left jab is slow but watch the uppercuts and right cross. He has power there."

Ian already knew all this from his sparring sessions with Bonecrusher. He nodded as Lefty smeared petroleum jelly into his eyebrows.

Around the ring, five rows of chairs had been set up at all four ends. A crowd of 200 people was expected. The front rows were already taken when Zhanna and Erika arrived, so they found two seats in the second row. Cigarette and cigar smoke hung heavy as nefarious looking men in cheap suits, most of whom wore Bowler hats, walked around gathering money placed down as wagers.

Without asking each other, both Zhanna and Erika took out some money. Erika flagged down one of the bookies.

"Leave me alone, Chickee, can't you see I'm busy," he grumped.

"We want to place a bet," Erika told him.

The man looked at her queerly. He had a cigar in his mouth and severely pockmarked cheeks. There were normally a few women spectators, all on the arm of a man, and the man placed the bet, not the woman. These two were by themselves. He couldn't recall seeing that before.

"What are the odds?" Erika asked him.

"No odds. It's a straight up pick."

Erika gave the man two five-pound notes, one for her and one for Zhanna. "This is on Ian Minton," she said.

He took the money and handed them each a blue-colored betting stub denoting the bet was five pounds. Bonecrusher's betting stubs were green. The stub color would tell the bookies who a bettor had laid his money on when it came time to pay out after the fight. "A five-pound bet will earn you four pounds profit if your fighter wins. The other pound is my cut, Chickees."

Some Friday nights saw multiple fights between various weight classes, but tonight there was just this one heavyweight bout.

Before the fighters appeared from the locker room, Zhanna saw Cyrus enter. He limped and walked with a cane. Their eyes locked and Cyrus immediately turned around and left the gym. Last Sunday night, when Zhanna returned to the East End pub on her own, she had flirted and lured Cyrus out of the pub and into the alley. *"You embarrassed the man I was with,"* she said to him. Zhanna roughly turned the drunk man around and drove her dagger deep into his buttocks. Cyrus screamed and collapsed, knocking over a trashcan. *"If you ever tell Ian I did this, you won't be alive the next day."* Zhanna used Cyrus's shirt to wipe the blood off the dagger then calmly walked out of the alley.

"You've had two dates with my cousin, Zhanna. What do you think of him? Like you, I didn't meet him until the dinner at my grandparents' home. What kind of man is he?"

Zhanna shrugged. "How should I know?"

"You've spent more time with him than I have in my whole life. You must have some opinion of a man you've gone out with twice, and you're here tonight."

"It's something I do to relieve boredom."

"That's all?"

"That's all, Erika."

"Have you kissed him?"

"Why would I do that?"

Erika just looked at her. This was certainly going nowhere so Erika dropped it after saying, "He's my blood relation, Zhanna. Don't forget that." Erika knew all too well how most men in Zhanna's past had fared. The majority hadn't coped well with the Russian killer and had physical scars to prove it. "My cousin thinks you are a refined and gentle lady, at least that's what he told my grandfather. Don't drag him down a dark hole, Zhanna."

Seemingly oblivious to Erika's caution, Zhanna said, "I wonder if they have popcorn here?"

Finally, the boxers appeared. Since neither was a champion or the favorite, they came out at the same time. Their respective corner men entered the ring first and stretched the ropes for the fighters to enter. Ian wore a white robe with 'Sandman' embroidered on the back. 'Bonecrusher' was embroidered on his opponents red robe.

"Sandman, what is that, Erika?" Zhanna asked.

"My grandfather told me Ian has not won all his bouts, but many of his wins were by knockout—putting his opponents to sleep, in other words."

"I still don't understand," the Russian said.

"Sandman is an English word used for someone who can put people to sleep."

"How can sand put people to sleep?"

"Never mind, Zhanna. Let's just watch the fight."

"How about that popcorn?"

"Will you forget about your damn popcorn!?"

The ring announcer had no microphone that dropped from the ceiling. The gym could not afford a sound system. Instead, he used a hand-held bullhorn.

"Good evening, ladies and gents! I'm your announcer, Morris Smythe. Your referee tonight is Herman Moad (booing ensued). Welcome to tonight's heavyweight bout between two of our fighters who train here at Druid's Gym. In the green corner and wearing red trucks, from London, standing six feet and one inch tall and weighing in at 15 stones with a record of 17 wins and 4 losses — Stan "Bonecrusher" McGrew!"

The spectators who had placed bets on Bonecrusher clapped and hooted.

"In the blue corner wearing the white trunks, originally from Cheltenham, standing at an even six feet and weighing in at 14½ stones with a record of 11 wins and 3 losses — Ian "Sandman" Minton!"

The applause was less. Apparently more of the crowd was betting on Bonecrusher.

Zhanna asked Erika about Ian's weight, "How much is 14½ stones?"

Erika did a quick calculation in her head. "About 203 pounds. The other man is about 210 pounds."

The fighters took off their robes and met in the center of the ring. It was the first time Zhanna had seen the hard-muscled and sculpted Ian without a shirt. The referee gave instructions, the two boxers touched gloves and returned to their corners for last minute instructions from their managers. Ian's corner man shoved a mouthpiece into his mouth just before the bell rang.

The bout was scheduled for a grueling 15 rounds, the first three of which were mostly uneventful. Both men landed and suffered some punches but it seemed most of the early three rounds were spent sizing up the opponent and trying to avoid being the first to be on the receiving end of a devastating blow. So far, no one had drawn first blood.

It wasn't until the fourth round when Bonecrusher's glove laces sliced open a cut in Ian's left eyebrow that the crowd came to life. After that round, as Ian sat on the stool in his corner, he glanced at Zhanna. She was watching him but with little expression. His corner man, also known as the cut man, taped the bleeding brow, and applied more petroleum jelly.

It was two rounds later, near the end of the fifth round, when Ian finally staggered Bonecrusher with a right uppercut to the jaw after working his body as his manager had instructed. Ian immediately went into full attack, but Bonecrusher was saved by the bell.

This time between rounds when Ian looked at Zhanna she was smiling at him. Seeing Zhanna's interest, Ian was determined to put Bonecrusher away as quickly as possible. However, after being staggered, Bonecrusher's corner felt their fighter should go more on the attack.

The next four rounds were vicious. Both men suffered set-backs and cuts. Ian's eyebrow was opened up again in round eight and his nose was bloodied. Blood streamed down his face when the bell rang. In the next round, Ian landed a hard right and blood spurted from Bonecrusher's mouth. An earlier left hook from Ian had swollen Bonecrusher's right eye nearly shut.

Midway through the 10th round, Bonecrusher landed a solid right that sent Ian to the canvas, but the count was only four when Ian was back on his feet. Bonecrusher, sensing the kill, moved in quickly and flailed away. Ian leaned back against the ropes and used his gloves to protect himself until the bell rang. As he walked exhaustedly to his corner, he saw both Zhanna and Erika on their feet cheering him on. This gave him renewed strength.

As his cut man again did his best to staunch the bleeding, Ian told his manager, "Fook the body, I'm going for the head."

"He has a two-inch reach advantage, Sandman, don't do it. Just hang in there. We might get a decision if you don't go down again. Try to back him into a corner and stay with the body. You can build up points that way."

The 11th round would be the last. Pugilistic strategy was abandoned by both competitors. This round would be a no-holds barred brawl. Ian ignored his manager's advice (unknown to Ian, his manager had placed his money on Bonecrusher) and went on the offensive, ignoring Bonecrusher's swings and delivering blow after blow to his opponent's head. With less than a minute left in the round, a missile of a left jab sent Bonecrusher to the canvas. He got to his feet by the count of eight but staggered about like a drunken sailor so the honest referee called the fight.

Ian won by a technical knockout.

Zhanna and Erika screamed wildly and rushed into the ring along with others—mostly those who had placed their money on Ian and were happy that they would leave the gym with some extra cash in their pockets. Ian tried to hide his beaten and bloodied face from Zhanna but she ignored his efforts, hugged him, and kissed him on the lips. Erika wasn't shocked. She had a feeling Zhanna was hiding her feelings for her cousin. Erika had never known Zhanna to go out on a second date with a man, let alone a third if tonight could be considered a date.

Zhanna asked Ian to take her out for a late-night meal, but the utterly exhausted and bloodied fighter refused. He didn't want a delicate woman like Zhanna to see him this way.

"How about tomorrow, Zhanna?" Ian said as he turned his face away from her.

Zhanna Rogova turned his head back toward her and kissed him again. "Tomorrow," she said. "Don't disappoint me, moy dorogoy. Call me at my hotel."

Erika stood nearby and witnessed all of this.

◊ ◊ ◊

After the fight, Erika and Zhanna piled into a taxi. Instead of going straight home to her grandparents' house, Erika walked with Zhanna into the hotel where they found a table at the bar off the lobby. Erika ordered a brandy, Zhanna her usual—a straight vodka. The finest hotel in London carried Zhanna's favorite brand—Stolichnaya.

"Good fight tonight," Erika said. "Have you ever been to a boxing match before?"

"Many times," Zhanna answered. "They were held weekly in the Red Army camps during the war."

"I'm glad Ian won. I think he would have been very embarrassed to have lost in front of you."

"Why do you say that?" Zhanna asked.

"Come on, Zhanna. He kept glancing your way, and you kissed him after the match. You can't kid me."

"You are wrong. It is common in my country for the victor to receive a kiss."

"You kissed him twice."

"No, I didn't."

"Yes, you did."

"If I did, then fuck you, Erika."

Erika laughed at the Russian's funny response. "Did you forget I speak Russian, Zhanna? You also called him 'moy dorogoy.'" (It was a Russian expression for "my dear.")

"Another Russian custom for the victor."

Erika grinned. "Okay, Zhanna. Whatever you say."

After the drinks were delivered, Erika turned serious. "I'm leaving London with Ada. We'll disappear."

Zhanna looked at her. "Why? You're with your daughter now."

"For how long? You know as well as I do that Leroy Carr allowed us to escape Washington. He has to know I would come here to see Ada. How long will it be before someone shows up on my doorstep—probably Al Hodge wanting to send me on another mission and again separate me from my daughter for who knows how long. Maybe forever if I get captured or killed."

This was the first time Zhanna Rogova had heard Erika Lehmann express concerns about her own death.

"When are you planning to do this?" Zhanna asked.

"Soon."

Chapter 9

Black Ram

London
Next day—Saturday, 02 October 1948

Louis and Marie Minton's part time cook did not report for work unless notified in advance of a formal dinner with guests, and the part time maid worked only for four hours on Monday, Wednesday, and Friday. This morning's breakfast had been prepared by Marie and Erika. Erika, Ada, and Erika's grandparents were only halfway through their English breakfast when the knock on the door came. Marie started to rise but Erika relieved her.

"I'll get the door, Grandmama," Erika said.

Erika knew a knock on the door would come eventually. She expected to open it to Al Hodge, but, instead, Kay Carr stood on the doorstep.

"Hello, Erika. May I come in?"

[that afternoon]

Kay placed the call to her husband at four o'clock in the afternoon London time. In Washington, it was late morning. Kay knew Leroy worked on most Saturdays, so she called his office first. She was right, he was in at E Street. Leroy's secretary patched her through immediately. Leroy now had a temporary secretary. His executive assistant, Army major Sheila Reid, was in Walter Reed Hospital. Reid, one of the Shield Maidens (a team of CIA field agents) included Erika as team leader, Zhanna, Kathryn Fischer and her sister Stephanie. Sheila was recovering from a gunshot wound sustained during a recent Shield Maiden mission in Austria. Kathryn was in the States working as an instructor at the Naval War College in Rhode Island—her assignment whenever she was not on a mission. Stephanie was at Fort Huachuca in Arizona undergoing training.

"Hello, Leroy."

"Kay! Is everything okay?"

"More or less," Kay said from a phone in the American Embassy.

"What do you mean, more or less?"

"I went to Erika's grandparents' home this morning. She was there. As you instructed, I went by myself. Al was not with me. She and I went into a separate room and talked privately for two hours."

"Was Zhanna there?" Leroy knew Erika did not fully trust Al, or himself for that matter. That's why Kay was in London.

"No, Erika told me Zhanna is staying at the Savoy."

"The Savoy! How can Zhanna afford that?"

"I don't know, but after I got back to the embassy, Al checked it out and Zhanna has a room there."

Kay continued. "Leroy, Erika told me she is going to disappear with her daughter."

"She told you that?" Leroy was astonished.

"Yes, she trusts me, Leroy. She told me she thinks you are not pursuing her American citizenship as earnestly as you can. She feels she has no choice."

"Kay, she can't become a citizen of the U.S. until charges against her in this country are dropped. You know I have been pestering the State Department to give her an avenue to citizenship but she keeps getting in trouble with the law."

"I know, Leroy, but I'm certain she's not going to accept this mission without a firm guarantee she'll get citizenship so she can take her daughter to the States. I promised her you would get this done if she accepted the mission."

"What? Why did you promise her that? The final decision is not mine, or anyone at the CIA. It has to come from the Department of Justice, or the White House with a Presidential pardon."

"I promised her," Kay responded. "Leroy, you have to guarantee her you can get her citizenship processed if you want the mission concerning Henry Wiltshire to start. Otherwise, she'll disappear and you'll lose her forever. That's the bottom line. You know she deserves this, darling. What's your answer?"

"It takes a lot of money for someone like Erika Lehmann to disappear, Kay. Did she tell you anything about her resources?"

"No, but remember, Zhanna is staying at the Savoy."

"I'll get back to you," said Leroy. "I want you safe. Tell Al I want you to stay at the embassy for now with no more contact with Erika."

"Leroy, it's too late for that. I'm going to dinner tonight with Erika, Zhanna, and Erika's cousin—some man Zhanna has been seeing."

"Zhanna is seeing a man?" Leroy was getting one surprise after another. Zhanna had a history that suggested she didn't like men. "And this guy is Erika's cousin? What's his name?"

"I don't know, but Erika told me he's a local boxer here in London."

[that evening]

Al Hodge had objected to Kay leaving the embassy but his protests fell on deaf ears. Al was stuck. He knew putting a tail on Erika Lehmann would fail. The former Abwehr spy was expert at spotting a shadow. If that happened, she would suspect Kay of betraying her and it was essential to the mission that Kay remain in Erika's confidence. Leroy Carr's wife would be on her own tonight.

Kay now sat at a table in a West End pub named The Black Ram with Erika, Zhanna, and Erika's cousin. Kay had already been introduced to Ian. The fruits of his bout the previous night were clearly evident. Three stitches held closed the cut in his left eyebrow, and tape did the same for a cut on his cheek. This, in addition to his already mashed nose and cauliflower ear left little doubt about what was his passionate part time occupation.

Tonight, Ian wore his best trousers and a white shirt. All three women wore slacks and blouses. Zhanna, of course, wore a neck scarf. Ian had never seen her without one.

Ian had chosen this West End pub. He would never again make the mistake he made on his first date with Zhanna when he took her to the Last Leap. He thought her too refined for a place like that and he was sure she had been frightened.

All four people had a Newcastle ale sitting in front of them. Food had not yet been ordered.

"Kay," Ian said. "You said you are a friend of Zhanna and my cousin. Where did you all meet?"

"In the United States. My husband works at the State Department. He oversees the section of foreign language translators that employs Erika and Zhanna. I speak Spanish so I'm occasionally involved in that section."

Ian nodded. "Sounds grand. You all must travel a great deal. I've always wanted to travel. I had a fight in Scotland once, but I've never been off this island other than during the war. Being shot means you've probably picked the wrong holiday getaway."

The women politely smiled at his joke. Zhanna patted his hand and said, "You're so clever."

This made Ian feel good. Most people considered boxers to be brainless brutes. Erika looked at Zhanna. *What is she doing?* Erika knew Zhanna had been with both men and women but seemed to prefer the latter. She herself had a physical history with Zhanna, although it was against Erika's will when Erika was a prisoner in Moscow during the days the German and Russian were mortal enemies.

The waitress returned and everyone ordered the pub's specialty—fish and chips. Zhanna asked for a double vodka to chase her ale.

"I was told the fish here is haddock," Ian told the ladies. Haddock was generally considered an upgrade from cod, the other species of fish used in England for its famous fish and chips, although both were probably equally enjoyed by locals when prepared properly.

"So, Ian, what are your hopes for the future?" Kay asked.

"I hope to be a fulltime boxer, but I'm twenty-eight. If that is to happen, it has to happen soon. I will keep trying to prove myself and with any luck move up the ranks. It's my dream to get a match someday with your American boxers Joe Louis or Ezzard Charles."

Erika abruptly said, "If you will all excuse me, I need to use the loo. Zhanna, would you like to come with me?"

Zhanna knew that meant Erika wanted to talk. She rose and followed Erika to the ladies' room.

"What are you doing, Zhanna?' Erika asked as soon as the door closed behind them. "Are you interested in my cousin or not? If you are, you need to be honest with him."

"Why is this any of your business?"

"Because Ian is my blood, that's why it's my business."

"Your blood that you never met until a week ago."

"That doesn't matter," Erika replied. "What are your intentions with my cousin?"

Zhanna shrugged. "I'm just having a bit of fun. What do you want me to do, Erika, tell him I work for the CIA?"

"Don't be ridiculous. I'm talking about stringing him along. Clearly, he has feelings for you. Have you any for him?"

"No."

"So encouraging my cousin is a lark for you?"

"I guess you could say that. And I will add, stay out of my fucking business, Erika."

"We're not in Moscow, Zhanna. I'm not your prisoner and you don't have Riika and bodyguards to back you up like the night you ordered me brought to your apartment. You know I can beat the shit out of you one on one. Have you forgotten our fight in Juárez?"

"If you attempt a repeat, make sure you kill me this time. Otherwise, it will be the biggest mistake you ever made," said the black-hearted assassin.

Once back at the table, Zhanna increased her fawning over Ian. Occasionally, she would glance at Erika and grin.

Kay Carr, a keen observer, knew sometime was wrong.

Chapter 10

Kay's Call

Washington, D.C.
Next day—Sunday, 03 October 1948

"Al told me you went out with Erika and Zhanna last night," Leroy Carr said from his office phone at E Street. Even though it was Sunday, he had gone to his office to make the call to London on a secure line. Carr had his home swept for bugs weekly; still, he preferred to use the home phone only in case an important call came in during the middle of the night. "Why did you do that, Kay, after I had asked you to have no more contact with Erika until further notice?"

"Leroy, you have to give me some freedom to make a decision now and again when I feel it's necessary. I'm doing the best I can to get done what you sent me here to do."

"I just want you to stay safe. After South America, I guess I'm a bit gun shy about having you get in deep with those women. You're more important to me than any damn mission."

"Thank you, dear. That's sweet, but remember I feel the same way about you when you leave on an assignment, yet that's never stopped you from doing whatever it takes. And, as it turned out, I think me going to dinner last night with them was important."

"Did you get a chance to take Erika aside and talk to her any more about the Wiltshire project?"

"No, not last night, but the name of the man Zhanna is seeing is Ian Minton."

"Okay, we'll check him out. Anything else?"

"Believe it or not, after the dinner ended, Erika, Zhanna, and I went to Zhanna's room at the Savoy and had girl talk."

"You're joking."

"No. They even opened up about their personal lives. There's some tension between them right now. Erika doesn't mind Zhanna dating her cousin—this Ian fellow—but thinks Zhanna is deceiving the man. Erika said Zhanna is stringing him along and her cousin believes Zhanna is

some sort of fragile, chaste damsel. She wants Zhanna to come clean with him."

"What did Zhanna say about all of that?"

"She told Erika to stay out of her business, with a few vulgar words mixed in. Some of it was in Russian so I didn't understand it all."

Leroy thought for a moment. "This isn't good. We need to get this Ian out of the picture. But that's not your concern; I'll put Al on that. Anything new about the Wiltshire dealings?"

"I have a meeting with Erika in an hour for more discussion on Wiltshire."

"Call me as soon as it's over."

"I will. I miss you, darling."

"I miss you, Kay. Please don't let Erika or Zhanna put you in harm's way."

"I'm certainly planning on avoiding that, Leroy. I'll talk to you later today, or tomorrow morning at the latest. Are you taking care of yourself? Where have you been eating dinner since I've been gone?"

"I eat at Jocko's most nights." Jocko's Pub in Annapolis was a favorite place for Leroy and Kay Carr. "Don't worry about me, just take care of yourself and keep up your guard with those women. Bail out immediately if things get sticky and come home. Forget the mission. Al will clean up any mess. Promise me you'll do that, Kay."

"Tell, Joey, I said hello," Kay said before the phone went dead. Joey was the bartender at Jocko's.

As soon as Leroy heard Kay hang up, he placed a call to Al Hodge at the American embassy in London. The call took about twenty minutes to be processed overseas, but finally, Hodge was on the telephone.

"Al?"

"Yes, Leroy," Hodge answered.

"I just got a phone call from Kay. I'm worried that things are going sour and I want you to send Kay back home immediately."

"Why? Is Lehmann starting her same old shit again?"

"There's static between Erika and Zhanna and I'm afraid Kay's going to end up in the middle of it. I just want Kay off the mission for her own safety," Carr replied.

"Static about what?"

"Zhanna is seeing Erika's cousin."

"Cousin! What cousin? A man or a woman?"

"A man. Some second cousin on her maternal side."

"So, Lehmann doesn't want Rogova seeing her cousin. Probably can't blame her. The first time the guy complains that she overcooked the eggs he's liable to end up with a fork stuck in his ear."

"It's not that. Kay told me Erika thinks Zhanna is just doing it for jollies to mess with the guy's head."

"Better his head than something else. What's this guy's name?"

"Ian Minton. Evidently, he's a local boxer. Ask MI-6 to run a background check on him. Stay in London but get Kay on the first flight home."

"Okay, will do."

[30 minutes later]

This time, it was Al Hodge in London who called Leroy Carr in the States.

"Leroy," Hodge said. "Kay didn't make that phone call to you from the embassy. I don't know where she called you from but most of her things are gone from her room. Looks like she packed a suitcase and left the embassy before she called you."

Leroy Carr dropped the telephone receiver to the desk, lowered his head, and massaged his temples.

Finally, Carr lifted the telephone and told Hodge, *"I'll get back to you, Al."*

As soon as the line was clear, he called his secretary.

"Alice, this is Leroy. I'm sorry to bother you at home on a Sunday, but as soon as you get to the office tomorrow morning, I need you to start the process of getting Kathryn Fischer, her sister Stephanie, and Axel Ryker to report to my office. I know they're scattered around the country but get them here to D.C. as soon as possible."

[that evening]

Originally, Kay Carr had agreed to meet with Erika at her grandparents' home but at the last minute, Kay telephoned Erika and asked for the meeting to instead be held at The Black Ram, the pub where Ian had taken them the previous night. Kay also asked Erika to bring Zhanna along—another change.

The deviation from the original plans meant the meeting began an hour later than originally scheduled, but at a few minutes past eight o'clock all three women were seated together at a table and already had their drinks. Sunday night was the slowest night at the pub. There were empty tables around them and they could talk freely.

"First off," Kay said, "it's nice to see you both and I want to thank you for being honest and frank with me last night after we left Ian. I appreciate you taking me into your confidence. The clash over Erika's cousin worries me. We have a 300-pound gorilla in the room. Before we go any further, I need to know you two can work closely together as you have done in the past."

One thing both Erika and Zhanna shared was commitment to an assignment. This trait dated back to long before they first met one another.

"Your husband knows I see missions through to the end, Kay," Erika replied. "But I haven't accepted this mission you talked to me about the other day. I told you I'm leaving with Ada."

Kay looked at Zhanna. She hadn't yet spoke with Zhanna about the Wiltshire mission. Zhanna looked at Kay briefly as if she were totally disinterested then lit a cigarette.

Kay redirected to the German. "Erika, disappearing with your daughter would be an injustice to her. What kind of life would that be for Ada—constantly moving from country to country."

The comment angered Erika. "I don't want to hear that shit, Kay. If your husband would have kept his promise he made to me over a year ago to get charges against me dropped I could have applied for American citizenship by now and wouldn't have to concern myself with running. I'm fed up with your husband and I'm starting to get fed up with you!"

"You and Zhanna said last night you trusted me when you opened up to me. You'll be wise to keep that trust. I've told my husband that if you agreed to this mission, he has to guarantee charges against you in the States be dropped, and right away. He'll do that, Erika."

"Did he say he would do it?"

"I won't betray your trust and lie to you. No, he didn't say he would, but you have my promise. I know Leroy has manipulated you on occasion in the past, but he's a good man and did what he did because he felt at the time it was best for his country."

Now Erika lit a cigarette.

Kay continued. "I left the American embassy this afternoon. I told my husband about the problem between you two knowing he will order Al Hodge to send me home. It's me who is on the run. I need a place to stay. You'll have to help me."

The two Shield Maidens stared at Kay Carr.

"Can we talk about Henry Wiltshire now?" Kay asked.

Chapter 11

A Visit from an Old Friend

London
Next day—Monday, 04 October 1948

This afternoon, Henry Wiltshire had written his letter of resignation from MI-6. Instead of sending it to Sir James by courier as he had originally intended, he would deliver it tomorrow personally.

His overseers must be madmen to consider asking him to work with the German Abwehr spy who had kidnapped him and smuggled him to Germany aboard a U-Boat where he sat out the last three years of the war a prisoner at Stalag Luft 2 outside Barth, Germany, near the Baltic Sea.

Maggie Harrison had seduced him and made a fool out of him. He had cursed himself countless times since 1942 (especially during the long days in the Stalag) for believing a beautiful young woman like her could be romantically attracted to a divorced, middle-aged and balding former college professor. He should have seen the red flags right away, especially because it was war time and he at the time had been recruited to a position within His Majesty's government that gave him access to top-secret information. Now he realized he had been nothing more than a silly old buffoon who had succumbed to a woman's charms and therefore let himself be duped. Only because during his long time in German hands had he, under interrogation, given the Germans only mis-information or low-level intel that served the Nazis no useful purpose was he was allowed back into government service after the war. It was the only thing in the entire, sordid affair in which he could take a small measure of pride.

After a long day at work in his office at MI-6 clearing up as many loose ends as he could on his ongoing endeavors for His Majesty's Secret Service, Wiltshire finally arrived at his flat well into the evening. He used his key to unlock his door on the third floor. In the darkness, he laid the key on a table beside the door. Before he flipped on the light switch, he heard a voice from the darkness.

"Hello, Henry. You have a beautiful flat."

Wiltshire jerked violently, nearly falling backwards into the hallway. His heart racing, he grabbed the door jamb to steady himself and fumbled in the dark until he found the switch and turned on the light.

Sitting in a chair across the small living room was Margaret Harrison smoking a cigarette.

Erika Lehmann smashed out the cigarette in a glass ashtray sitting on a small end table next to her chair. "It's nice to see you again, Henry."

Wiltshire thought he might faint but, determined to stay lucid, he opened a drawer in the table by the door where he kept a handgun. He jerked it out of the drawer and, shaking violently, aimed it in her direction.

Erika smiled sweetly. "Henry, do you really think the bullets are still in that gun?"

Wiltshire hurriedly opened the revolver's cylinder. It was empty.

"The cartridges are in your bedroom under your pillow. You can reload after I leave." Erika pulled out her Berretta Brevetatta, but instead of aiming it at Wiltshire, who she could tell already had frayed nerves, she ominously rested it on the end table. "Sit down, Henry my love. We have business to discuss. What are your thoughts about taking me on a romantic trip to Paris?"

"I'd rather you put me in prison again."

"Really? Are you sure about that?"

"Most sure."

Erika stood up and put her gun in the holster inside the back of her pants then walked toward Wiltshire. He thought for a moment that she was planning on again plying him with her charms, but she simply walked past him and said, "I'll see you soon, Henry," before walking out the door.

Henry Wiltshire found the nearest chair and collapsed into it.

Part 2

**"I can't go back to yesterday,
because I was a different person then."**

— *Lewis Carroll*

Chapter 12

A Shock from Kay

London
Next day—Tuesday, 05 October 1948

Al Hodge answered the eight o'clock in the morning telephone call in his room at the American Embassy expecting it to be Leroy Carr. Instead, it was Leroy's wife.

"Kay! Where in hell have you been? More importantly, where are you now? Leroy's about ready to send in the 101st Airborne and the 2nd Ranger Battalion to find you! Are you trying to get me fired?"

Hodge heard Kay laugh quietly over the phone.

"Leroy will never fire you, Al. He'd fire himself or divorce me first."

Hodge ignored her humor. "What's going on, Kay? Please be honest with me. It's Lehmann, isn't it? Or Rogova? They're both bad news."

"I'm fine. I know my husband, and I knew he would tell you to send me home after I told him about the friction between Erika and Zhanna. I was right, wasn't I?"

"Leroy loves you. You can't blame him for not wanting you in the middle between Lehmann and the Russian lunatic. Please come in."

"I can't do it, Al. Leroy sent me here to do a job and I'm not abandoning it until I see it through. I think I proved that in South America."

"Dammit, Kay, please don't do this. If you don't come in, Leroy is going to send Ryker and those two crazy Fischer sisters to find you." As soon as he said it, Hodge felt like punching himself. He knew he said the wrong thing.

"Thanks for letting me know that, Al. Please tell Leroy I'm safe and give him my love."

The phone went dead.

All incoming phone calls to the embassy were automatically put in trace mode. Hodge knew the conversation had taken enough time to be traced. He called the embassy switchboard and asked for a report.

After a moment, the embassy operator said, "Sir, the call came from a phone booth on the corner of Brewer Street and Denman Street in Piccadilly Circus."

Goddammit! Hodge cursed to himself. He knew Erika Lehmann had decided on a public phone booth in a busy area. Kay would be long gone before he could get a car there.

The embassy operator was still on the line. Hodge knew it was his duty to call Leroy. It was the middle of the night on the East Coast. He gave the operator the Carr's home telephone number.

[same time]

Erika and Kay had already walked three blocks from the telephone booth and now waited at a bus stop. Erika knew Kay's call would be traced by the embassy switchboard, and also knew taking a taxi would be a bad idea. Hodge could check cab companies for their driver's daily records and interrogate drivers for descriptions of their passengers and where they were dropped off. They stood off from the other waiting passengers so they could talk.

"Well, how did it go?" Erika asked.

"Al said Leroy might send Axel Ryker and the Fischer sisters here to find me."

"Kay, I think you should walk into the embassy and let Al send you home. You've been a big help but I can handle it from here."

"What about Zhanna?"

"Zhanna is a professional. She'll do her duty."

"Erika, apparently you learned nothing about me in South America. I realize I have no training, but I'm not going anywhere until I've seen this through. I don't appreciate you, Zhanna, or even my husband trying to protect me as if I'm some child."

Erika looked at her. She had admired Kay ever since they had first met during the war, even though Kay had plenty of reasons to hate her back then and did so for a long time.

"If your husband sends Ryker, Kathryn, and Stephanie here to find you, they will find you. If your mind is set, I have to get you out of this country. You speak Spanish. How does Barcelona sound?"

"The mission requires you and Zhanna to accompany Henry Wiltshire to the upcoming summit in Paris. What use will I be in Spain?"

"When we get to Paris," Erika said, "I'll contact you, then you can make your way there."

[shortly afterwards]

Al Hodge now had Leroy Carr on the phone. Even though it was middle of the night in Washington, Hodge hadn't awakened Carr from sleep. The CIA Deputy Director was sitting in the kitchen drinking gin and tonic. Sleep for the last few nights had been nothing but a brazen flirt for Leroy Carr, tempting him and then suddenly turning her attention elsewhere.

"Kay's not coming in, Leroy. I screwed up. I let it slip that you might send over you know who—the three."

There was a long pause. He knew Hodge had indeed made a big mistake, but decided to take it easy on his faithful, longtime comrade. Carr finally said, "Don't worry about it, Al. That doesn't change anything. If Kay refuses to come in, Erika knows how to make it hard on us regardless of whom we send."

Carr knew what he said was true. Erika Lehmann had hardened experience working for both the Nazis and the CIA and knew all the tricks.

"Is it really necessary to assign finding Kay to the Fischer sisters and Ryker?" Hodge asked. "We have other people."

"Are you forgetting that Erka's involved here," Carr said. "We're not going to find Kay without finding Erika first and she'll be using her Abwehr training. She always falls back on that when she goes dark. We don't have anyone that is familiar with the real nuts and bolts of Abwehr modus operandi besides the Fischer sisters. As far as Ryker, he's the only one who has ever succeeded in finding her when she's under the radar. We've never been able to do that. He found her in Evansville in '42, remember?"

◊ ◊ ◊

[that afternoon—Washington, D.C. time]

It had taken two days to assemble the search team. Axel Ryker lived on the Fort Dix Army Base in New Jersey. Kathryn Fischer had to be brought in from Rhode Island, and her sister, Stephanie, from Fort Huachuca in Arizona. All three were German, and they had all had worked for the Third Reich during the war. The Fischer sisters had been agents of Abwehr—German military intelligence. Stephanie as an oversees field agent like Erika Lehmann. Her sister Kathryn had been assigned by Abwehr head Wilhelm Canaris to infiltrate the Gestapo. Kathryn had been so successful that she had risen to the officer rank of Kriminalkommissar (a major). Axel Ryker was a different matter. His name was still on lists of hunted war criminals. He had been Heinrich Himmler's favorite henchman because of his skill at apprehension, interrogation, torture and murder. Despite their pasts, all three now worked for the CIA.

The three now sat before Leroy Carr in his E Street office as a light rain gently tapped his two office windows. He had already briefed them on their duties without revealing anything about the Wiltshire mission.

Carr ended with, "Your only assignment is to find my wife and bring her home safely. The reason Kay has disappeared is not important for you to know as far as accomplishing what you are tasked to do. Your job won't be easy; Erika knows you're coming. You'll all fly out to London together first thing tomorrow morning. Al Hodge will be waiting for you at the airport when you land Thursday. He'll have further instructions at that time."

[late this night]

Kathryn and Stephanie Fischer shared a room at the Mayflower Hotel. As Carr had told them, they, along with Axel Ryker, would fly out for London tomorrow. Ryker had a room on another floor. Both women were asleep when the ringing room telephone woke them. Kathryn sat up on the edge of the bed and picked up the receiver.

"Hello," she said.

"Hello, Kathryn, it's me. I assumed Leroy would put you up at the Mayflower."

"Your plan worked, Erika. Mr. Carr is sending me and Stephanie to London. As you suspected, he's also sending Ryker."

"We can't talk longer than 40 seconds, Kathryn. (In London, Erika was timing the call on her wristwatch.) *You and Stephanie should be in London sometime Thursday morning or afternoon, right?"*

"If there are no unforeseen delays. I assume you have already left your grandparents' home."

"Yes, I'm dark. You and Stephanie meet me at a café in Soho called Skip's at noon Friday."

"Skip's in Soho?" Kathryn confirmed.

"Yes. We have to hang up now," Erika said.

Both receivers, one in Washington and one in London, were placed back on their cradles simultaneously.

Chapter 13

King's Cross

Washington, D.C.
Next morning—Wednesday, 06 October 1948

Erika Lehmann wasn't finished with her phone calls to the States. It was two o'clock in the afternoon in London, making it mid-morning in Washington when her call was patched through to Leroy Carr's office.

"Leroy, before you start ranting and raving, I want you to know Kay is safe."

"Erika, I want to speak to Kay right now!"

"Sorry, Leroy. Kay is no longer in England. She's on the continent. Listen to me carefully. You know I respect you and I consider you an honest man at heart. Nevertheless, you have promised me a path to American citizenship for over a year with little or no progress."

Carr interrupted. "And who's to blame for that? You've made it very difficult for me with your actions during that time."

"Let's not argue. Kay has promised me that you'll ensure any current charges against me are dropped if I complete the Wiltshire mission. She told me she informed you of this and I trust Kay. If I promise you Kay's safety, and complete the mission, I want my American citizenship so Ada and I can be together in the States. What is your answer?"

Carr fumed. "Does Kay know you are manipulating her for your own purposes?"

"I need your answer now, Leroy."

"If anything happens to Kay. It's all over for you, Erika, and in the worst way."

"I accept that. Is that 'yes'?"

Carr didn't respond.

"By your silence," Erika said, *"I will assume you agree. Call off Al Hodge. I need him off my back. Tell him to cooperate with me. Call him as soon as you and I get off the phone. There is no time to waste. Goodbye, Leroy."*

Carr heard the dial tone.

◊ ◊ ◊

It wasn't long before Leroy Carr had Al Hodge on the telephone at the American embassy. Carr filled in Hodge about the conversation less than a half hour ago with Erika Lehmann.

"Leroy, none of this surprises me," Hodge said from London. *"What do you want me to do?*

"As soon as you find Erika, I want her arrested on the spot."

This was what Hodge had hoped to hear. *"ROGER that."*

[that afternoon]

I didn't know you were such a good actress, Zhanna," Erika said. "You sold it to Kay that you and I are at odds."

Last night the women stayed in a flea bag hotel near the East End docks.

Zhanna shrugged. "It was an easy matter. Have you spoken with Kathryn?"

"Yes. The 'friction' between you and me worked." During their brief, real confrontation in the loo at the The Black Lamb, Erika saw an opportunity and exploited it.

After their 'girl talk' with Kay that evening after the pub meal with Ian, Kay reported to her husband that some of the argument between Erika and Zhanna was in Russian that she didn't understand. Erika understood Russian and knew Kay didn't speak that language, so she and Zhanna used it to act like they were arguing but in reality were confirming to each other what they would say next in English in front of Kay.

Erika continued. "Kay called Leroy and he's sending both Kathryn and Stephanie over."

Zhanna was surprised. "Stephanie, as well? She has just begun training."

"Yes, for the CIA, but Leroy knows her background with Abwehr. Unfortunately, he's also sending Ryker, but I expected as much. Leroy knows Ryker is the only one who has ever successfully tracked me down when I've gone below ground on a mission."

"How did things go with your daughter?" Zhanna asked.

Erika had been forced again to say goodbye to Adelaide.

"I'd rather not talk about it."

Zhanna could tell her friend was glum. "If your plan works as you hope, and charges against you dropped, then you can take your daughter to America."

"And if it doesn't work, I'll have more charges against me."

"The Americans can't charge you with treason; you are not a citizen of that country."

"True, but Leroy can charge me for disobeying orders and kidnapping his wife."

"Kay Carr is not kidnapped," Zhanna replied. "She decided to disappear on her own."

"That's not how Leroy will see it."

Erika changed the subject. "Tonight you can say goodbye to Ian. I know you don't care anything about him, but he doesn't know that, and you can't just disappear. He might go to the police. What are you going to tell him?"

"I haven't thought about it. I'll come up with something."

"Have you called him for a meeting?"

"He called me for another date yesterday before I checked out of the Savoy. He's cooking us dinner tonight at his flat. Have you things worked out with your mark?" Zhanna still occasionally used odd word orders in English, but she referred to Henry Wiltshire."

"Not totally. I plan on seeing him again tomorrow, even though he doesn't know it yet."

Zhanna smiled. "This is the second time that man has been your mark. The last time he spent in one of your stalags three years. Do you think you can for a second time fool him?"

"I'll find out tomorrow."

◊ ◊ ◊

[same evening]

Ian Minton's flat lied in the King's Cross district of London. An area with many industries, King's Cross was home to many blue-collar workers because of its many apartment buildings offering affordable housing—humble flats, but clean and efficient. Ian lived in one such flat.

Like the East End docks, because of its industries, King's Cross had been a major target of German bombers during the Blitz, but the hardworking Brits had by now mostly rebuilt the area. Only a few piles of rubble that used to be buildings could still be found here or there.

Yesterday, when Ian called her at the Savoy he had told her he would pick her up in his car. Zhanna, knowing she would not be at the Savoy today, insisted she would take a taxi. She knocked on his door at seven o'clock.

When Ian opened the door he was wearing an apron. The sight of an apron on this large, muscular, tough boxer still sporting scars from his last fight made Zhanna smile and comment as she entered his flat, "You look like that American cook on the cake boxes in the stores. What's her name? . . . Betty Crocker."

Ian laughed. "That's the first time someone has compared me to her. Have a seat, Zhanna. Dinner will be ready shortly."

"What's on the menu?"

"Spaghetti. I'm afraid it's the only dinner I know how to cook. I'm pretty good at breakfast, but I'm limited on dinner. I hope spaghetti is agreeable to you."

"I like spaghetti," Zhanna lied. She hated spaghetti, but it didn't matter. The only reason she was there was to invent an excuse to say farewell that would not encourage Ian to search for her.

"I didn't buy wine because I would have picked the wrong one," Ian said, "but I know you like vodka. I bought some for you."

The flat was small. The kitchen and living area were basically the same room, separated only by a waist high counter. Zhanna sat down on a small sofa. Ian went into the kitchen, poured a dram of vodka and picked up a small bouquet of daisies and brought the drink and flowers to Zhanna.

No one had ever given Zhanna Rogova flowers.

Ian walked back into the kitchen to finishing the cooking. After 20 minutes of chit chat from the short distance of the tiny kitchen to the small living room, the food was ready. Ian held a chair at the small counter for Zhanna.

"I like your flat," Zhanna said as Ian laid the plates on the table. He also sat down the bottle of vodka and an ale for himself.

"It's not much, but it has a loo. Many flats at these apartment buildings in King's Cross require a floor of people to share a loo in the hallway."

They both started eating and more small talk ensued. The spaghetti had no meatballs or sausage but rather was topped by ground beef in canned marinara sauce.

"Everything is imported from the Yanks," Ian said, referring to the ingredients. England had not yet recovered from the severe rationing of wartime. "Even the vodka was made by the Yanks. You've spent time in the United States, Zhanna. Tell me about it."

"They are a strange people," Zhanna said. "They talk too much. No matter where you are—a store, a restaurant, a pub—an American might talk to you like he, or she, has known you for years. It can get, what is the English word . . . tiresome or tiring?"

"I would say either word works. During the war, when I was with the 22nd Dragoons, we went through several battles with the Yanks in Sicily and in northern France. I got the same impression. But they impressed me as a hardy lot, and good soldiers."

Ian downed a swig of ale.

"Zhanna, I've been meaning to ask you. I know nearly nothing about my cousin. What can you tell me about Erika?"

Zhanna was again forced to lie. "I know little more than you, Ian. Like me, she is translator for foreign dignitaries for the American Department of State. That is all about her I know."

Ian nodded, then suddenly stopped the small talk. "Zhanna, I've never met a woman like you. I have grand feelings for you." He seemed embarrassed and diverted his eyes to what remained of his meal.

There was a lengthy pause where Zhanna did not reply, making Ian even more discomfited.

"I'm sorry, Zhanna. I shouldn't have said that."

"Ian, I'm leaving England soon."

"Leaving? Why?"

"Erika and I have been ordered to Helsinki by our bosses at the State Department. Seems there is some sort of summit meeting with German and Russian officials and they need more translators."

"When can you come back to London?"

"Ian, it's best for you that you forget about me. You are too good a man for a woman like me."

"I don't understand."

"I am not the woman you think I am. I have done things in my life that would shock you and make you regret even knowing me." She removed her neck scarf, revealing the hideous, nearly two-inch wide purple and red scar that totally encircled her neck.

"The German SS bestowed this on me when they captured and hanged me during the battle of the Korsun Pocket in 1944. I survived only because the SS relished in hanging Russians slowly. My comrades were nearby, overtook the camp, and cut me down before I was dead."

"So that's why you always wear a scarf."

"Of course."

It took Ian no time to reply, "Look at me, Zhanna. I look hideous to most women. Do you really think I would care about a neck scar? You are beautiful to me."

"It's not just about the scar, Ian. It's about my past."

"Zhanna, we have all done things for our country during the war that haunt us."

Chapter 14

Maidens and a Monster

London
Next day—Thursday, 07 October 1948

Zhanna was still asleep when Erika awoke just after 6:00 a.m.

When she walked out into the small living area of the seamy hotel room, she saw a small bouquet of daisies standing in a glass of water.

◊ ◊ ◊

A bit later that morning, Henry Wiltshire sat at his desk at MI-6 finding it hard to concentrate on the work at hand; instead, being preoccupied with the events of the past three days.

Two days ago, the morning after Erika Lehmann surprised him in his flat, instead of delivering his resignation papers to White Hall as he had originally planned, Henry Wiltshire told Sir James about what happened the previous night and that Erika told him as she left that she would "see him soon." Sir James immediately called Al Hodge who made a beeline to White Hall.

Hodge had explained that Erika Lehmann had disobeyed orders and had disappeared. A plan was devised. If Erika contacted him, Wiltshire was to set up a meeting with her. During the meeting, Erika would be apprehended.

It all sounded good to Wiltshire. If he could play a part in getting the woman who was responsible for him spending three years in a German Stalag what was coming to her, he was more than happy to play a part. He tore up his resignation papers after the meeting.

"Mr. Wiltshire," the American, Hodge, had told him Tuesday, "If she contacts you, it's important to make her think you're reluctant to meet. If you agree right off the bat, she'll know it's a trap. Eventually agree but take your time and try to sound hesitant."

"I can do that," Wiltshire promised.

Now it was two days later and Wiltshire still had not been contacted by the woman who in 1942 he had known as Maggie Harrison.

[that afternoon]

The United States Air Force plane carrying Axel Ryker and Kathryn and Stephanie Fischer squealed down under a clear fall sky at the London Airport just after lunchtime. Al Hodge was waiting.

Ryker and the Fischer sisters would billet in an American safehouse. All three were too well known by the Soviets who kept the U.S. embassy under around-the-clock surveillance. If the Russians saw all three CIA operatives coming and going from the embassy they would seek to find out why. The mission at hand didn't concern Russia, but both Leroy Carr and Al Hodge felt it prudent to avoid any additional issues they would have to deal with.

[that evening]

Henry Wiltshire picked up the handset to his ringing telephone.

"Hello," he said.

"Hello, Henry."

It was Erika. Wiltshire wasn't listed in the telephone book, and the phone wasn't even in his real name so no one could get it from an operator. This was standard procedure for employees of MI-6. But he realized she got it easily from the round paper disk in the center of the dial when she had been waiting for him to arrive home Monday night.

"I'd like to meet with you Henry but not at your flat. I assume you reported our meeting Monday to your supervisor."

"Bloody right I did."

"Then your flat is being watched and you'll be followed. Tomorrow, the postman will deliver a letter to your box downstairs in the entryway of your building. I know you'll show the letter to your supervisor, so I won't waste my time asking you not to. In the letter will be instructions for both you and the American, Al Hodge, whom I'm sure you've met by now. Goodbye, Henry."

She never gave Wiltshire the chance to work on his acting skills.

[just after midnight]

Government safehouses were not jails. People were housed in such places for their own safety or to lie low. The safehouses included a military chaperone around the clock—usually an Army sergeant—but his duties were as a buffer, a lookout, and a guard to protect those housed there if the need arose.

It was an easy matter to escape from a safehouse.

Kathryn and Stephanie Fischer did so by simply going out the window of the bedroom they shared. The window faced an alley and in moments they disappeared into a pea soup fog London was famous for.

Chapter 15

A Note

London
Next day—Friday, 08 October 1948

Al Hodge again was forced to awaken Leroy Carr. Although it was 7:00 a.m. in London, it was the wee hours in Washington.

"It's me, Leroy."

"Yes, Al."

"Late last night, Henry Wiltshire called Sir James after receiving a phone call from Erika."

"What did she say?" Carr asked.

"She told him he'd receive a letter in the post today, giving him and me instructions. But that's not the main concern, Leroy. The sergeant-in-charge at the safehouse reports that the Fischer sisters disappeared last night. Ryker is the only one still there. So now Kay is missing, and Erika and the sisters have disappeared on us. What do you think is going on?"

Carr had to think for a moment. *"I'm not sure. Did you ask Wiltshire when his mail arrives?"*

"Of course. He said usually just after lunchtime."

Carr remained calm, or at least he gave that impression. *"Be waiting with Wiltshire at his mailbox and as soon as the letter arrives, read it and call me from the embassy on a secure line. Make sure Wiltshire is with you at our embassy when you call. The letter might give us a clue to Erika's end game."*

"What about MI-6? Wiltshire called them, not me, so they know about it."

"Okay, instead of our embassy, take Wiltshire to White Hall and call me from Sir James' office. You're right, Al, there's no way we can keep any of this from them. That would lead to a cock fight between us and the Brits. We don't need that."

"What do I do about Ryker?" Hodge asked.

"Keep him on ice until we know what's in Erika's letter."

Leroy Carr didn't bother to say goodbye. He lowered the phone for a moment then hung up. He knew there would be no more sleep tonight. He rose from the edge of the bed and went to the bathroom to shave.

[noon]

Erika's gamble had paid off. By disappearing, she assumed Leroy Carr would send at least Kathryn Fischer and Axel Ryker to try and hunt her down. Stephanie was a bit of a surprise. She had just begun CIA training so Erika couldn't assume Carr would send her, but then again it made sense on Carr's part and Erika was glad both sisters were sent over.

It had been agreed to with Kathryn that the day after Kathryn arrived in London, she would meet with Erika and Zhanna at a café in Soho called Skip's. Erika had spent much time in London before the war visiting her grandparents and knew of this place, as well as many others that could serve as out-of-the-way places for a furtive meeting. When Erika arrived in London two weeks ago one of the first things she did was make sure Skip's had survived the Blitz. She assumed her former German comrade-in-arms, Herman Göring, had held little interest in leveling an arts district, that's why she went out on a limb and chose this place in Soho. She was relieved to find out she was right and Skip's still stood.

Zhanna, Kathryn, and Stephanie now sat with her at an indoor table. It was a cool but beautiful fall day. The café had tables outside on the walk, but they all realized that sitting outside in plain view would be less than cautious.

Their lunch orders had been placed.

"Does anyone have a cigarette?" Zhanna asked.

None of the three did.

"Kathryn and Stephanie," Erika said, ignoring Zhanna's tetchiness that no one could hand over a smoke, "I owe you both so much already, I don't know quite what to say."

"Then don't say anything," Zhanna interjected. "Where's that fat-ass waiter with our lunch?"

Zhanna Rogova was funny sometimes, even if it wasn't a conscious attempt. The other three women laughed.

Erika, the Shield Maiden leader, got down to business.

"Kay is now in Barcelona," Erika said. "She's backing us in this. Barcelona is where you're headed, Stephanie. Nothing bad can happen to her. You'll be her bodyguard. Here is the hotel where she's staying." Erika handed Stephanie a piece of paper. "You leave tonight. I've arranged for a freighter to take you to Calais, France. That journey will take only a couple of hours. After that, it's up to you to find a flight to Barcelona. The important thing is you get to Kay as quickly as possible."

"Does she know I'm coming?" Stephanie asked.

"No. But Kay knows you. Just fill her in on our plans. I don't have guns for you or Kathryn but we'll get them after this afternoon. I know of a black marketeer."

Erika continued. "It's important for all of you to get out of London as soon as possible. Kathryn, you and Zhanna will leave tonight with Stephanie for Calais. Then you'll make your way to Paris. If things work out, I'll be able to meet you there in a few days. Stay at the Hotel Napoleon. It's on the right bank in the 8th Arrondissement. Go to the Eiffel Tower every night at eight o'clock and wait underneath it for half an hour until I meet you there. If I don't show up within a week from today, consider the mission over and do what you think is best for you after that. This money should be enough for all of you to start a new life somewhere."

Erika gave each woman a generous amount of money in British pounds. "You can convert this money into whatever currency you need."

"What about you, Erika?" Kathryn asked.

"My grandparents are in their seventies. They can't take care of Ada much longer. If what we're doing doesn't succeed, it's all over for me. I have talked to Ian about taking Ada to his family in Cheltenham." Erika stopped there. She didn't tell them that if the plan failed and she had no hope of ever being a mother to her daughter, she had a bullet reserved for herself.

◊ ◊ ◊

[an hour later]
Al Hodge and a member of MI-6 assigned by Sir James Ashworth were waiting with Henry Wiltshire when the mail carrier stepped into the entryway of Wiltshire's apartment building. Hodge beat Wiltshire and the MI-6 agent to the punch and grabbed Wiltshire's mail. He thumbed through a few innocuous letters until he found one with no return address. Hodge ripped it open and read it. At the bottom, Erika had signed it with her codename. Without waiting for Wiltshire or the MI-6 operative to see it, Hodge said, "Let's go. You both can read this in the car on our way back to White Hall."

Dearest Henry,
Since I have no doubt that you have informed your superiors about this letter, please make sure they deliver this to Al Hodge of the CIA.

Hello Al,

I'll keep this as brief as possible. As you know, Kay has disappeared. She has done this of her own free will and is not a captive. She can return to the States whenever she wishes. Zhanna, Kathryn, and Stephanie are out of your reach and have joined with me. Here's my offer. If I am guaranteed in a letter from the U.S. government that charges against me in the United States have been dropped, opening a path to me for citizenship, the assignment you sent me here to complete will go forward. He also has to agree that none of my fellow Shield Maidens suffer any consequences.

Furthermore, I know the anti-Bolshevik French, the British, and the Americans are trying to coax Charles de Gaulle to return to French politics to help stem the tide of the strengthening communist wave in that country. If Leroy doesn't agree to my offer, Charles de Gaulle will be assassinated. I will also release to the world press the truth that the CIA has in its employ, and are protecting, Axel Ryker, a man wanted by the international tribunals for war crimes. Tell Leroy I will call him at his home Sunday evening Washington time. We will talk less than 40 seconds so any attempt to trace the call will be useless.

All my love,
Your Lorelei

Chapter 16

Stephanie awaits

Barcelona, Spain
Next day—Saturday, 09 October 1948

The trip to Barcelona took Stephanie Fischer longer than expected. She disembarked from the freighter at 2:00 a.m. to find there were no flights from Calais to Barcelona, forcing her to wait until morning to board a bus for Paris, then take a flight to Barcelona from there. She finally arrived in the Spanish city in the mid-afternoon. From the airport, she hailed a taxi to take her to Kay Carr's hotel.

Kay was staying in the Gothic Quarter at the Hotel Catalonia Portal de L'Angel in the heart of the city center. Stephanie stepped up to the desk clerk. The man didn't speak English so he summoned a teenage girl from the office that did.

"I'm here to see a friend of mine. She's a guest here at your hotel. Lauren Jones." It was the alias Kay had registered under.

The girl translated and the man looked at the key board behind him. After speaking to the girl in Spanish, she turned to Stephanie.

"Señora Jones has apparently stepped out. Her key is on the board."

"That's fine," Stephanie replied. "I'll wait here in the lobby. Gracias."

[Paris, France—same time]

Zhanna and Kathryn's journey to Paris had taken much less time than Stephanie's trek to Spain. After disembarking the same freighter in Calais, they, too, had to wait until morning for a bus to Paris. All three rode the same bus. At the Paris bus depot, the two sisters hugged and parted ways. A half-hour later, Kathryn and Zhanna walked into the Hotel Napoleon.

◊ ◊ ◊

[Barcelona]

Stephanie Fischer wasn't forced to wait long. Less than a half-hour after she found a seat in the lobby, Kay Carr walked in. Kay stopped in her tracks when she saw Stephanie, but then walked over to her.

"Stephanie, what a surprise," she said.

"It's nice to see you again, Kay."

"I was just out on a walk. Erika should have told me you were coming."

"We had no idea when I would make it here," Stephanie said.

"Well, I imagine you have things to tell me. Are you hungry?"

"Starved."

"They have a good restaurant here in the hotel, but I found a nice cantina only four blocks away. I'll take you there."

The two women left the hotel and fifteen minutes later entered the O'Centrollo cantina. Kay had already eaten here twice, so the Catalonian man at the bar recognized her. He told them in Spanish to choose any table they wished. Kay spoke fluent Spanish and chose a table.

Stephanie said, "I see now why you went with Erika, Zhanna, and my sister to Central and South America last year." Stephanie had not been part of that mission to those Spanish speaking areas, but Kathryn had told her about it.

"Yes. Erika, besides German, speaks fluent English, Russian, and French. Zhanna speaks Russian, of course, and is getting much better at English and German. Your sister speaks German and has mastered English. Yet, none of them speak enough Spanish to get by in a Spanish speaking country. You're right, that's why my husband asked me to accompany them as an interpreter last year."

"How did you learn Spanish?" Stephanie asked.

"I studied it in college for four years. It was my minor, but I badly wanted to learn a foreign language so it was important to me. I spent a semester in Mexico City as an exchange student during my college days. How did you learn English?"

"I went through an extensive, two-year English program at Quenzsee, the training school outside Berlin where Abwehr agents received instruction. We weren't allowed to speak German, only

English. One can, and has to, learn a language quickly that way." Stephanie Fischer spoke English with the British accent in which she had been trained for her mission during the war.

The bartender brought to the table a bottle of red wine that Kay had ordered when they arrived. He poured two glasses. Stephanie took a sip.

"I'm not a wine connoisseur, but it tastes very good."

"What do you want to eat?" Kay asked. "I'm getting the paella. It's a rice and seafood dish—very Mediterranean."

"That sounds fine. I'll have that."

Kay caught the eye of the bartender and he returned to their table.

"Tendremos dos órdenes de paella, por favor," Kay said to the man. He nodded and left.

"There's a reason Erika sent you here, Stephanie," Kay said. "What is that reason?"

"I'm here to ensure your safety, Kay."

"So you're my bodyguard?"

"That's right. None of us want anything to happen to you. We all respect you, Kay."

Kay paused and took a sip of wine. She knew what Erika Lehmann was capable of and wasn't sure if Stephanie's comment should be considered as comforting or disturbing.

After the pause, Kay said, "What's the latest on the mission my husband sent me to London to tell Erika about?"

"That's hard to say. It all depends on your husband."

"What do you mean?"

"Kay, Erika is determined to get the American citizenship your husband has promised her for nearly two years. If that doesn't come about, I'm afraid bad things will happen. But this doesn't concern you. I'm here to protect you because Erika respects you. She wants you to go home to Annapolis. I want you to call your husband and tell him you're coming home."

A stunned Kay Carr replied, "I'll call Leroy when we get back to the hotel."

After the phone call Kay made to her husband later that evening, it would be Stephanie who would be shocked.

[three hours later]

Stephanie was now on the telephone to Erika at her hotel in London.

"Erika, Kay just got off the phone to her husband. I told her to go home, but instead she sideswiped me. I was standing next to her when she made the call and she told Leroy she wasn't coming home until you receive the letter you demanded from the government. You have a way to contact my sister and Zhanna, right?"

"Yes, I'll let them know, Steph."

Erika hung up, knowing this compounded their problems.

Chapter 17

The Day of the Telephone

Washington, D.C.
Next day—Sunday, 10 October 1948

After receiving Kay's phone call yesterday telling him she wasn't coming home until the standoff concerning Erika's path to U.S. citizenship was resolved, Leroy Carr had to give Erika credit. Then again, she *was* his best agent. Erika had planned this well, even duping him into sending over two of the Shield Maidens. Carr, who had hoodwinked more than just a few skilled adversaries in his clandestine world over the years, was not a man easily fooled and he didn't like the taste of it.

He refused to believe that Kay was a willing accomplice in all this. She told him during her phone call yesterday that Stephanie Fischer was with her. Stephanie might have forced Kay to say what she did under threat of harm.

Carr had already taken action. Now, still morning, he had just gotten Al Hodge on the telephone in London. Hodge already knew about Kay's call.

"Any new developments since last night?" Carr asked.

"Nothing on my end," Hodge answered.

"Have you briefed Ryker on any of this?"

"No. He knows the sisters went on the lam from the safehouse because he billets there, but he knows nothing else."

"Brief him and take him off the leash, Al. Give him what he needs to track down Erika. I'm sending over Houchen and Stephen Floyd. They'll be in the air within the hour, and you have additional agency men already stationed in London and Paris you can enlist as needed."

Earl Houchen was Hodge's top man on his CIA team, and Stephen Floyd was a tough U.S. Army Ranger, highly decorated during the war, who was expert with explosives and a bevy of firearms.

"It won't be easy finding Lehmann, Leroy. That time Ryker found her in Evansville he knew what city she was in and it wasn't a large city like

London. And who's to know if she's even still here. She might be in France by now."

"I understand that, Al," Carr uncharacteristically snapped at his old friend. "Do you have a better plan? Maybe we should just keep Ryker in the safehouse or send him on vacation to Bermuda. Is that what you want?"

"Calm down, Leroy. Kay is going to be alright. As much as I think Lehmann and those other broads are a pack of gangsters, I don't believe she would ever hurt Kay. With that said, I think she's serious about cancelling de Gaulle. And she's got Rogova with her, one of the best long-range snipers in the world. Are we going to tell the Froggies?" (It was the word Hodge used when referring to the French.)

"I don't know yet. I have a meeting with Hillenkoetter first thing in the morning where we'll talk about that. There are big problems with telling an ally that a group of CIA field agents have plans to assassinate one of their national heroes."

Roscoe Hillenkoetter was the director of the CIA and the only person in the agency that Deputy Director Carr answered to.

"I can imagine that might prove to be a bit awkward."

"Until a decision is made," Carr said, "it's up to us to end this."

"Are you coming over here to London?"

"I don't know yet, Al. Erika said she would call me tonight. I'm going to demand I speak with Kay."

"What about Lehmann's demands for her criminal slate to be wiped clean."

"A lot of that hinges on my conversation with Roscoe tomorrow. I've been working on that for well over a year. No one knows that better than you. Erika hasn't made it easy. She thinks I have more influence with the Department of Justice than I really do."

Then Al Hodge said something Leroy Carr thought he'd never hear from his longtime sidekick who, over the past four years, had had numerous conflicts with Erika. *"Lehmann deserves a clean slate, Leroy. She's done a lot for our country. I agree with Kay."* He ended with, *"I'll fulfill your orders. I'll brief Ryker today and let him loose."*

Then Al Hodge hung up on his boss.

[London—two hours later]

A large man wearing a black porkpie hat tilted toward the right side of his head entered the room.

Axel Ryker sat down heavily in the chair facing Al Hodge across a table in a soundproof room at the American embassy in London. They were the only ones in the room.

During the war, Ryker, a repatriated German from Lithuania, was a man called upon by Heinrich Himmler from time to time for "special" tasks. Ryker possessed several qualities that augmented his usefulness to Himmler and the Gestapo. He spoke fluent Russian (his native tongue), acceptable Slovak and Czech (most speakers of Slovak had few problems with the similar Czech), and German. Ryker had even managed by now to learn English, although his English consisted of a hodgepodge of Russian, Czech, and German accents.

He could also snap a man's neck as easily as a chicken bone, which he had proven on more than one occasion. For Axel Ryker, liquidation, torture, and murder were job skills honed sharp, and sometimes even pleasant diversions.

Ryker was a full six-feet tall (probably a little more) with a wide, heavily muscled torso, a shaven head, and dark, pitiless eyes. His protruding brow gave him a caveman countenance. Adding to his already grisly genetic features was a nose that had been broken but never properly repaired, and three noticeable scars on his right cheek. The nose was a souvenir from the twenties, courtesy of a pipe swinging communist who crept up on him during a street brawl. Ryker was a teenager at the time.

To frighten women and intimidate men, Axel Ryker simply had to enter the room.

Yet Ryker was no mindless automaton dusted off only during the Gestapo's murder and maim hour. In addition to his impressive language skills, Ryker possessed an innate craftiness, including an almost supernatural ability to discern when someone was lying to him. These qualities allowed him to ferret information when others failed. He was also particularly proficient in finding persons who had gone underground, something he had proven time and again during his years with the Gestapo.

He now worked for the CIA and had to this date completed two missions for the Americans. One mission in Denver, Colorado, and a second in Europe where he was assigned to work with Erika and her Shield Maidens to help free Stephanie Fischer from the Soviets. Ryker was well acquainted with all the players.

Al Hodge filled Ryker in on all the events of the past two days—about Kay, about the Fischer sisters, and the last contacts they had received from Erika.

"Ryker, your job is to find Erika, plain and simple. And we want her with a pulse when you bring her in, is that clear?"

Ryker stared at Hodge. "If she's gone rogue and is such a threat, why do you want her alive?"

"Deputy Director Carr wants it that way, that's why, and so do I. He's sending over some specialists to help you, but they won't arrive until sometime tomorrow. We have men here in London presently that are at your immediate disposal if you decide you need them. I'll requisition you a car and driver."

"Do we have reason to believe the Abwehr slut is still in London?" Ryker asked, referring to Erika.

"We have no way of knowing. Are there any other questions?" Hodge asked. Ryker repulsed him.

"I understand my orders, Herr Hodge."

[that evening in Annapolis]

"Hello, Leroy. How's the weather there?"

"Cut the crap, Erika. I want to speak to Kay now!" Carr demanded loudly from his home telephone.

"I'm not with Kay. She told you she is with Stephanie. Stephanie is keeping her safe."

"That makes me feel a whole lot better," Carr said sarcastically.

"Leroy, we can end all of this and proceed with the Henry Wiltshire mission like nothing has ever happened if you give me your word I'll get that pardon I asked for."

"I know you don't believe me, but I have been working on that for quite some time. But every time I get close you do something stupid such as getting arrested after a stupid bar fight in Denver or getting drunk and stealing a boat in the Chesapeake Bay, going for a joy ride, and getting arrested for piracy by the Coast Guard sets me back, Erika. Your poor decisions during your down time makes it tough on me. And those kinds of crimes pale in comparison to the murder charge in Cincinnati filed against you during the war."

"I admit I have made some dumb mistakes with petty arrests, but you very well know I never killed anyone in America unless it was in self-defense or to save an innocent victim. Is your answer to my pardon yes or no, Leroy?"

"I want to talk to Kay. I expect a phone call from her within the hour."

"Very well. I'll call you back after you talk to your wife."

[Barcelona—an hour later]

After ending the Washington phone call. Erika called Kay in Barcelona. Kay placed the international call through to her husband and waited as the phone rang in Annapolis. It rang only once.

"How are you, darling?" Kay said after her husband picked up.

"Kay! Are you okay?"

"I'm fine."

"Where's Stephanie Fischer? Is she listening in?"

"I'm calling from a phone booth. Stephanie is standing outside the booth. She is not monitoring what I say."

"Where are you, Kay?"

"I'm on the continent, but I'm not going to tell you the country."

"Kay, I don't believe this! Have you been threatened?"

"I have not been threatened, Leroy. Both Erika and Stephanie have encouraged me to return home, but I'm not going to do that until our government does the right thing and grants Erika a pardon. If that doesn't happen, Stephanie told me of their plans. She has been very honest with me. Bad things will happen Leroy. Things that can be easily avoided by our government doing the right thing. Erika has nothing to lose."

There was a pause. When Kay came back on the phone she said, "Stephanie tells me I have to hang up now so the call cannot be traced. Goodbye, darling."

[Annapolis—an hour and a half later]

"You should have had time to have heard from Kay by now, Leroy," Erika said from London.

"Yes, I heard from Kay."

"Are you convinced she is not our hostage and is in no danger?"

"Knowing you, Erika, no, I am not convinced. But regardless of if she is or not, I want her sent back home immediately."

"We have offered her that option, Leroy, and have even done our best to encourage her to do so."

"How do I know Stephanie wasn't holding a gun to her head, forcing her to say those things?"

A pause ensued. *"Okay, to prove this to you, I'll have Stephanie deliver Kay to the closest American embassy to where they are staying. After that, our plan goes forward to eliminate Charles de Gaulle unless I'm guaranteed my pardon."*

"The attorney general doesn't have the power to pardon you Erika. Only the President of the United States."

"You have forty-eight hours, Leroy, to give me an answer."

"If you kill de Gaulle, you're a dead woman. Every democratic country on earth will be searching for you and anyone that is involved with you. Surely you realize that."

"Zhanna and I know that and I accept it. The Fischer sisters will not be involved in the assassination."

"Too late for that. They're already involved."

"Forty-eight hours, Leroy. I'll call you at home Tuesday evening your time."

Chapter 18

Monster comes Calling

Barcelona, Spain
Next day—Monday, 11 October 1948

As Kay Carr's bodyguard, Stephanie Fischer now stayed with Kay in her Barcelona hotel room. After breakfast at the hotel restaurant, Stephanie told Kay, "Let's go for a ride around the city."

Stephanie asked the hotel desk clerk to summon a taxi. Fifteen minutes later both women were in the back seat of a cab as it made its way through busy Barcelona streets.

Stephanie had received a phone call last night from Erika and gave the driver an address.

"Where are we going?" Kay asked.

"We'll be there soon."

The taxi stopped in front of the American embassy in Barcelona.

"Get out, Kay," Stephanie ordered sternly. "You're going home."

"I don't understand."

"Go up to the guard at the gate and tell them who you are and that you want to return to the United States. Now get out."

Arguing with a formidable person like Stephanie Fischer was not an argument Kay considered she could win. She got out of the cab and it immediately drove away.

Left alone, Kay had to think quickly. She walked up to a U.S. Marine guard patrolling just inside the locked gate and got his attention. She pulled out her passport and showed it to him through the bars of the gate.

"My name is Kay Carr. I'm an American. Please look at my passport, then look at me."

The Marine corporal did so.

"Would you agree I am this woman?" Kay asked.

"Yes, ma'am." The armed Marine started to unlock the gate. Kay stopped him.

"I'm not coming in, corporal. Please tell your commanders you identified me and that my husband is Leroy Carr." Kay stopped short of telling the young Marine that her husband was second in command at the CIA. "He's affiliated with the Department of State."

Kay walked away.

◊ ◊ ◊

Two hours after being dropped off at the American embassy, Kay Carr walked back into her hotel room. Stephanie Fischer, who had already started packing to leave for Paris, stopped what she was doing and looked at Kay. Kay ignored her as she walked past.

[London—that evening]

Marie Minton answered the knock on the door. Opening it, the sight of the man standing on the landing shocked her. He was a large, grisly-looking man with multiple scars on his face.

"Yes," Marie said hesitantly.

"Hello, Madam. My name is Ryker. I am an associate of your granddaughter. May I come in?"

"My granddaughter?"

"Erika Lehmann is your granddaughter, is she not?" The man spoke acceptable English, but with an odd accent.

"Very well. Yes, please come in."

Axel Ryker stepped through the doorway and removed his porkpie hat.

"My husband and our nephew are in the study," said Marie. "This way, please." She led Ryker to the study. When she opened the door, Ryker saw an elderly, dignified looking gentleman smoking a cigar and a young man of sturdy physique.

"Louis and Ian, this is Mr. Ryker. He says he is an associate of Erika's."

Both men stood and introduced themselves. "Come in, please." Erika's grandfather said. "Anyone who is a confederate of Erika is most welcome."

"Let me take your hat," Marie said. Ryker handed it over and Marie left the room.

"Please have a seat, Mr. Ryker," Sir Louis said. "Would you like a brandy or a whiskey? Perhaps a cigar."

"A whiskey and a cigar," Ryker said as he studied both men.

Louis Minton poured the drink and handed Ryker a cigar. "The whiskey is from America. They call it Bourbon and it's made in the Yank state of Kentucky. The cigar is from Cuba."

All three men sat down. A gold lighter and a cigar guillotine sat on the small coffee table separating Ryker from the two men. Instead of using either, Ryker bit off the end and lit the cigar with a match from a book of them in his jacket pocket.

"So, how is it that you know my granddaughter?" Sir Louis asked.

Ryker knew that Erika's grandparents had found out near the end of the war that their granddaughter was, at that time, a spy for Nazi Germany, having a German father and being born it that country. Al Hodge had also told him her grandparents now believed she was an interpreter for the American State Department.

"Like your granddaughter, I work for the State Department. I was sent here to contact her and offer my assistance. I was told she was staying here." Ryker knew she wasn't there.

"She was until about a week ago. She was ordered to Helsinki to serve as an interpreter at an international conference."

The canny Ryker knew immediately this was a cover lie Erika must have told her grandparents. One thing he knew now was that Erika was not in Helsinki.

"And the woman that came to London with her—a woman named Zhanna Rogova. Have you seen her?"

Ian spoke for the first time. "Zhanna was also assigned to the Helsinki conference."

Ryker switch his lifeless gaze toward the young man. "So, you have met Miss Rogova?"

"Yes," Ian replied. Neither Ian nor Sir Louis had reason to suspect Ryker was there because he was hunting Erika.

Ryker continued to look at Ian. When he mentioned Zhanna's name, the young man was quick to jump in.

"I notice you are not drinking or smoking with your grandfather," Ryker probed.

"I'm in training. I box."

"A worthy vocation," said the massive Ryker. A highly skilled interrogator, he knew he had gotten as much information from the two men as was in their power to give him. He pulled a small package out of his suit jacket pocket.

"I have a gift for Erika's daughter," Ryker said. "I understand she lives here. May I see the child?"

"Of course," Sir Louis replied. He stood, walked to the study door, and summoned his wife. Three minutes later, Marie Minton brought Ada into the study. The seven-year-old had been in her upstairs room playing with her dolls. Ryker gave the young girl a wrapped gift—a small necklace.

Even though her father was a deceased Nazi SS officer, Erika had elected to keep her daughter's last name unchanged to honor her father. Axel Ryker stared at Adelaide Faust as she happily opened the gift.

Chapter 19

Less than 40 Seconds

London
Next day—Tuesday, 12 October 1948

This time, it was Leroy Carr who awoke Al Hodge in the wee hours.

"Al, our ambassador in Barcelona just called me. Kay apparently showed up this morning at the embassy gate and identified herself to the guard."

"What??"

"The guard is sure it was Kay. She showed him her passport."

"Thank God. So she's safe at the embassy?"

"No, after she identified herself, she walked away."

"What??"was a word Hodge repeated. "Why?"

"I'm sure she wanted to prove to me that she wasn't being held hostage. It's apparent now that Erika has drawn Kay into her web."

"Why did it take the ambassador so long to call you?"

"He's a bureaucrat who doesn't want to lose his job. He went through the State Department first. Do you have any updates from Ryker?"

"He visited Erika's grandparents. Apparently Zhanna told that guy who is Erika's cousin some bullshit story that she and Erika were being sent to Helsinki to translate at an international conference. Ryker says he thinks the cousin and Zhanna have established some sort of relationship."

"That's it?"

"For now, but Ryker also reported that he met Erika's daughter. What do you want me to do, Leroy?"

"Erika told me Stephanie Fischer is protecting Kay. Reassign Ryker from hunting Erika to finding Stephanie Fischer in Barcelona. At least we have a city to narrow it down."

"Roger that," Hodge replied.

◊ ◊ ◊

[Paris, France—very early that morning, Paris time]
Zhanna Rogova and Kathryn Fischer had been in Paris for three days. Staying at the Hotel Napoleon on the Champs-Elysees two blocks from the Arc de Triomphe, they had just returned to their hotel room from a night out at the Moulin Rouge. They bided their time in Paris while they waited to hear from Erika. After a long night on the town, both women needed sleep.

[that evening, Washington time]
CIA telephone call tracking experts, and technicians with recording equipment, were set up inside the Carr home in Annapolis. Leroy Carr fully expected the phone call from Erika would be too short to trace—she was too experienced to allow that to happen—but at least the call would be recorded. Perhaps the eggheads in the CIA analysis department could magnify any background noise and come up with a clue on location from where the call originated.

Everyone had been prepared and waiting since mid-afternoon. Finally, at a few minutes before eight o'clock. The phone rang.

It was Kay's mother in Illinois asking for her daughter.

"Kay's not here, Verla," Carr said quickly, trying to end the phone call as quickly as possible in order to keep the line free. "I'm sorry but I just got a call from work and I have to head into the office. Some sort of emergency on a case now before the court of appeals." As far as Kay's mother knew, Leroy was an attorney for the Department of Justice. He even had false I.D.s proclaiming as much (among several other false I.D.s). Carr had been an attorney before joining the OSS and this served as a good cover vocation for family and friends. He used it often. "Can I call you back later tonight or tomorrow?"

The call ended. Carr knew he'd have to call her back with some concocted story about Kay being out of town, but he'd concern himself with that later.

Another fifteen minutes passed, maybe twenty, when the phone rang again. Carr again made sure all the technicians were ready before he picked up.

"Hello," Carr said.

"Good evening, Leroy."

"Unless you've returned to the States, Erika, it's not evening where you are."

"That's true. I'm not in America but I know it's evening in Annapolis. We have only a short time to talk. What is your answer? Will I get my pardon?"

"Erika, the United States is not going to be intimidated into giving anyone a pardon. You're not going about this the right way."

Erika talked quickly. *"What other way would you recommend, Leroy. I've been patiently waiting two years and still nothing has come about. In that time, I have fulfilled all my orders faithfully."*

"That's not true," Carr countered. "You went rogue for weeks in South America, and for a short time also in Denver."

"In South America, you told me I was being sent there to search for the Führer when in truth it was Axel Ryker you wanted found so you could employ him. The press would be very interested in that story, Leroy. You manipulated me. In Denver, I went dark for a few days in order to accomplish the mission. Both missions were successful from the CIA standpoint. We're at the end of our time. I'll call you back in ten minutes."

Carr heard the dial tone and hung up. He looked at the tracer, who shook his head and said, "Thirty-eight seconds. Not enough time."

They waited.

"Yes," Carr said when the phone rang ten minutes later.

"So your answer is 'no.' Is that what you're telling me?"

"Right now that's the only honest answer I can give you."

"Very well, Leroy."

"Don't hang up," Carr said. "We have more time. Where is Kay?"

"Stephanie told me she dropped Kay off at the embassy in Barcelona. I know they have contacted you by now. Kay's actions have to prove to you that Kay is not a hostage, and by her own free will decided to not walk in ('walk in' was CIA jargon for turning oneself over). *By the way, you'll be wasting your time searching for Kay in Barcelona. She and Stephanie left that city eight hours ago. Good bye, Leroy."*

The phone went dead. Carr didn't comment to the CIA technicians sitting in his living room, but the thought that Erika Lehmann still referred to Adolf Hitler as the *Führer* wasn't lost on him. Kay, who hated everything Hitler stood for, was now in league with this woman.

Chapter 20

Valencia

Washington, D.C.
Next day—Wednesday, 13 October 1948

After studying the taped telephone calls from Erika Lehmann last night, the report from the analysts included nothing more than that they devised the call had come from a telephone booth because of traffic noise discernable when the volume was magnified. They picked up no background voices, which might have indicated a language and therefore possibly a country. Leroy Carr expected as much.

Carr called in Sheila Reid to his office. Sheila, one of the Shield Maidens and the only American amongst that group, had been seriously wounded by a gunshot to her shoulder in Austria during the last Shield Maiden mission. She was now out of the hospital, yet still recovering and had not yet returned to work.

Sheila had proper clearance and Carr filled her in on what was happening on Erika's current assignment—Erika's demand for a pardon under the threat of assassinating Charles de Gaulle, Kay's apparent backing of Erika along with the other Shield Maidens, the phone calls—everything.

"You probably know Erika better than I do," Carr said to the U.S. Army major. "Tell me what you think."

A long pause ensued. "Hard to say, Leroy, but none of this sounds like it might end well to me. No one knows better than you the ruthlessness Erika is capable of, then add to that the element of Zhanna Rogova being along for the ride."

[Valencia, Spain—same day]

After contacting Erika yesterday about Kay refusing to walk in to the American embassy, Stephanie now had Kay in Valencia, another large, Spanish city on the Mediterranean coast, this one about 225 miles south of Barcelona. Large cities were always preferred to small ones when the focus was on remaining covert.

They had checked into the Caro Hotel in the city center using aliases. Stephanie was now Ann Kellenberger. Kay again used the name Lauren Jones.

Instead of eating dinner at the hotel, Stephanie asked the hotel concierge about a venue for Gypsy Flamenco. She had spent time with a band of Gypsies in Austria during the previous Shield Maiden mission. He recommended a place and after a 20-minute taxi ride, Stephanie and Kay arrived at the Cordobes Tablae Flamenco. It was here they paid for dinner and a show. The Cordones impressed one more as a large cave than a conventional restaurant. A dark-haired, swarthy man greeted them and led them to a small table.

"That man who seated us looked surprised to see us," Kay commented after the man walked away.

"We're the only two women in here without a male escort," Stephanie said.

Kay looked around. She was right. "That must be spy stuff."

"We call it situational awareness. The ratio of men to women is about three to one. Surprisingly there are more Catalonians than Roma."

Spanish Catalonians were almost always lighter skinned than Gypsies.

Kay was impressed. She didn't know a lot about Stephanie Fischer, even though she spent a night in jail with her after they were arrested along with Erika, Kathryn and Zhanna. Last month, after the Shield Maidens returned from Europe after finding Stephanie, Kay made a bad decision. Leroy was still overseas and one-night Erika coaxed Kay into a night of drinking. All the women ended up intoxicated, and Kay was with them when a speed boat was stolen for a joy ride in the Chesapeake Bay. They were arrested by the Coast Guard for piracy. Kay was released the next day. Erika, Zhanna, and the Fischer sisters spent four days in jail, not being released until Leroy pulled some strings.

"I know spending three years in a Russian gulag had to be horrible," Kay said.

"It was." Stephanie stopped there.

A waiter arrived with the wine and poured two glasses, telling them the meals would be delivered shortly. There were no menus. The Cordobes cook and his staff decided on what customers would eat depending on the day of the week. One meal was decided on and that was what each customer received on that particular night with the price of the dinner and Flamenco show ticket. Even the wine was chosen for the diners. Tonight it was a sweet white wine in a clear glass decanter with no label. The Cordobes bought its wine by the barrel from a family-owned vineyard outside Valencia.

Kay Carr had a mid-level CIA clearance and could be told things without breaking the rules of protocol, but Stephanie didn't offer up any more information about her imprisonment by the Soviets. Kay was aware of the treatment captured Germans received, and were still receiving, at the hands of the Russians and decided not to question her further on that matter.

"What made you join Abwehr, Stephanie? Why did you decided to become a spy? Everyone knows how dangerous that is."

"For obvious reasons. I wanted to serve my country. My sister and I joined together."

"There are safer ways one can serve. Why a spy?"

"You don't know how it was in Germany before the war, Kay. One didn't choose. Kathryn and I both spoke basic English we had learned growing up. She and I had jobs at the Berlin zoo in the thirties when Kathryn was in Gymnasium and me in university. We learned rudimentary English because of all the American and British tourists. The Abwehr was in need of English-speaking agents so we were assigned to rigorous English classes and eventually the choice of how and where to serve was made for us."

Kay nodded. "I see."

The meals were delivered. Tonight, it was Sea Bass with citrus salsa, and a cup of assorted vegetables and chickpeas sautéed in olive oil and poured into a broth. The Roma called it 'Moosewood' soup. A basket containing several thick slices of a hard crust bread and a generous slice of locally made white cheese accompanied the meal.

Both women were hungry and tucked in. After a few bites it was Stephanie's turn to ask questions.

"How long have you been married?"

"Leroy and I will be married for twenty-one years this summer—August 22nd."

"How did you meet your husband?"

"Leroy was an attorney and I worked as a legal assistant at the same firm. This was before he opened his own practice. Why do you ask?"

"I was just wondering what it's like to be married."

"It's wonderful if you find the right man." Kay looked at Stephanie, who looked away. "Would you like to marry someday, Stephanie?"

The Shield Maiden took a sip of wine. "How can I marry with a job like mine? It's not meant for women like me, Kay."

Kay detected melancholy in her reply and said no more; instead, she changed the subject.

"You seem to know a great deal about identifying the Romani, Stephanie. How is that?"

"You bewilder me, Kay. Your aware that they prefer to be called Roma or Romani. They have learned to live with 'Gypsies' but consider 'Gyps' a vulgar insult. How do you know about the Roma—most Americans don't."

"I speak Spanish, Stephanie, and have spent time in countries with a significant population of Romani. I might ask you that same question."

"A family of Roma helped me escape from the Soviet occupied area of Austria this past summer. That was just before I found my sister in Salzburg, in the American sector."

Both women continued eating.

Once in a while, truth proves greater than fiction. As they neared the end of their dinner, the Flamenco band and dancers appeared on the stage. It was Raval and his family—the Gypsy clan that had helped Stephanie in Austria.

Kay, whose back was to the stage, saw Stephanie's expression and turned around.

The dinner and Flamenco show would turn into a long night of drinking and dancing for Stephanie Fischer with Kay Carr along for the ride.

Chapter 21

News about Ada

Washington, D.C.
Next day—Thursday, 14 October 1948

This morning, Sheila Reid walked into Leroy Carr's office.

"I'm going stir crazy, Leroy. I'm coming back to work." She wore her Army uniform, her left arm in a sling.

"It's been only three weeks since you were shot. The doctor said six weeks before you're cleared to work."

"I don't care what he said. I've already sent my replacement back to the records sector where she normally works. I'll be in my office."

He felt he should object, but he didn't. It was a relief to have Sheila back.

Carr's meeting with CIA Director Roscoe Hillenkoetter on Monday went as Carr had expected. The French and other allies were not to be informed of Erika's threat against Charles de Gaulle, at least not yet. Hillenkoetter agreed to this only because Carr laid out a plan that might hopefully end this standoff between the agency and Erika Lehmann.

That was two days ago. Carr expected to receive a phone call today.

[London—same morning]

Erika was the only one of the Shield Maidens still in London. Tomorrow, she would leave for Paris to join Zhanna and Kathryn. She had called Stephanie and Kay's hotel in Valencia an hour ago to check on their status but no one answered the phone in their room. She asked the switchboard operator to have a desk clerk check the board for their keys, and the keys were there. They had not returned to their room last night. This didn't particularly concern her. Erika knew Kay was safe with Stephanie. If they had stayed out all night, good for them. Someone should be allowed to enjoy themselves amidst all this disarray.

[Washington—around noon]

The telephone call Leroy Carr was expecting came through just before lunchtime. The buzzer on his desk sounded.

"Yes, Sheila."

"A call from Erika's grandfather in London. It sounds urgent."

"Put it through."

After a couple of clicks, Carr said, "Hello, Sir Louis. It's nice to speak to you again. What can I do for you?"

The father of Erika's mother was obviously in a panic. *"Mr. Carr, my granddaughter is missing!"*

"Ada!"

"Yes!"

"Does Erika know?"

"No, I haven't seen her in days and don't know how to reach her. You're the only one I could think of to call besides the police."

"When did the child disappear?"

"Marie went to her room this morning to awaken her for breakfast. Her window was open and the kidnapper left a note."

"What does the note say?"

"It's addressed to Erika. For the safe return of her daughter, the kidnapper demands she immediately turn herself in to an American embassy in whatever city she is currently in. It's signed 'Ryker.' This man came by the house two days ago. Marie let him in because he said he was a colleague of our granddaughter. He had identification showing he worked for your Department of State."

"Odd that a kidnapper would sign the note. Unfortunately, I've never heard the name, Sir Louis," Carr lied. "But if Erika contacts you, encourage her to do what the note demands. Ada is what counts. Is there anything else you can tell me? Did Erika ever call to speak with Ada?"

"She calls every night before Ada goes to bed but doesn't speak long."

Carr knew why, so her call couldn't be traced. "I'll put a team on this, Sir Louis. Reassure your wife. We'll get to the bottom of it. I'll be in touch."

As soon as the phone call ended, Carr buzzed Sheila. "Get me Al Hodge at our London embassy."

This call went through a little quicker than normal, taking only 15 minutes. After he identified himself to the embassy operator she put Carr though.

"I thought you'd call sooner, Leroy," Hodge said from London. *"Did Sir Louis call the Bobbies?"*

"Yes, of course. Anyone would."

"Good. Should I make sure Ada's picture is posted as kidnapped in the London newspapers in case Erika is still in this area?"

"Let's wait one day. Sir Louis told me Erika calls Ada every night. Is Ada safe at the embassy?"

"Yes, I got her a nanny, a puppy, and some dolls."

"Who did the job?" Carr asked.

"Earl Houchen and the Ranger, Steven Floyd. Floyd climbed up and went through the girl's window. It was a piece of cake for him, the guy scaled the cliffs of Pointe de Hoc on D-Day. He handed her down to Earl. Floyd left the note we had Ryker scribble."

It was now Leroy Carr's time for a high-stakes gamble, a game of chance Erika had forced him into.

"Al, keep on your guard. When she finds out about her daughter, de Gaulle will go to the back burner. That's what we want, but she knows Ryker is under your charge, so you and Ryker will now be her targets. Watch your back, old buddy. I'll get to London as soon as I can."

[London—8:00 p.m. that evening]

Erika made her nightly phone call to Ada just before the girl's bedtime. Mother and daughter would chat briefly, Erika would say good night prayers with Ada over the phone, then when the little girl was tucked in, Erika would sing part of a German lullaby, always being conscious of how much time the call was taking. If the time limit expired, Erika would hang up and call back. It was the highpoint of Erika's day.

"Hello, Grandpapa," Erika said to Sir Louis. "I'm ready to talk to Ada."

"Erika! Your grandmother and I have been waiting for your call! Ada is not here. She was kidnapped from her room sometime during the night

last night by a man named Ryker. This 'Ryker' called on us Monday here at our home and claimed he was an associate of yours. He left a note."

A long pause ensued.

"Erika, are you still there?" Sir Louis asked.

"What's in the note, Grandpapa?"

"This Ryker wants you to turn yourself over to an American embassy. What is happening, Erika? Are you in trouble?"

After another pause, she asked, *"I assume the note is written in English. Read it to me, Grandpapa."*

Louis Minton read the short note word for word.

"Good bye, Grandpapa. I love you and tell Grandmama I love her."

[Washington, two hours later]

When the telephone rang at his home at 2:30 a.m. East Coast time, Leroy Carr expected it to be either Al Hodge or Erika Lehmann. These middle-of-the-night phone calls were getting commonplace. It was neither Hodge nor Erika, but Sheila Reid.

"Erika just called me, Leroy. She said she didn't want to talk to you."

"And."

Sheila said, "She told me to tell you that you can wave goodbye to Axel Ryker, and if anything happens to her daughter, she'll take out Al Hodge and some MI-6 people for good measure."

Nothing Sheila said surprised Leroy Carr, but at least his plan to remove Erika's focus from de Gaulle was so far working.

"Sheila, get me a plane out to London in the morning. You're going with me. We'll take along an Army doctor to watch over you."

Part 3

As you sow, so shall you reap.
— Galatians 6:7

Chapter 22

Saving Lorelei

Paris, France
Next morning—Friday, 15 October 1948

Zhanna Rogova and Kathryn Fischer stepped up into a train from a platform at the Paris station. Last night, Kathryn answered a telephone call from Erika. She and Zhanna were being recalled to London.

[Valencia, Spain—same time]
"Erika called last night, Kay," Stephanie said. "You were in the bath. Our orders have changed. We're staying here until further notice."

"We're not going to Paris?"

"Not for now."

"Why?"

"Erika will be sending us a couple of guests. It will be our job to look after them."

[London—that morning]
Al Hodge was on the phone with Leroy Carr in Washington.

"What time will you arrive in London, Leroy?"

"I fly out from Andrews in two hours. I should be there early-afternoon London time tomorrow. Any word on Kay?"

"None, I'm assuming Kay is still somewhere on the continent."

"How's Erika's little girl?

"The nanny is taking great care of her. She cries for her grandparents at night."

Carr winced. He hated what he was doing, but it was all in an effort to save the child's mother. If Erika were to be implicated in a plot on de Gaulle's life, even if it failed, it would be the end for Erika and there would be nothing he could do about it. Carr was grateful to Roscoe Hillenkoetter for agreeing with him that the French and other allies were not to be informed of the plot. Yet, Carr knew Hillenkoetter had him on the clock with a limited time frame to get this resolved.

"She's hunting Ryker as we speak, Al. He's still at the embassy, right?"

"Yes. I have him under orders not to leave."

"Rescind those orders," Carr said. *"Tell Ryker we still want him sleeping at the embassy, but during the day he can come and go as he pleases."*

"Are you sure about that, Leroy?"

"I'm sure. I'll see you sometime tomorrow. Don't bother picking me up. Sheila is coming with me. She has an embassy car lined up to meet our plane and take us to the consulate. I'll see you there."

"Sheila's back at work?"

"Yes, thank Heaven. Erika isn't going to trust any of us. We'll need Sheila as a liaison. Watch your back, Al. Erika also threatened you."

[London—late that evening]

The cross-Channel ferry delivered Zhanna Rogova and Kathryn Fischer to the eastern coast of Great Britain at 5:00 that afternoon. After a bus ride to London, the two women now sat with Erika Lehmann in the same room in the flea bag hotel near the East End docks she and Zhanna had spent nights together before the Russian left for Paris. It was a good location to lie-low and at that point Erika had seen no reason to change it.

Erika had already filled in her two fellow Shield Maidens on the current situation: mainly that Ada was missing.

"This is the second time my daughter has been used as a pawn to get to me," Erika said. "The first time was by Heinrich Himmler during the war. Rescuing Ada cost Stephanie three years in a Siberian gulag, and nearly cost her life. Leroy believes I'm hunting Ryker, but I know Ryker isn't behind this."

"What makes you think that?" Kathryn asked. "It certainly sounds like something Ryker is capable of."

"Ryker weighs 270 pounds. A stiff, musclebound man like him could not climb up two storeys on a flimsy ivy lattice to my daughter's bedroom window. Secondly, I had my grandfather read me word-for-word the ransom note supposedly left behind by Ryker. Ryker still struggles when writing English. He could not have written such grammatically correct sentences unless he was coached what to write. Al Hodge is behind this, and Al wouldn't have done it without Leroy Carr's permission."

"We have Carr's wife," Zhanna said. "Let's arrange a trade. His wife for your daughter."

Erika countered. "Kay's not part of this and is on our side; we won't betray her. Better to strike at the heart of the beast. We're going to take captive two men: Al Hodge and an MI-6 analyst named Henry Wiltshire. That will send a wakeup call to both the CIA and MI-6 that we're serious."

Chapter 23

Henry meets Ekaterina

London
Next day—Saturday, 16 October 1948

To his relief, Henry Wiltshire had heard no more from Erika Lehmann for a week and a half. This passage of time, along with the fact that he had been assured by his superiors at MI-6 that the woman who was responsible for him spending three years in a German Stalag was now out of his life forever, loosened him up to a night out at his favorite pub.

He was on his third pint when an attractive woman sat down beside him.

"Hello, my name is Ekaterina."

She spoke with a strong Russian accent and wore a neck scarf.

◊ ◊ ◊

Al Hodge had just finished his meal at the Sherlock Holmes Café eight blocks from the American embassy. As he handed the waitress his money, he saw Erika Lehman walk in.

She sat down at his table and said, "Hello, Al."

Kathryn Fischer stood outside the café. She had just taken Hodge's embassy driver out of the picture. The man sat unconscious behind the wheel in the driver's seat.

◊ ◊ ◊

Two hours later, the three Shield Maidens sat in Erika's hotel room. Al Hodge and Henry Wiltshire were bound and gagged in her bedroom.

Kathryn asked the obvious question. "Where are we going to store these guys? It can't be here in London."

"While you and Zhanna were making your way here from Paris, I spoke with your sister. Stephanie recommended a place outside Valencia—a Gypsy camp. These people helped her in Austria and she trusts them. They will guard our hostages for a reasonable amount of money to help their family. Kathryn, I have a small plane reserved for you. The pilot is being paid well and will ask no questions. You'll leave with Al and Henry tonight for Valencia. Zhanna and I will remain here in London for a time."

Chapter 24

Carr in London

London
Next day—Sunday, 17 October 1948

Erika called Leroy Carr's office in Washington this morning and was told that Carr and Sheila Reid were in London. Alice was back on the job in Sheila's absence and released this information to Erika on Carr's orders.

"Contact Leroy with these instructions," Erika told her. "He is to meet me at a pub called the Black Ram in the West End at exactly eight o'clock this evening. He should not arrive early or late. Tell him to bring Sheila. Leroy knows I will be watching. If anyone is shadowing them, I will not appear."

[that evening]
Leroy Carr decided to stay at the Savoy instead of the American embassy. Protocol would require him to brief the ambassador on why he was in London if he stayed at the embassy. Carr wanted to avoid that. He had stayed at the Savoy in the past and was acquainted with the surrounding area. Two hours ago, he received the phone call from Alice telling him of Erika's message. Erika was right, Carr knew it would be useless to try and surveil the meeting place—the highly-trained and shrewd Erika Lehmann could spot surveillance in her sleep. Carr also billeted Sheila Reid at the Savoy. After hanging up from Alice, Carr called Sheila's room and told her of the plans for the evening.

Now, two hours later, Carr and Sheila walked into The Black Ram at exactly eight o'clock. Carr asked for a corner table and they sat down to wait.

"It will be a while before Erika arrives," Sheila said.

"I know," Carr replied. He had not ordered surveillance, but he and Sheila both knew Erika was out there somewhere watching for it. Only after she was satisfied it was safe would she join them. Carr spotted a waiter walking their way. "We might as well get a drink while we wait."

Carr ordered a gin and tonic, Sheila a dark ale from Wales that the pub had on tap.

"Leroy, you filled me in during our flight over about what's going on," Sheila said. "But you didn't tell me about the main issue that's causing the conflict. Is Erika going to receive her citizenship, or not? She deserves it, you know."

"That's what Kay said, and even Al."

"They're right," Sheila retorted.

"You know as well as anyone that Erika has been her own worst enemy. Every time she successfully completes a mission for our country—giving me something I can use to lobby for crimes during the war against her being dropped—she turns around and gets in trouble for something foolish like a bar fight or getting drunk and arrested by the Coast Guard for stealing a boat in the Chesapeake Bay. You're not in my shoes, Sheila. It's all about politics."

"Leroy, we've been together for quite some time. If you trust me, you need to heed what your wife tells you or this is going to end badly. I've been in the trenches with Erika. I know what she is capable of. You can end this tonight by promising Erika she can become a U.S. citizen and be with her daughter. If you don't, your 'politics' will suffer, and you'll have hell to pay which might include you never seeing Kay again."

Carr didn't like her comment but said nothing. It seemed no one understood his predicament, including his wife, Al Hodge, and now Sheila. Carr had what he hoped to be a solution. Tonight, Erika and Sheila would find out about it.

At a quarter to nine, Erika Lehmann walked into the pub. When she spotted them and walked over to their table, she ignored Carr; instead, hugging Sheila, being careful to avoid disturbing her left arm sling.

"How is your shoulder?" Erika asked her.

"The doctors tell me I should be able to remove the sling in a couple of weeks."

"Wonderful," Erika replied.

After she sat down, Erika finally directed her attention to Carr. "I want to see my daughter. I know you're behind all this, Leroy."

"Ada is safe at the American embassy and well taken care of. You can't be seen at the embassy. I'll have Agent Houchen meet you somewhere tomorrow morning. He'll bring Ada."

"Where?"

"You choose."

"Hyde Park. At the playground. Eight o'clock."

"Fine."

"I knew it was you behind taking Ada when my grandfather read me the note," Erika said with a grim look. "Ryker can't write sentences in English that well. And even if he could, he wouldn't do it without orders from you."

"Erika, believe it or not, I did it for you and Ada. It was the only way to flush you out. If you keep going on your present course, you'll be dead. A dead mother will do nothing for Ada. If you want Ada returned to your grandparents, I'll have Agent Houchen do that, but if I were you I'd leave Ada at the embassy. She's safer there."

"Why?"

"MI-6 knows of your threat against de Gaulle. They don't hesitate to do whatever they think necessary. They might come up with the same idea I did in order to make you surface. If that happens, you won't know where Ada is and neither will I."

"My grandparents have to be worried sick."

"Contact them and tell them you found the kidnapper and now have Ada at the American embassy for her safety. Tell them they can visit her anytime they wish. I'll let the embassy people know. What's your decision? Is Ada staying at the embassy or returning to your grandparents? It's up to you."

Erika stared at Carr for a long moment. "Embassy. I'll call my grandparents as soon as we're done here."

Carr nodded. "What do you want to drink—a brandy?"

"No, I'll have what Sheila is drinking."

Her ale was ordered.

"Leroy," Erika said. "I'm sure you know by now that Al and Henry Wiltshire have disappeared."

"Yes, I know that. You need to listen very closely, Erika. You are on a fast track to disaster. If it were to leak out to the French that a CIA agent even threatened to kill de Gaulle, Ada would be middle-aged before you get out of prison. If you actually attempted it, you would be hunted down and whatever country you were eventually found in, the French would insist on extradition back to France where you would be guillotined. I hated having to take Ada away from your grandparents, but is being on the run until you're caught what you want for Ada? I'm trying to save your life, Erika. Of course, I have some conditions. Kay remains safe. I accept the fact now that she is trying to help you and doing so of her own free will. Regardless, unexpected things can happen. Kay has to be protected."

"Both Kathryn and Stephanie are now with Kay. They won't let anything happen to her." Erika said.

"Then I take it Zhanna is here with you in London."

"That's right."

"This plan is going to be difficult and dangerous," Carr warned. "The odds are against us, and I don't mean slightly against us, but heavily against us. Yet, if by some miracle it would happen to work, my government will have little choice but to either drop all previous charges or grant a pardon."

The conversation at The Black Ram between Leroy Carr, Erika Lehmann, and Sheila Reid would last for three hours.

After Carr had laid out the plan and answered numerous questions, he ended with. "I want Al released. Tell him to call me. Sheila will stay here in London. Keep Henry Wiltshire captive for now. If he's released, he'll spill his guts and tell MI-6 where you have everyone holed up. I have to return to Washington for the plan to work, and if MI-6 finds out I'm in London they'll want to know why. Find Axel Ryker and give him his orders. I gave him freedom to leave the embassy during the day and I told him to cooperate with you. You won't have any trouble finding him, but he as yet knows no details about what we've just talked about. He won't believe those orders from you so tell him to call me when I get back to Washington and I'll validate."

"You're not demanding that Kay be released?"

"Kay doesn't want to be released. Demanding that would be useless. She can be as hard-headed as you. Plus, you're going to need her. You told me she is no longer in Barcelona but I'm guessing she and the Fischer sisters are still in Spain. Just ensure her safety, Erika. That has to be your first and biggest priority."

When they eventually parted on the street, Erika left bewildered by Carr's strange plan. The only thing she knew for certain was that she had to find Axel Ryker and release Al Hodge.

She would go along with any uncanny scheme if it offered even a remote chance of giving her the opportunity to make a life with her daughter. And there was another reason. She was more than willing to sacrifice her life to kill Charles de Gaulle but doing so would drag the other Shield Maidens down with her. She would give Carr's outrageous idea a try for her friends' sakes.

Chapter 25

Hyde Park and a Warning for Earl

London
Next day—Monday, 18 October 1948

The meeting between mother and daughter in Hyde Park was bittersweet. When Ada saw her mother she rushed to her, but as soon as she was in Erika's arms the child told her she wanted her Mumaw and Pap.

"They will visit you this afternoon, my angel."

Earl Houchen walked some distance away to give mother and daughter some privacy.

"It's best for now that you stay at the place the nice men have taken you. They are treating you well, I'm sure."

"Mummy, they gave me a puppy." Ada spoke with a British accent.

"That's wonderful. What did you name him?"

"It's a girl puppy. I named her Noodles because she likes spaghetti."

Erika smiled. "That's very clever, angel."

Erika took her time. After she and Ada had talked for a while, Erika pushed her daughter on a swing and watched her climb on the monkey bars. Adelaide had inherited athleticism from her parents along with her mother's bright blonde hair. It was as if Erika looked back in time at herself as a seven-year-old.

Finally, and reluctantly, it was time to part.

"The nice man will now take you back, angel. Remember, Mumaw and Pap will visit you this afternoon. Now, I want to talk to the nice man for a moment." Erika hugged her daughter tightly and kissed her goodbye, then drew Earl Houchen aside. Talking softly, so Ada could not overhear, Erika said, "You better do your job, Earl. If anything happens to my daughter, I'll slit you open from your asshole to your appetite."

◊ ◊ ◊

[Spain—same morning]

Al Hodge and Henry Wiltshire had just been delivered to the Gypsy camp in a forest ten miles outside Valencia. An airport wasn't needed. Kathryn had the pilot land the plane in a pasture. Back in London, when they were loaded into the small, four-seater, overhead wing plane, Kathryn held a gun on the two men until they were in the air. After they were airborne, she put the gun away. There was nothing Al Hodge could do at 8,000 feet, and Henry Wiltshire wasn't a threat.

When the plane set down, her sister Stephanie and Raval, the Gypsy king, and two other members of the clan (all well-armed) were waiting with mules. Most of the clan spoke only Romanian or Spanish, although Raval also spoke German. Kay Carr would have her work cut out for her as interpreter.

[London—same day]

Last night at The Black Ram, Leroy Carr told Erika that he had given Axel Ryker permission to leave the embassy during the day. Erika knew a man like Ryker would not be hard to intercept. Carr stressed that making the plan work was up to her, and for it to work, he had to return to Washington. The plan could not be successful if he remained in London, drawing suspicion from both his own embassy and MI-6. Sheila Reid would stay behind at the Savoy to act as liaison between Carr, Erika, and Al Hodge.

[Spain—that evening]

This was the second time Henry Wiltshire had ended up a captive because of Maggie Harrison—the woman he now knew as Erika Lehmann. He couldn't avoid the thought that the woman was a curse on his life. On this cool evening, he sat near the campfire. Besides the Gypsies who held him hostage was the American CIA agent he had met in Sir James' office, and two mysterious women. One had been on the airplane that brought him here from London. The other had not been identified to him but he thought he noticed some familial resemblance.

Wiltshire had no idea who they were but assumed they were CIA or affiliated with it.

[back to London—same evening]

The pouring rain that splashed on the red cobblestones gave the illusion of tiny electrical sparks exploding under the street lanterns as Erika kept an eye on the American embassy from a dark alley across the street. Watching the drops splash reminded her of her late father. When she was a child, he told her the splashing raindrops were dancing fairies.

At a few minutes after seven o'clock, Axel Ryker walked out of the front gate on the consulate grounds, opened for him by a U.S. Marine wearing a rain poncho. Ryker held no umbrella to protect him; instead, relying on a dark gray trench coat and his porkpie hat to keep the rain at bay.

Staying on the opposite side of the street and avoiding the street lanterns, Erika shadowed him under an umbrella for three blocks until she saw him enter a pub. Axel Ryker was easy to tail. The monstrous former Gestapo hitman rarely concerned himself with being followed. He had as little fear of an enemy following him as a killer whale had concern of being stalked by a porpoise.

Ryker had eaten dinner at the embassy, so food was not ordered. He had been in the pub long enough to order a pint, which had already been delivered. Ryker always sat facing the door and he saw her when she entered. He and Erika Lehmann spotted each other immediately. She collapsed her umbrella, shook it off, and walked to his table.

Not waiting for an invitation, Erika sat down across from him.

"I've been expecting you, Sonderführer," Ryker said. Sonderführer had been Erika's rank when she worked for Abwehr during the war.

"I've asked you not to call me that."

He ignored her and took a drink from his pint.

"Ryker, I know you had no part in taking my daughter from my grandparent's home other than writing the message you were instructed to write."

"I obey my orders, Sonderführer."

"Leroy also told me his plan, and that he ordered you to be at my disposal. Your orders from him are to obey my orders. Is that correct?"

"Yes. Now, as the Americans say, get to the point. I'm growing weary of you and I want to enjoy my ale in silence."

The waiter stopped by the table. Erika told the man she wouldn't be ordering. After he walked away, she told Ryker what she wanted him to do.

"I will confirm these orders with Herr Carr," Ryker said.

"By all means. Leroy left for Washington this morning," Erika responded. "He should arrive tomorrow morning Washington time. He expects your call."

Chapter 26

Workout Surprise

Valencia, Spain
Next morning—Tuesday, 19 October 1948

Kathryn stayed with Al Hodge and Henry Wiltshire at the Gypsy camp, while Stephanie, who had been charged with guarding Kay, returned to the Caro Hotel with her at night.

The call from Erika came shortly before 7:00 a.m. Erika told Stephanie that Kathryn was to take Hodge to the American consulate in Barcelona and release him (there was no U.S. embassy in Valencia). Then Kathryn was to return to the Gypsy camp where Henry Wiltshire was to remain the captive of Raval and his clan.

"What about Kay?" Stephanie asked.

"Nothing changes with Kay for now," Erika answered. "Stay with her, Stephanie. She has to remain safe. Last night I had a long talk with Leroy. I'll tell you and Kathryn what's going on but I don't want to do it over the telephone. I'll see you soon."

[Washington, later that morning]

Axel Ryker didn't like taking orders from Erika Lehmann, and as he had promised her, he called Leroy Carr. He reached the CIA Deputy Director at his E Street office.

Ryker filled in Carr about his orders from Erika and expressed his displeasure at being subject to a woman, especially Erika Lehmann.

"I confirm your orders she issued you, Ryker. Is there anything about her orders you don't understand?"

"Yes, I don't understand why I have to answer to one of Canaris's Abwehr embassy sluts."

"You're living in the past, Ryker. Canaris is dead and your beloved Nazi Party has been smashed. The only thing that you should concern yourself with now is the continued support of the CIA, which is the only thing that is keeping your neck out of a noose. My protection of you only continues as long as you obey orders to the letter. Is that understood?"

"I always fulfill my orders, Herr Carr. I did this for Reichsführer Himmler. Now, I do this for you."

"Ryker, you've said this to me before and I hate the comparison. Just do your job for the United States. Consider Erika your current Heinrich Himmler."

Tired from the journey, worried about his wife, and fed up with Ryker, Carr slammed down the receiver.

[late that afternoon]

Ian Minton had finished his day as a bricklayer an hour ago and was now working the speed bag at the Druid's Gym when Zhanna Rogova walked in. Concentrating on the frenzy of the speed bag, he didn't see her. She tapped on his shoulder.

"Hello, Ian."

He stopped his punches and, sweating profusely, turned to see who was interrupting his workout.

"Zhanna! I'm surprised. Is the conference in Helsinki over?"

"Yes."

Ian removed his gloves. "Brilliant! May I take you to dinner?"

"Very well. If that is your wish," Zhanna replied.

"I'll take a quick shower and get dressed."

An hour later, they were sitting at a table at The Black Ram with drinks on the table. Although Ian was at Erika's grandparents' house when Axel Ryker appeared at the door that day, he had not been back there since and had no idea of anything that had happened after that, including that Ada had been taken from the home.

When Zhanna realized this, she avoided mentioning it. He would want to know how she knew about it. She'd have to let him find out the next time he visited Erika's grandparents.

"How long will you be in London, Zhanna?"

"We have no way of knowing. Erika and I might be sent somewhere else together or separately depending on the languages they need translated. Or we might be ordered back to America if they have nothing more for us here in Europe at this time."

"Sounds like an exciting life—the travel, meeting important people and all that."

"Yes, sometimes it can be exciting, then sometimes it can be quite boring. Many times, long hours of sitting around with nothing to do happens while waiting for things to get started."

"I want to continue seeing you, Zhanna. While you remain in London, I want you go out with me every night. One night we'll have dinner, another night a movie or whatever you want to do." Ian grinned. "I'll buy you all the popcorn you can eat."

Zhanna looked at him, bemused.

[later]

It was late when Zhanna returned to the hotel in the East End. Tonight, when she and Ian parted, they kissed for the first time other than the brief kisses Zhanna had given him for winning the boxing match.

Erika was sitting at the kitchen table looking over some papers.

"Where have you been, Zhanna. I need to go over a lot of things with you concerning our change of plans."

"I went to see Ian at his boxing place."

"His gym?"

"Yes, his 'gym'."

"He couldn't have been training until this late hour."

"We went out to dinner. You're nosing in my affairs again, Erika."

Erika looked at her, grinned, and said good-naturedly, "You're full of shit, Zhanna."

"That's an insult and I don't like it."

"I don't care what you don't like. You tell me you have no feelings for Ian. It's obvious that you do. That means you're full of shit."

"He is nothing more than a distraction for me. Something to keep me from dying of boredom, that's all."

"Okay, whatever you say. Going over these plans can wait until tomorrow."

Zhanna replied, “As long as it’s not tomorrow evening. Ian is taking me to a movie.”

Chapter 27

Zhanna puts in a Request

Spain
Next day—Wednesday, 20 October 1948

Yesterday, Al Hodge was released. From the American consulate in Barcelona he called Leroy Carr. After receiving his orders, an airplane flew him to the main U.S. embassy in Madrid. A couple of hours later he was onboard another plane and on his way out of Spain. The Lockheed Electra carrying Hodge sat down outside Paris at four o'clock in the morning.

Henry Wiltshire was forced to remain behind at the Gypsy camp where he was never out of sight of Kathryn or one of Raval's men. Stephanie continued to stay with Kay Carr in their Valencia hotel room.

[London—that afternoon]
Earlier today, in the morning, Earl Houchen again brought Ada to Hyde Park to see her mother.

Now it was afternoon and Erika had been going over Leroy Carr's plans with Zhanna for two hours.

"Your target will be at least a quarter of a mile away, Zhanna," Erika said. "Can you make the shot?"

"That's four-hundred and forty yards. It will take the projectile 0.6 seconds to reach my target. From that distance, much depends on the weather, most of all any wind or rain. For example, a ten-mile-per-hour crosswind at four hundred and forty yards would require a scope adjustment of twenty inches. I will also have to consider . . . what is the English word for *vlazhost?*

"Humidity."

"Yes. Humidity—wind and humidity. If you can get me my old friend—a Mosin-Nagant 91/30 sniper rifle with a P/U scope, I'll make the shot."

[London—that evening]
Tonight's main feature at the Hippodrome was *The Ghost and Mrs. Muir* staring Gene Tierney and Rex Harrison. Although the film had been released nine months ago, it was still popular and continued to draw crowds to the theaters. Neither Ian nor Zhanna had yet seen the movie.

After Ian purchased their tickets, he didn't bother to ask Zhanna if she wanted popcorn. He bought her a large bucket from the concession stand along with an Orange Crush soda before they settled into their seats.

"I liked Gene Tierney in *Laura,"* Zhanna said.

"You've seen that movie?"

"Near the end of the war. We were allies with the Americans and they sent us Hollywood films. I saw it is Moscow during a leave from the front. I didn't understand English then so I had to read the subtitles. For this movie, I'll be able to understand her. What is this movie about?"

"A widow-lady falls in love with a ghost."

"A ghost?"

"That's what I read in the Times theater section."

It occurred to Zhanna that such a plot might apply to her relationship to Ian, only reversed. She was the ghost.

Chapter 28

Plausible Deniability

Washington, D.C.
Next day—Thursday, 21 October 1948

Leroy Carr's plane landed at Andrews Air Force Base yesterday. He now had Sheila Reid on the telephone. Sheila was headquartered at the Savoy under guise of being a tourist. The U.S. Army major was ordered by Carr to not have any contact with the American or British embassies, and to not wear her Army uniform while she was there.

Carr knew MI-6 had Savoy switchboard operators in its fold monitoring calls because of the significant number of foreign diplomats and political figures who stayed there when in London. For that reason, the conversation would necessarily be in code.

"Hello, Sheila."

"Hello, Uncle David."

"Are you enjoying your vacation in London?"

"It's wonderful. Everyone is so friendly."

"I received your post card yesterday." Carr said.

"I'm glad." This told Sheila that yesterday Al Hodge arrived in Paris.

"Have you seen the Tower of London yet." The "Tower' was Axel Ryker.

"Not yet, Uncle."

"You must see it as soon as possible—so much history there. Call me after your visit."

"I will definitely go there tomorrow."

"Have you heard from your cousin?" Carr asked. The *cousin* was Erika.

"Yes, she calls every day."

Carr had ordered Erika to check in daily with Sheila for any updates.

"That's good. How's the weather in London?"

"It's been very nice. A little cool in the evenings and foggy most nights, but nothing unpleasant."

This told Carr there were no new developments at this time.

"I'll let you go," Carr said. "I've taken up enough of your time. Give me a ring after you've visited the Tower."

He used the word *ring* instead of the more common American word of *call.* This told Sheila that the next time she called Carr (after she spoke with Ryker), she was to use a telephone booth in another part of London so they could talk freely.

[Paris—50 minutes later]

Al Hodge had now been patched through to Leroy Carr in Washington. They had talked briefly yesterday after Hodge arrived in France but the call was placed from the Paris airport and was not secure. Hodge was now on a pay telephone outside a café on the Left Bank.

"Tell me what you know, Al."

Hodge said, "Wiltshire and I were taken to a Gypsy camp outside Valencia. Apparently, these are the same Gypsies that helped Stephanie and Inka—that young girl she brought with her from Bratislava—escape from the Soviet zone to the American zone in Austria last summer. What are the chances of coming across this same Gypsy clan?"

"We've been in this business long enough to know stranger things have happened, Al."

"You're right there. Anyway, it was me, Wiltshire, and Kathryn at the camp. I didn't see Kay or Kathryn's sister."

"They have to be in the area. It's Stephanie's Gypsy friends. Erika said Stephanie would be watching over Kay. They have to be in town somewhere."

"That's what I figure. What's up next?"

"Just hold tight in Paris for now. Erika and Zhanna should join the group in Spain soon. Sheila will be in touch. From here on out I can't have any more contact with anyone other than Sheila. To save Erika, I have to have plausible deniability to the Senate and State Department when the shit hits the fan."

"Copy that, Leroy, and I agree. I'll contact Sheila from here on out. No one knows that Lehmann is a pain-in-the-ass more than me, but you're doing the right thing by giving her daughter a chance to have a real mother. Lehmann is a blonde thug, but from what I've seen in the past she's a good mother. The thing that haunts me, the thing I can't get out of my mind, is that Rogova is a key player in this scheme."

"Zhanna has a bond with Erika and the other Maidens," Carr replied.

"Rogova is as crazy as an outhouse rat. You know that, Leroy."

Carr didn't comment on the assessment. *"You're in charge from here on out, Al."*

"Alright, Leroy. You know what the chances of this succeeding are, but we'll ty our best."

"The key is that it has to be done on November 11th. Not a day before or a day after."

"ROGER."

Both men hung up their telephone.

[same day—five hours later]

It was late afternoon when Erika and Zhanna sat down to talk.

"Zhanna," Erika started out, "you and I are leaving for Spain tomorrow."

After an uncomfortable pause, Zhanna said, "I can't leave tomorrow. I am going on a date with Ian tonight, tomorrow, and Saturday."

"No, you're not. Tomorrow we leave for Spain. See him tonight and tell him you and I have been ordered to fly back to Washington tomorrow. Those are your orders."

"Orders from who?" (Zhanna never used *whom,* a word that she had yet to figure out the proper English language usage).

"From me. Go on your date with my cousin tonight and tell him you're returning to America." Erika softened, learned over and kissed the Russian on the cheek. "Please do this, Zhanna. We can't do it without you."

◊ ◊ ◊

[that evening]

A traveling carnival was spending a week in London, setting up in Greenwich Park. This is where Ian took Zhanna. They had stood in a long line but were now finally on deck to ride the Ferris wheel.

"I hope you're not afraid of heights, Zhanna," Ian said jokingly.

"I'm not," she said as they sat down in a two-person gondola.

When the wheel was fully loaded and began turning in earnest, Ian put his arm around Zhanna's shoulder. It was a clear night and when they reached the zenith, the lights of downtown London could be seen across the Thames. Big Ben insisted it was 7:55. Ian pointed out Ben, but other than that, little was said.

After the ride, they walked through the carnival. Children excitedly played the various carnival games hoping to win a stuffed animal or any toy, while parents or grandparents stood patiently nearby smiling.

"Are there carnivals like this in Russia?" Ian asked.

"Of course. Gorky Park in Moscow has a huge circus carnival every year. Other cities, as well. The city I'm from, Leningrad, has a Christmas festival and carnival that is very popular."

"I didn't know they celebrated Christmas in Russia. I thought the Soviets did away with anything having to do with religion."

"They try, but many people refuse to give up old customs and still go to church. The government allows Christmas festivities but insists it be called Winter Festival, but that's mostly ignored and most people still call it Christmas. The Orthodox church refuses to go away, and the Politburo doesn't want that conflict with the people at this point in time. The main focus now is rebuilding after the war."

After a few more steps, Zhanna asked, "Do you believe in God, Ian?"

"All I have to do is look up in the sky at all the stars and think of the people and creatures on this earth. Yes, I believe in God."

"So, as an Englishman, I assume you are a Christian?"

"Yes. What religion are you, Zhanna?"

"I don't deserve a religion or God's grace. I've told you about some of my past."

"None of us deserve it, Zhanna. Christ died so we can be redeemed."

As they continued walking, Ian suggested they get something to eat when he spotted a food stand. He ordered four hotdogs and two soda pops. He was breaking his training diet but being with Zhanna made it worth it to him.

"I thought hotdogs were an American food," Zhanna commented as Ian handed her two.

"I believe they are, but our little island swarmed with Yank soldiers in the year leading up to D-Day so we've had hotdogs ever since."

"Yes, I've learned that the Americans love their hotdogs and chewing gum," Zhanna added.

Ian put his hand on Zhanna's lower back to lead her away. His hand was where she normally carried her handgun in the waist of her pants. Because of that, she was glad she didn't bring it along tonight; though, she did carry her dagger strapped to her leg just above her right ankle.

When the hotdogs were eaten, Ian noticed a carnival booth where children used dart pistols to try and win prizes by shooting cardboard ducks. "Would you like to try this, Zhanna?"

"If you wish."

Ian paid the carnie and Zhanna picked up the dart pistol. Ducks dropped like flies until the carnie finally brought it to a halt. "Give me a break, lady,"

Zhanna walked away with the largest prize, a huge stuffed giraffe.

"I'd like some popcorn now," she told Ian.

◊ ◊ ◊

Four hours later, Erika Lehmann sat in the living area of the shabby East End hotel looking over paperwork when Zhanna Rogova walked in carrying a four-foot stuffed giraffe.

"Did you tell Ian you're leaving London tomorrow?" Erika asked.

"No."

"Why not? Those were your orders."

"Because I'm not going to Spain tomorrow. I'm staying here in London."

Chapter 29

Unforeseen Delay

Valencia, Spain
Next day—22 October 1948

Stephanie Fischer was expecting the morning call. Erika had told her that she would call her at the hotel in Valencia before she and Zhanna left today for Spain.

"Hello," Stephanie said.

"Hello, Steph. How's Kay?"

"She's getting dressed. Everything is fine. What time will you be here? Kay and I will meet your plane."

"There's a problem and we're not coming today."

"What is it?"

"Zhanna is in love with my cousin and refuses to leave London."

"You must be joking! Zhanna told you she loves him?"

"No. She would never admit that to me or anyone else. She probably wouldn't even tell Ian because she won't admit it to herself, but she's in love with him."

"What are you going to do?" Stephanie and Kathryn did not yet know of Leroy Carr's maneuver that Erika had agreed to try. The sisters still thought Erika and Zhanna were set on killing Charles de Gaulle if Erika didn't receive a pardon.

"Zhanna and I will be there, but it might take a couple of days. I'll contact you when I can tell you something more. How is Henry Wiltshire holding up."

"Poor man. He probably feels like he's on a different planet at the Roma camp, but he won't be harmed, and he won't escape. When you get here, bring more money for Raval and his clan. Their time at the Flamenco cantina has ended and they are ready to move on. It will take more money to keep them here. The money you gave me is disappearing faster than planned."

"Okay. I'll be there with Zhanna as soon as I pry her away from my cousin."

[Paris, France—that afternoon]

Al Hodge was on the phone with Sheila Reid in London.

"Have you heard from Lorelei?" Hodge asked.

"Nothing yet," Sheila answered.

[London—that evening]

Erika gave Zhanna an ultimatum but included a compromise with the demand—Zhanna could have her dates with Ian tonight and tomorrow night, then on Sunday the two women would leave for Spain. Erika reminded Zhanna that they were no longer rogue and were back working for Leroy Carr. If she refused orders, the Americans would withdraw her protection. Erika didn't like threatening Zhanna but felt the Russian had backed her into a corner. Her daughter's future was at stake. Zhanna reluctantly agreed, knowing if the Americans pulled the rug out from under her, she would be at the mercy of the Soviets.

Chapter 30

The Date is Confirmed

London
Next day—Saturday, 23 October 1948

Sheila Reid finally received a phone call from Erika this morning. The two women had just finished lunch in the busy Savoy restaurant where, because of the close proximity of other diners, they refrained from discussing topical matters. Now they sat in Sheila's hotel room.

"I'm glad your shoulder is healing," Erika said to her fellow Shield Maiden.

Sheila had removed the sling (against the doctor's advice). She still had very limited mobility in her left arm.

"It's fine, Erika. We can talk shop now. Leroy said he filled you in on what you have to do."

"Yes, he did."

"And it has to be done on November 11th."

"That's right," Erika replied.

"My duty is liaison with Al Hodge. Leroy cannot be contacted, so fill me in. What are your immediate plans?"

"Zhanna, Ryker, and I will leave for Spain tomorrow. Kay, Kathryn, and Stephanie are already there. We'll train for the mission there until it's time to leave for Paris."

"Is there anything I can do? I want this to work out for you, Erika. I can channel you funds through a secret CIA account in Cuba that the Senate oversight committee will never find out about."

"Thanks, Sheila. I have money but getting paid back if I'm alive at the end of this would be nice. Other than that, there's nothing I need right now. I found Zhanna the rifle she wanted on the black market. If we need anything, I'll let you know."

"Where are you staying in Spain?"

"Zhanna and I will stay at a hotel in Valencia called the Caro. That's where Kay and Stephanie are right now. Kathryn is with Henry Wiltshire at a Gypsy camp outside of town. I'm going to send Ryker to the Gypsy camp to relieve Kathryn. She can join us at the hotel where we can all work together on the plan."

"Okay, Al is already in Paris. I'll contact him and fill him in. Keep me up to date."

"I will. Tell Al I'll contact him as soon as we get to France."

[that evening]

Last night, Ian took Zhanna to another movie. Tonight, it was dinner at his flat and then a trip to a dance hall in the London borough of Camden. Zhanna had to take charge of guiding Ian through the dances. When the band took a break, it gave them a chance to sit down, much to Ian's relief because his lack of dancing skills embarrassed him.

The dance hall served only ale or Coca-Cola, so ale was the drink before them on their table.

"Where did you learn to dance, Zhanna?"

"Watching American movies, and your cousin, Erika, taught me some steps. We have traditional dances in Russia, but they are much different from this American swing music."

"Tell me about your parents and your growing up days in Leningrad."

"I never knew my parents," Zhanna responded. "I was raised in a state-run orphanage, which I fled from when I was fourteen years old."

"Why?"

"Girls were discharged from the orphanage at age sixteen. Most became prostitutes to survive."

"What did you do at age fourteen after leaving the orphanage?"

"I lived on the streets of Leningrad by doing whatever it took to endure. Six years later, when the war broke out, I joined the army."

Ian dropped the subject. She had already told him about her wartime duties as a sniper for the Soviet military. (She had not told him about her time near the end of the war as an assassin for SMERSH.)

Zhanna would honor her compromise with Erika. She had little choice.

"Ian, I'm leaving London tomorrow."

The disappointment in his face was palpable.

"Where are you going?"

"I can't tell you." Erika had told her to tell Ian she was being recalled to Washington, but she decided not to lie.

"When will you return?" he asked.

"I don't know."

"How can I get in touch with you, Zhanna?"

"I will call you when I can."

"When will that be?"

"I don't know, Ian."

Chapter 31

A Promise from Maggie Harrison

Spain
Next day—Sunday, 24 October 1948

At mid-afternoon, the same airplane manned by the same pilot that flew Kathryn Fischer, Al Hodge, and Henry Wiltshire to a pasture outside Valencia now dropped out of low clouds and landed on a packed gravel runway at the small Valencia airfield. Erika, Zhanna, and Axel Ryker were onboard.

Being hired for two flights to Spain within a week's time was something new and unusual for the British pilot, and he didn't care that during the first flight a woman had held a gun on the two men until they were in the air. To be honest, he didn't care who these people were or why on this second flight their luggage included something that to him looked like a case for a hunting rifle. The rough-looking, scarred-face man onboard weighed as much as two normal passengers so his fuel costs would be more than the first trip, but he was happy with the agreement. For what he was being paid he would have flown Scar Face Al Capone and his Tommy gun to Valencia.

Stephanie and Kay met them at the airfield with a rented car. With only an approximate time of when the plane might arrive, they had waited for five hours. They lingered for all that time because Erika wanted to visit the Gypsy camp before going to the hotel so Ryker could relieve Kathryn.

◊ ◊ ◊

As with many Gypsy clans, this one was made up mostly of relatives: fathers, mothers, brothers, sisters, cousins and their wives or husbands with their children. Raval, the king of this clan, sat just outside one of several canvas-covered wagons and looked at the woman and man as they sat around the campfire eating rabbit stew from wooden bowls with wooden spoons. Raval spoke German—the only one in the clan that spoke a language other than Romanian or Spanish. Since the woman spoke German all communication had to go through her. The middle-aged man spoke English and French, but Raval didn't understand those languages.

The reason he had agreed to guard the man was because of the woman's sister who he knew from a time in Austria not long ago. That, and his family was being paid. Roma clans were outcasts and moved often from town to town around Europe where they sang and danced, offering fortune telling to local engaged women, games of chance for men, and other things that could earn money. It was common for the Roma to steal chickens and vegetables from farmers in order to eat. Some clans even prostituted their women to remain together, but Raval refused to do this. His family getting paid to guard this man from England was a stroke of luck.

As dinner neared its end, an automobile appeared, bumping over the forest trail his wagons had used to reach this clearing outside of town. Five people had crammed into the car and when the doors opened, Stephanie, the clan's friend from Austria, emerged from the driver's seat. A large man got out of the front passenger door. From the back seat, three women emerged, one was a blonde; one was a raven-haired woman wearing a neck scarf; and the other was a woman wearing a hat and jacket that looked somewhat like the style Raval had seen worn by American women in some of the larger European cities.

Stephanie introduced the people to the clan king. Their stay would be brief, but before leaving, Erika walked over and sat down on a log beside Henry Wiltshire.

"How are you, Henry?" She spoke in the British accent she used as Margaret Harrison.

He ignored her.

"Kathryn will be leaving you tonight. That large man over there will take his place. He'll help the Roma keep you safe."

Henry finally spoke. "You mean Axel Ryker the war criminal will keep me safe? That's a kind way of saying I'm a prisoner."

Erika had to think fast. She wasn't expecting Wiltshire to recognize Ryker but then Wiltshire worked for MI-6. She couldn't tell Wiltshire that Ryker now worked for the Americans.

"I ran into him in Argentina last year. He's still on the run and works as a mercenary to whomever will hire him. The Americans are hunting him, as well. I hire him when I need him but keep it quite hush hush. You won't betray me, will you darling?"

"Please don't call me *darling*. If you don't murder me in my sleep and I make it home, I'll tell Sir James everything."

"Of course you will. You are steadfast for your country. Yet, it's not time to concern ourselves with that, is it now?" She stood up. "I have to leave you but will visit now and then. Don't try to escape from Ryker and the Gypsies, Henry. I promise that you won't be harmed if you do not try to escape."

"A promise from Maggie Harrison—that's certainly a jewel."

"Don't try to escape," she warned again, this time more ominously. "It won't end well for you, Henry."

[Two hours later—the Caro Hotel]

The Shield Maidens and Kay Carr were now back in Kay's hotel room. From a street vendor, Erika bought everyone Valencian paellas. This was a popular, local rice dish with shrimp, squash, and beans. Stephanie and Kay had bought them from this particular street vendor before. They were similar to the paella's the two women had enjoyed in Barcelona. The helpings were generous but everyone was very hungry so Erika bought everyone two. The vendor served up each paella in a thin, disposable tin plate covered by tin foil.

In the hotel room, Kay watched the four hearty Shield Maidens engulf their food like slobs. All of them consumed their two paellas before she had finished her first. In fact, one was enough for her.

"I can't eat another one of these," Kay said. "Is anyone still hungry?"

Kay's second Paella was quickly divided and disappeared within seconds. If someone were to ask Kay to describe the Shield Maidens, she wasn't sure what adjectives she would use. All were attractive women and could display feminine charms when needed, but many times acted more like hardened male convicts than ladies. And she had seen with her own eyes in South America how cruel they could be.

"Kay," Erika said, "would you mind going to your bedroom while I speak with Zhanna, Kathryn, and Stephanie?"

"I'm not going anywhere," Kay said strongly. "I went against my husband's wishes in order to support you. I want to be included. I've earned that much."

Erika looked at her for a moment. "You're right, Kay."

Erika started the briefing. Zhanna already knew of the change of plans, the Fischer sisters and Kay heard it for the first time.

It took Erika about forty-five minutes, maybe fifty, to give everyone the basics about Leroy Carr's alternative to killing de Gaulle. When she finished, she said, "Leroy cannot be contacted by any of us from here on out until the plan either succeeds or fails." Erika then looked at Kay. "Kay, that includes you. You asked to be included."

After hearing the plan, the old saw immediately went through Kay's mind—*Be careful what you ask for.*

Erika ended with, "We begin training tomorrow."

Chapter 32

Secret Phone Call

Paris
Next day—Monday, 25 October 1948

Al Hodge had a room at the Hotel Napoleon, the same hotel Zhanna and Kathryn had stayed at two weeks ago. He chose that hotel for the same reason the two Shield Maidens did. It was within easy walking distance to the Arc de Triomphe.

Hodge was back in his room after breakfast when he received a phone call from London.

"Hello," Hodge said.

"Al, it's Sheila."

"Yes, Sheila."

"Erika called me this morning. They are all now in Spain and she said they would start training today."

"Anything else?" Hodge asked.

"Erika said Kay insisted on being included."

"Erika told her no, right?"

"I'm afraid not."

"Holy Mother of God!"

"We can't contact Leroy," Sheila said. *"What are you going to do about it?"*

"I want to talk to Lehmann ASAP."

"I can't do it, Al. Leroy's orders."

Hodge had no other ideas except, "Next time you talk to Lehmann, tell her to call me at the Hotel Napoleon in Paris."

"I'll tell her, but I know Erika and she won't do it, Al. She's not going to contact you until the team gets to Paris. Those are her orders from Leroy; you know that."

"We go through this crap with Lehmann on almost every mission. Now she has Kay mixed up it this. I'm so tired of her shit." He paused, then said, "Next time she contacts you, call me immediately. That's all we can do for now."

When they hung up, the injured Shield Maiden had to smile. Erika had put Al Hodge through the wringer so many times it was becoming comical.

[Valencia, Spain]

It was Kay Carr's habit to take a daily walk. Of course, Stephanie's job was to walk with her. Kay, Sheila Reid, and the Fischer sisters knew something Erika, Zhanna, and Ryker did not. Far from ignoring her husband's wishes, Kay now worked with the Fischer sisters to save Erika from herself. It was Erika's threat against Charles de Gaulle that made them go into action. They knew Erika, and knew she wasn't bluffing. Any attempt on de Gaulle's life, even if it failed, would end Erika's life either by death or life imprisonment. The Fischer sisters felt that if they didn't intercede they would be abandoning their friend. To put it simply, Carr, Hodge, Sheila, and the Fischer sisters had entered into an intrigue to save Erika. Carr felt he couldn't trust the erratic behavior of Zhanna Rogova, or the menacing comportments of Axel Ryker so they were not included.

Only after he had the Fischer sisters onboard could Leroy Carr propose his alternate scheme to Erika. He managed to meet with Kathryn and Stephanie privately during his brief stay in London, which was the reason for that trip from Washington. Both sisters realized Erika had set her course for disaster, and at that meeting they agreed to work with Carr.

After a five-block walk from the hotel, Kay found a phone booth. Stephanie waited outside. The tedious wait to be connected to the United States took longer than usual. Luckily, Kay had brought along plenty of Spanish coins. Finally, she got through to her husband at his E Street office.

"Hello," he said.

"Hello, David. It's Lauren," Kay said.

"Yes, Lauren."

"I'm in," Kay said, which told Leroy that Erika was including her in the plan.

"I understand. Is Ann there?" (Stephanie's codename for this mission.)

"She's here, do you want to talk to her?"

"Yes."

Kay opened the folding phone booth door and handed the receiver to Stephanie who stepped inside.

"This is Ann."

"Is the man with the porkpie hat with the Brit?" The 'Brit' was Henry Wiltshire. Axel Ryker always wore a porkpie hat.

"Yes. Can we release the Brit and send the hat back to you? This would help simplify things."

"No. If the Brit returns home he'll tell everything then we'll have his mother scouring your area." 'Mother' was MI-6. *"We're nearing the end of our time. Put Lauren back on."*

"Yes, David," Kay said after Stephanie handed her back the receiver.

"We have only nine seconds. Stay safe, Lauren, and stay in touch. If things get dicey, bail out."

"I'm going to see this through, David. Regardless of her checkered past, Lorelei has proved to us all that she has earned a chance to be a mother to her child."

The response from his headstrong wife did not surprise Leroy Carr. With only one second left, both were forced to hang up without saying goodbye.

Chapter 33

Taking Practice

Outside Valencia, Spain
Next day—Tuesday, 26 October 1948

Since Erika had agreed to Leroy Carr's alternate plan, Charles de Gaulle was no long in danger.

In the woodland west of the Gypsy camp, it was a thirsty and smoky autumn of reds and golds; the roosting wrens, disturbed by the women walking through the trees, whirled into the air like ashes from a chimney. Today was the second day of training but the first day for Zhanna with her Mosin-Nagant rifle and P/U scope. Yesterday it was handgun target practice for all of them. Kay asked to be included even though her duties for the mission would not require being armed. Erika let her fire a few rounds from her Berretta.

Although Zhanna's target would be at nighttime, she wanted to first practice during the day to learn about her scope's optical quirks that could vary slightly with any hand-assembled item. She had used this brand of scope during the war, but any experienced shooter would take the time to carefully calibrate rifle and scope. This was especially important for a target that would be 400 to 500 yards away and possibly moving.

Zhanna, Erika, and Kay were together atop a small hill three miles west of the Gypsy camp. Kathryn and Stephanie had stepped off 500 yards and were now in a meadow below. The women had kept the tin plates from their paella dinners the other night and Kathryn had nailed one to a tree on the far edge of the clearing. Stephanie had made sure the tree was in line of sight for Zhanna then, on the Russian sniper's instructions, made her way halfway back to the hill carrying a flag, stopping at 250 yards.

The bolt-action Mosin-Nagant held five rounds of 7.62x54mm rimmed cartridges in a non-removable magazine. Cartridges had to be loaded one-by-one or with a stripper clip such as used for the American M-1 Garand infantry rifle. Erika had gotten Zhanna three stripper clips when she bought the rifle and scope from the black marketeer in London, but she and Kay watched Zhanna load the rifle a cartridge at a time.

"I don't like stripper clips," Zhanna said. "Occasionally a cartridge doesn't seat well. The thumb does a better job."

A curious Kay Carr asked a question. "Zhanna, will you tell me what Stephanie is doing?"

"The wind or breeze at the target makes little difference," Zhanna said as she started adjusting the scope. "By that time that late in the flight the bullet has decided its course. And wind at the shooting point, like where we are now, is also a minor consideration because the velocity after leaving the barrel is enough to negate any interference. It's halfway to the target that the mischief is done. That's when air movement affects aim.

"Rules of thumb, as you Americans say, is if you can feel a breeze at the halfway point the air is moving at three to five miles per hour. If the leaves on the trees are moving, it's five to eight miles per hour. If loose papers blow, the wind is eight to twelve miles per hour. If small trees are swaying, it's twelve to fifteen. That's why Stephanie is halfway to the target holding a flag; it's a better gauge."

Erika added, "Watch Stephanie, Kay. In Paris you'll be the one holding the flag. Don't worry, you won't stand out. The Champs-Élysées will be crowded that day and many people will be holding flags."

"I'll aim at the middle of the target before we have Stephanie raise the flag," Zhanna told them. "I see some leaves moving where Stephanie is standing, so this will be a miss." She took a long moment and adjusted the scope a couple of times. The rifle cracked. Erika, looking through binoculars, confirmed that it was a miss.

"Signal Stephanie to raise the flag," Zhanna said. Erika pointed her Berretta toward the sky and fired a shot. Stephanie could plainly discern the sound of the handgun from the powerful sniper rifle and raised the flag.

Zhanna watched the flag move for a long moment with the naked eye, then pointed the rifle at Stephanie, zooming out just enough to also see the flag. After another minute, Zhanna said, "A 7.62x54mm cartridge will take 0.6 seconds to reach a target 500 yards away. The wind at the halfway point where Stephanie is standing is six miles per hour. That means a wind drift of twelve inches." She adjusted her scope.

Down in the valley, Kathryn Fischer stood about 30 yards away from the tin pan. She saw the pan blow off the tree before she heard the crack of the rifle. To hit a stationary target over a quarter of a mile away, it had taken Zhanna Rogova only one practice shot. Kathryn nailed a second pan to the tree.

[three hours later]

After Zhanna was satisfied with her first day of training with her rifle, the women headed to the Gypsy camp—the trunk of their car loaded with groceries. Items that would not spoil after spending an autumn afternoon in the trunk of a car: many loaves of hard bread; sacks of certain vegetables like carrots, potatoes, and onions along with bottles of wine, brandy, and hard spirits including gin, vodka, and Scotch. Also included were ten cartons of cigarettes and several boxes of matches for the clan.

Kay was especially interested. She had come across Gypsies in Mexico City during her semester there, but they were all in the city. Mostly they begged or played music for tips on street corners. She was fascinated by the Roma camp.

As they neared the encampment, Stephanie said, "Kay, as you know, none of Raval's family speaks English. He understands German, but the others speak only Romanian or Spanish. When we get there, tell them we have food."

"Okay," Kay replied.

After the car finished bumping over the forest trail and entered the camp, they were greeted by shotgun toting men. The men recognized Stephanie first and slung their guns back onto their shoulders. Everyone got out of the car and Kay said, "Venimos con la comida." (We come with food.)

A nearby Roma women overheard, shouted to other women, and they rushed to the car.

◊ ◊ ◊

[that evening]
Everyone had enjoyed a satisfying meal. Added to the bread and vegetables brought by the foreign women was mutton from a sheep stolen from a farm by the Roma men. With bellies full, Raval's clan was in the mood to celebrate.

Axel Ryker considered Gypsies to be Untermenschen (less than human) and Henry Wiltshire sat with a glum look on his face so Erika and the other women ignored them both. Time to celebrate just being alive.

Even Kay took part. With enough alcohol in her, she had gotten over the shock of Axel Ryker and joined with the Shield Maidens and the Roma girls as they danced around the campfire.

Chapter 34

Flamenco

Reykjavik, Iceland
Two days later—Thursday, 28 October 1948

Neither Leroy Carr or Al Hodge would be spending the night in Iceland. After their meeting both would fly back: Al to Paris and Leroy to Washington. Carr chose Reykjavik for the meeting. The flight was several hours longer for Carr coming from Washington than it was for Al coming from Paris; still, it would let Carr avoid the full flight to France.

Since the meeting would take less than two hours, they met inside Carr's Air Force DC-3 as the airplane sat on the tarmac being refueled and undergoing a maintenance check.

Both men spent time filling each other in.

"How's Sheila doing," Carr asked.

"She's following your orders, Leroy. She won't tell me shit over her phone at the Savoy." Both men and Sheila knew MI-6 listened in to Savoy phone calls.

"I knew we could count on Sheila," Carr replied.

"What about those Fischer sisters?" Hodge asked. "Are you sure they can be trusted?"

"We have no choice but to trust them. This won't work without the sisters working with Kay. It's Zhanna Rogova we have to worry about. Ryker will obey orders, but Zhanna is a wild card. You don't know what you're going to be holding until the other cards are dealt."

Both men took a drink of coffee an Air Force corporal had brought them earlier, before the airman retreated to the rear utility room of the plane.

Carr said, "I want to know how you're doing, Al, now that Erika and Zhanna's target has been changed. Are you still behind this? You can pull out anytime."

Hodge didn't hesitate. "We don't have any other options, Leroy. We can't let de Gaulle be the target. And we certainly can't warn the French government that a CIA agent has threatened to assassinate him."

[that afternoon]

Because of her ability to communicate with the Gypsies, Kay Carr seemed to be spending more and more time at the camp.

At present, the Shield Maidens were farther west at the area where they trained. For the past four hours of this afternoon, Kay had been alone with Axel Ryker and Henry Wiltshire at the clan's campground.

During her time in the camp the past couple of days, Kay tried to avoid Ryker, yet this proved difficult. He was always watching over Henry Wiltshire and it seemed the frightful man kept his second eye on her. When she had no choice but to converse with Ryker, he presented a polite façade, but it was obvious to Kay that the acting was hard for him. To Kay, Ryker seemed the archetypal savage brute.

Finally, Ryker had to walk into the woods to answer nature's call. This gave Kay a chance, for the first time, to talk to Henry Wiltshire without Ryker leering nearby. Kay sat down beside the Englishman.

"Henry, I can only imagine how you feel," Kay said, "but be confident you're protected."

"Protected from what—being murdered if I make a false move?" Wiltshire said snidely. "Erika sent me to a German Stalag for three years. I don't believe anything that woman says. For that matter, I also don't believe you because it's obvious you're in league with her."

"Erika cares about you as a person, Henry. It would be in your best interest to trust her."

Wiltshire didn't want to hear it. "You're lying."

[that evening—Valencia]

One of Raval's nephews had found some work for the musicians and dancers at a Flamenco club in Valencia. The job started tonight and would last through Saturday night. Several men of the clan with shot guns would be left behind to guard the camp. The Shield Maidens and

Kay Carr went with the entertainers to the cantina. Erika even told Ryker he could go while Raval's men watched Henry Wiltshire at the camp.

"I've watched these thieves and whores dance every night," he replied. "Why would I go someplace to watch them dance more? I will accompany you into town then I will find my own cantina."

"Very well," she said. "Just be back at camp tomorrow morning. That's an order. Tell me you will comply."

Ryker grunted irascibly, "We learned in the Reich to never walk away from a mission, Sonderführer. You and those sisters served the Führer and should know that." A dark grinned appeared on his scared face.

"Fuck you, Ryker. Just be back at the camp in the morning."

◊ ◊ ◊

All the women got drunk except the Russian, Zhanna Rogova, who seemed to possess some unnatural faculty to consume an absurd amount of alcohol with few side effects. Kay Carr, the slightest among them, was the worst off. She passed out in the cantina and the other women had to prop her up when loading her in the cab that took her and Stephanie back to the hotel. Erika, Zhanna, and Kathryn left the cantina an hour later.

Chapter 35

Dinner for Old Times Sake

Valencia, Spain
Two days later—Saturday, 30 October 1948

For the past two days Ryker had been training with the Maidens and Kay while the Roma men watched over Henry Wiltshire. During Zhanna's target practice it was now Kay who raised the flag halfway to the target. Zhanna had long ago shredded all the tin pans so now the targets were six-inch square pieces of cloth cut from a roll of material Erika bought from one of the Gypsy women.

Zhanna also practiced on moving targets engineered by the Fischer sisters. Placing the cloth at the middle of a 30-foot-long rope, each sister would take an end and walk slowly, each being only 15-feet from the target. Dangerous perhaps, but they had confidence in Zhanna's marksmanship. As Zhanna pulled the trigger, a last second shift in wind at Kay's halfway position might cause the Russian sniper to occasionally miss the small target a quarter of a mile away, but it would be by a matter of inches, not feet, so the Fischer sisters where never in any real danger. Nevertheless, any miss would bring on a vulgar diatribe spoken in Russian by the woman looking through the scope. Zhanna Rogova had killed Germans a half-mile away during the war, and she didn't like missing at a quarter of a mile even though the current target was much smaller than a man.

Other training they all participated in were runs up hills and over rough terrain, handgun target practice, and hand-to-hand combat. All were skilled in every aspect, yet everyone had their forte. "That's what makes for a good team," Erika had commented. "Everyone has their own specialty."

Of course, Zhanna was the expert long-range sniper. Both Fischer sisters excelled with handguns and knives. Erika was also a dead-eye shot with a handgun and she was the queen of hand-to-hand combat. At Quenzsee, the German spy school outside Berlin, Erika had trained in hand-to-hand fighting with the men because none of the other women plebes could give her any competition and the instructors felt it demoralized the other women to be beaten so quickly by the woman codenamed Lorelei.

Kay insisted on taking part in all the training, even though her job in Paris would be simply to raise a flag. The Maidens took it easy on her in hand-to-hand which made Kay angry, but she knew commenting would serve no purpose. The running was another matter. Kay wasn't the fastest of the group in short sprints, that was Erika, but during the long-distance runs Kay finished ahead of the heavier and more muscular Shield Maidens. She took pride in that.

And then there was Axel Ryker. The 270-pound behemoth was terrible at both speed and endurance running and Erika took pleasure in taunting him as all the women left him behind in both the sprints and the long-distance runs. But when it came to weapons, Ryker was highly skilled, and in hand-to-hand he was unparalleled. Ryker could snap a man's neck like a strand of spaghetti and enjoyed doing so. Erika was well aware of this, so she kept Ryker out of hand-to-hand combat training, not trusting him to not go overboard. The women gave each other bumps and bruises from the hand-to-hand between themselves, but she couldn't afford to have anyone seriously injured by Ryker.

Even though it was a pleasant fall day, everyone was perspiring profusely after the runs, which were always the last facet of each day's regimen.

Before they returned to the Gypsy camp to drop off Ryker, Erika called a meeting in the forest.

"Everyone gets this evening off to do what they want. We'll have one more day of training tomorrow here, then Monday we leave for Paris. Al Hodge is supposed to find us a place outside Paris to continue training until the mission day comes. As you all know, that's November 11th so we'll have more training days in France. That's everyone but you Ryker. I'll pay Raval to keep his family at their camp until November 12th. By that day, the mission will have either succeeded or failed. Regardless, it will be over. On the 12th you will take Henry back to London, release him unharmed, then fly back to Washington and report to Leroy Carr. Any questions?"

"Why do I have to spend another two weeks with the vermin Gyps? I can take the Englander back to London and guard him there until the date you say."

"Because I want it done just as I told you. That's why."

Ryker glared at her, wishing he would have succeeded in eliminating her in Evansville during the war.

◊ ◊ ◊

After the forest meeting, they returned to Raval's camp to drop off Ryker. Erika couldn't help but notice Henry Wiltshire's shaking left hand. She decided to give him a night off from the gruesome former Gestapo henchman and the captive aura of the Gypsy camp. She'd take Wiltshire with her tonight into Valencia.

[that evening]

Erika Lehmann and Henry Wiltshire sat together inside a cantina three blocks from the Flamenco club where the musicians and dancers of Raval's clan worked the last night of their agreement with the club's manager. Kathryn, Stephanie, Zhanna, and Kay were already at the club. Ryker had come into town with them, but, as he had done on Thursday, he went off by himself.

After capture, Wiltshire had been relieved of any possessions, including money and even his wristwatch. Erika would pay. She bought them both a Fideuè, a locally popular Mediterranean dish of noodles and fish in a garlic and olive oil sauce. The meal sat before them on the table along with a small carafe of white wine. Erika poured them each a glass.

"How did you come to this point, Maggie." Henry asked. "Or I presume I should say Erika."

"I felt bad about my role in you spending those years in the Stalag, Henry, but you must understand. I fought for my country during the war just as you did."

"That doesn't answer my question."

"You know I now work for the Americans."

"You still avoid my question."

"What do you want me to tell you, Henry?" she asked impatiently. "Why I'm working with a man like Axel Ryker?"

"That would be a start," Wiltshire replied.

"I can't tell you anything, other than I have no choice in the matter. Can we enjoy our dinner now?"

"Maggie, I'm an MI-6 analyst. Until you showed up at my flat that night in London, I didn't know if you were alive or dead, but I knew about your daughter. I don't like or appreciate my situation here in Spain, but I've had days to think about it and I believe I've figured out why you're doing this, and I can't say in all honesty that I wouldn't do the same."

Erika looked at him. The middle-aged man she had seduced during the war was indeed a skilled analyst for his country.

Part 4

"The die is cast."

— *Julius Caesar (100—44 B.C.)*

Chapter 36

Sheila Changes the Plan

Paris, France
Monday, 01 November 1948

Late in the evening, Al Hodge was on the telephone with Sheila Reid in London.

"Sheila, Kay and the female gangsters got here about an hour ago. They're all checked in at the Napoleon where I'm staying. Tell Leroy that Kay is okay."

"Thanks, Al. That will be a great relief for him. He'll want to know how they got there," Sheila said. *"Train or airplane?"*

"The felons stole a car in Valencia early this morning, drove to Madrid, then flew in on a commercial flight. They had a rental car while in Valencia but they didn't want to drive it to Madrid and leave a trail."

Sheila wanted to laugh about the stolen car but didn't. "That's good procedure on their part, Al."

Hodge continued. "I was going to book Kay a room of her own, but the pain-in-my-ass Lehmann refused to have her separated from her bodyguard. So Kay and Stephanie room together. Erika, Zhanna, and Kathryn share a suite.

"Erika is making sure Kay stays safe, Al. That's point number one of her agreement with Leroy. I'll contact him right away. What about Henry Wiltshire?"

"Lehmann told me he's safe. She left Ryker with him in Spain and ordered Ryker to take him back to London and release him on November 12th. I'll call you tomorrow after I've had time to sit down with them."

It was time to hang up.

[30 minutes later—Washington]
It was still afternoon when Carr received the call from Sheila Reid.

"Al called me, Leroy. Kay and the ladies are in Paris. Kay is fine." Sheila heard a pause. She couldn't hear it, but knew the pause was a sigh of relief from E Street.

"What's up with Henry Wiltshire? MI-6 is scrambling about trying to find him."

Sheila told Carr about Wiltshire's situation.

"Okay, Sheila. Contact Al and tell him to let the Maidens train as they are expecting but use MPs we have in Paris to take them all into custody on November 10th. He can call a meeting with them all and have the MPs waiting. We can't let them go through with the plan for the 11th."

"ROGER that, Leroy," Sheila said. When she hung up the phone, the Army major knew she could not betray her comrades-in-arms and fellow Shield Maidens, even though disregarding orders from Leroy Carr could lead to her court-martial and most probably prison time.

[midnight in Paris]

Sheila's call woke Al Hodge in Paris.

"Al, Leroy was glad to hear about Kay. He told me to tell you the plan for November 11th is a go."

"Leroy said that?"

"Yes."

"I don't know what to say other than I'm shocked, but he's the boss. Tell him I received his orders."

"I will," Sheila said, knowing Hodge had gone dark on Carr's orders and could not contact his boss. She would lie to Carr about the orders she relayed to his top lieutenant.

Chapter 37

MI-6 gets Lucky

Paris
Next day—Tuesday, 02 November 1948

The Shield Maidens, Kay Carr, and Al Hodge breakfasted in the Hotel Napoleon restaurant and then proceeded up to Hodge's hotel room. He stayed in a single room, so it was crowded. Some of them found a seat on the bed or in the one chair; others stood.

"I've secured a place for you to train," Hodge told the Shield Maidens. "It's southeast of Paris, outside Saint Maur des Fossés. It's a forty-minute drive, so not very far away. I have one car for the four of you, no driver. You bandits don't have to steal a car."

"That's five of us, Al," Kay interjected without consulting Erika. "I'm going along to train. We can all crowd into one car."

[London—same time]
A man wearing a tweed suit sat in Sir James office at MI-6.

"How did you come about this information?" Sir James asked.

"I must admit it was dumb luck, sir. During his off-duty hours, one of our men overheard a conversation in a pub. A pilot was telling some bloke about how much money he had made recently after being hired twice in October by women with guns to fly people to Valencia, Spain. We brought the pilot in and showed him a photograph of Henry. The man confirmed that Henry was on the first flight along with an American man (Al) and a woman that spoke English with a German accent (Kathryn). I questioned him further. His passengers on the second flight were a blonde woman who spoke with a British accent, a woman who spoke with a Russian accent, and a quite large man with jagged scars on his face. He claims the second flight he landed at the Valencia airfield, but the first flight, the one Henry was onboard, the woman directed him to land in a pasture west of town. Perhaps they are holding Henry at a farm outside the city."

“Perhaps. Send a team right away” Sir James ordered.

“Of course. Do you have any thoughts on who is behind this?”

“Yes, I have thoughts. But when we get Henry back in our fold we’ll know for sure, won’t we? Find Henry and get out of Spain quietly. I don’t want to notify the Spanish government of this operation on their soil. MI-6 is not on the best terms with Franco and he’ll make it difficult for us.”

Chapter 38

La Vie en Rose

Spain
Two days later—Thursday, 04 November 1948

For the past two days, a team of six MI-6 agents posing as wine merchants had checked several farms and vineyards outside the city. The men split up into two separate cars in order to cover more ground. They had come up dry. Next, they would begin the tedious task of checking hotels in town. As the sun began setting, they headed back to their hotel after a long day of driving around the countryside. An agent in the front passenger seat of one of the cars suddenly directed the driver to stop. Something in a valley in the far distance drew his attention.

"What's that?" he asked. "Blackmore, check it out."

An agent in the back seat rolled down his window and raised his binoculars.

After a moment he said, "It looks like a Gypsy camp."

"It's getting dark, we'll have to wait until the morning."

[Paris—that evening]
The three days of training in the woodland southeast of Paris, and three nights of being good girls and staying close to their hotel in the evening, convinced the Shield Maidens they were ready for a night on the town. After all, it was Friday night and this was Gay Paree.

They ended up at the Moulin de la Galette. Kay went along. This nightclub, much smaller and much less famous than the world-renowned Moulin Rouge, was located in the 6th Arrondissement on the Left Bank. Erika had been at this club before—during the war. It was a very popular club for men because it offered a special perk over its much more famous competitor. While the showgirls at the Moulin Rouge performed topless, the girls at the Moulin de la Galette did their stage routines totally nude except for large, colorful, feather hats and high heels.

After the women were seated in the smoke-filled room they looked around. As would be expected, there were more men, but still a noticeable number of women were scattered about in the crowd. Some with men, some without. Many French women also enjoyed the cabarets and were tonight of various ages, from young women to some who looked like middle-age had deserted them a while back.

The next show was to start in fifteen minutes. A waitress wearing a bustier took their drink orders. After the waitress walked away, a cigarette girl, also in a bustier, stopped at their table. Zhanna purchased a pack of American Lucky Strikes which came with a free book of matches. Zhanna lit one up and threw the pack on the table to share. Everyone, including Kay who smoked only two or three cigarettes a year, took one from the pack.

"I think training is going well," Erika said. "Zhanna, tomorrow start looking for your location." She was referring to the place Zhanna would use to fire the all-important shot on November 11th.

The Russian nodded.

Besides what she just told Zhanna, Erika felt no need to discuss further any specifics. Since the beginning of training in Spain, they had discussed everyone's role ad nauseam. Everyone was aware of their part.

The drinks were finally delivered and the show started. Instead of showgirls, who would appear next, five naked ballerinas danced slowly and elegantly on stage as a chanteuse in a green dress sang *La Vie en rose,* a cabaret song made popular by the French singer Édith Piaf.

Chapter 39

Ryker admires a Car

Spain
Next day—Friday, 05 November 1948

The MI-6 agents decided to approach the Gyspy camp as they had done the farms—just one car with three men posing as wine buyers and sellers.

Sadly for them, this was the wrong strategy. Axel Ryker saw the car coming and hid Henry Wiltshire in one of the covered wagons. Ryker followed him in.

[same day—London]
Sheila Reid was once again reporting in to Leroy Carr in Washington.

"What's the latest, Sheila," Carr asked.

"The women continue their training. That's all I have from Al."

"Al knows the Shield Maidens are to be arrested on November 10th, right?"

Sheila lied. "Yes, he knows that, Leroy."

[Spain—same day]
One of the MI-6 agents spoke Spanish and now conversed with Raval who told him he had not seen an Englishman.

"Really," said the agent. "It was our understanding that a colleague of ours was supposed to visit you about selling you some wine."

Raval's family was being paid to hide Henry Wiltshire. "I will tell you again; we have seen no Englander."

The MI-6 agent produced a fake I.D. showing he had approval from the Spanish government to conduct searches. He had used this same I.D. at many of the farms.

Raval gave him a sharp look. "So, you lie about this wine business."

"If you and your men will stand aside, we'll finish our business quickly and then leave you in peace. We don't care if you have illegal contraband in the wagons. We only look for our colleague."

Four young men holding rifles or shotguns standing behind Raval came forward and pointed the business end of the weapons at the Englishmen. "Hold up your hands," Raval ordered.

Axel Ryker stepped down out of the wagon, spoke to Raval in German, then walked up to the MI-6 agents. "Nice car," Ryker said.

[late that afternoon]

The other three-man team of MI-6 agents became concerned when the other men hadn't returned. Travel to and from the Gypsy camp, and adding to that time for a search, should easily have been accomplished in three hours. After all, they were looking for a man, not some small item that took a comprehensive search. Four more hours had passed since the others should have returned to the hotel in Valencia.

So now it was the second car of the MI-6 team that bounced over the rough forest trace to get to the camp. When they arrived, the Gypsy women were preparing dinner over the campfire.

Raval and the gun-toting men met the car when it pulled into the camp. By necessity, each of the three-man British Secret Service teams had at least one agent who spoke Spanish.

These men also produced false papers stating the Spanish government had issues them search warrants.

"We have nothing to hide," said Raval. "You may search the wagons." He signaled his men to drop their weapons.

"Gracias."

It didn't take long to look through the eight wagons. No one was in any of the wagons other than a few of the Roma children playing games. The agents had seen no sign of a car on their way into the camp.

"Thank you for your cooperation, sir. We'll leave you now. Good luck."

As the three MI-6 men drove away, the leader of this group told the others, "Something fishy here, lads."

"What makes you say that?" asked the man driving.

"Gypsies allowing strangers to come into their camp and search wagons? During the war, I spent three years undercover in Bulgaria and came across many Roma. They are suspicious of all strangers and have reason to be. A large portion of them were sent to the extermination camps by the Nazis. A Roma king is not going to let strangers waltz into his camp and search the wagons, paper or no papers, unless he has a reason to let them do so. The Roma are poor people who live from day to day, never knowing where their next meal will come from. Did you notice all the store-bought food in the wagons? I've never seen that before. The Roma hunt, fish, or steal livestock and vegetables from local farmers. Rarely do they have canned goods, fruit like oranges, and liquor that we saw in those wagons. Even if the Roma have money, they usually can't get those items because they're not allowed in most stores.

"Let's get back to the hotel. We'll hope the other team has returned by now."

[same evening—Paris]

The Shield Maidens had arrived in Paris six days ago and each day had continued the training they started in Spain. Now, it took place in the woodlands southeast of Paris, outside Saint Maur des Fossés. Thursday had seen some rain, but they welcomed the chance to train in adverse weather. After all, it might occur on November 11th. No one knew. The only Shield Maiden concerned about rain was Zhanna Rogova.

"Even in a light rain," she told the others, "one cannot know how many rain drops the projectile will have to pass through, all of them affecting the flight. Rain is the sniper's worst enemy for a long-distance shot, even more so than wind."

Each day after they returned to Paris, Zhanna Rogova would head out on her own, exploring the buildings along the Champs-Élysées to find the location that she felt would give her the best line of sight with her old friend, the Mosin-Nagant.

Each afternoon, after Zhanna returned to the Napoleon, Al Hodge would gather them all for a meeting to review that day's work before he released them for dinner. Because of Sheila Reid, Hodge still thought the November 11th target was a go. As did everyone else in the room.

The day of reckoning was but five days away.

Chapter 40

Zhanna's Surprise

London
Next day—Saturday, 06 November 1948

The MI-6 second team leader in Spain was on the telephone with Sir James in London.

"Sir James, I regret to say that Walker, Blackmore, and Massey have disappeared."

"What? What do you mean they've disappeared?"

"They told us they were going to investigate a Gypsy camp. They were very late getting back so we went there to look for them."

"And?"

"We didn't find them and they never returned to the hotel. I have an uneasy feeling about this, Sir James. I think Henry Wiltshire was there when Walker's team arrived."

"Return to the Gypsy camp immediately and demand more information. Apply pressure if you must."

"Yes, sir."

◊ ◊ ◊

An hour later, after receiving their orders from White Hall, the car containing the second team of MI-6 agents in Spain emerged from the forest into the clearing. The Gypsy camp was deserted—nothing left behind other than the rocks that surrounded the dead campfire.

[Paris—that evening]
The Shield Maidens and Kay went to dinner this night at the Bofinger. Founded in 1864, it was credited with being the oldest brasserie in Paris. Located near the Place de la Bastille where the Bastille prison stood until its storming and destruction in 1789 during the French

Revolution, the Bofinger was now a place for the upper-crust of Paris society, foreign diplomats, and rich tourists. Erika would treat.

It was near the end of dinner when Zhanna dropped her bombshell.

"Erika, I invited your cousin to Paris. He's never been off the island."

The blonde leader of the Shield Maidens dropped her fork onto her plate and glared at the Russian.

"What's wrong with you? Are you mad?" Erika said angrily. "As soon as we return to the hotel, call him and tell him not to come."

"It's too late for that," Zhanna said. "He left London earlier today. If the ferry and the trains are on time, he might be waiting for us back at the hotel when we return."

Kay and the Fischer sisters remained silent, watching the seething Erika.

"Zhanna, you're jeopardizing any chance I have to live with my daughter. When we get back to the hotel I'm going to kick your ass. Your neck scar won't be the only scar Ian will be looking at."

"Don't threaten me, German," Zhanna said, the assassin-look in her eyes. "You'll regret it. It would serve you to remember that I am the only one among us who has a chance to make such a precision, surgical shot at a quarter of a mile. My shot will be for the benefit of you and your daughter unless you interfere any further in my personal business. If you do, I can always change my target."

"You'll have a difficult time making any shot with two broken wrists."

Kay, the peacemaker, tried to interject. "Can we calm down a tad? Nothing will be accomplished . . ."

Kathryn Fischer caught Kay's eye and shook her head, signaling that she should stay out of it. One should not step between two angry jungle cats, unless it was someone who knew the beasts better than anyone.

"Erika," Kathryn said. "What is the harm? I'm sure Zhanna will tell your cousin nothing about our undertaking. Isn't that right, Zhanna?"

Zhanna was now irked with Kathryn and shot her a frown. "I consider it an insult that anyone would even ask me that question. Of course I will tell him nothing."

Kay, refusing to be silenced, interposed, “Erika, I know you’re the boss, but we should all be allowed to add our opinion. I agree with Kathryn. Zhanna won’t tell your cousin anything, so what is the harm?”

The blond Tigress and the raven-haired Tigress continued to glare at one another.

Stephanie tried to lighten the crushing mood. “I think the grapes of this wine were stomped by a Frenchwoman with feet unwashed for a fortnight.”

Under the current conditions, no one felt like ordering dessert so Erika paid the bill and they left. Thirty minutes later, when they walked into the lobby of the Hotel Napoleon, Ian Minton sat in one of the lobby chairs waiting for Zhanna.

Chapter 41

View from the Top

On a freighter in the Mediterranean Sea
Next day—Sunday, 07 November 1948

Axel Ryker had Henry Wiltshire drive the MI-6 agents' car. With MI-6 on their tail, Ryker knew it was time to leave the Gypsy camp. After two hours of driving, the three bound, gagged, and blindfolded British agents were roughly pulled from the car on a remote forest road and thrown down an embankment by Ryker, who didn't bother to untie them. That was two days ago.

Ryker and Wiltshire spent the night in Barcelona then yesterday Ryker bribed a freighter captain to take them along on the ship's journey to Marseille, France.

[Paris]

Erika still steamed over Zhanna inviting Ian to Paris, but it was too late now for her to do anything about it now. In a way, she was happy for Zhanna who, as far as she knew, had never had a meaningful relationship with a man. Her cousin seemed to fill a void in Zhanna's empty heart. Nonetheless, Ian now being in Paris was at a very inopportune time for them all. At the morning briefing with the Shield Maidens and Kay, she avoided mentioning the subject of her cousin.

"Today will be our last day of training outside Saint Maur des Fossés. Starting tomorrow we'll spend the next two days surveilling the area on the Champs-Élysées. Zhanna, have you found the place from where you'll take the shot?"

"I'm undecided. I've identified three locations, but much will depend on the weather forecast for that day. I can't make a final decision until the night I pull the trigger. And by the way, I need some more money Erika. I'm taking Ian to the Bofinger tonight. He will never admit it, but he can't afford it. I told him I insisted on treating. Give me some money."

Erika looked at the Russian assassin, decided to say nothing, and handed her some francs. "This should be enough, including a good bottle of wine."

[that evening]
After dinner, Zhanna and Ian hired a taxi to take them to the Eiffel Tower. Instead of waiting in the long queue for the lift, they climbed the stairs all the way to the top. Standing high over the City of Lights, they gazed at the shimming man-made stars on the ground and at those made by God blinking high above in the heavens, happy to proclaim their creator in the cloudless night sky. A fall breeze supplied a bit of chill atop the Tower.

Ian had been in the lobby yesterday evening when the women returned from the restaurant. "Who were the three other women with you and Erika last night?"

"Colleague interpreters for the Americans."

Ian nodded. "How long will you be in Paris, Zhanna?"

"Just a few days," she answered.

Ian removed his blazer and draped it over her shoulders to guard her from the nippy autumn gusts over 900 feet above the city.

Chapter 42

The Green Fairy

Paris
Next day—Monday, 08 November 1948

Erika met alone with Zhanna over breakfast in the Hotel Napoleon restaurant.

"How was your date with Ian?"

"Fine, after dinner we climbed to the top of the Tower."

"That will certainly walk off a meal."

"Yes, it was a good work out for both of us."

"Where is Ian staying?" Erika asked.

"A cheap hotel in the 17th arrondissement," Zhanna answered.

"Tell him to move to our hotel tomorrow, Zhanna."

"He can't afford the Hotel Napoleon."

"Tell him I'll pay for his room."

"He's a proud man and won't welcome charity, Erika."

"Then think up some reason to get him at this hotel so you can keep an eye on him."

"What are you talking about?" Zhanna asked.

"You bringing Ian to Paris has backed me into a corner. My only consideration is the mission, so please just do as I ask. Don't give him any details, just tell him you're here on an assignment. Then I want everyone except Ian to assemble for a meeting tonight."

[White Hall—London]

Sir James Ashworth was on a secure line with Leroy Carr in Washington.

"Leroy, a couple of hours ago I was informed that men we had sent to Spain to search for Wiltshire were tied up and deposited on a lonely woodland road. After several hours of struggling to unbind themselves, they eventually made it to a village. It's time to be honest with me. I know you Yanks are behind Henry Wiltshire's disappearance."

"Sir James, I have no knowledge of that. It certainly was not on orders from this office." Carr was technically telling the truth. Erika had captured Wiltshire on her own. "But, as you know, the CIA is willing to help our great friends at MI-6 anyway we can."

"Does that include allowing us to bring in Erika Lehmann, Axel Ryker, and Zhanna Rogova for questioning? Yes, Leroy, we know Ryker now works for you Yanks."

Leroy hesitated. MI-6 was surely worthy of its reputation.

"I won't deny Ryker works for us, Sir James, just as the Nazi war criminal Horst Kopkow now works for MI-6. You Brits even faked his death to get the war crimes tribunals to close the books on him."

"Touché, old friend," the Englishman said. "Let's not get into a pissing game. I don't know what you have going on here, Leroy, and I realize asking would be a waste of time, but I want Wiltshire returned safely—and soon."

[early evening]

Stephanie and Kay had the largest hotel room of the group so that's where the team met. In the room was Al Hodge, Kay Carr, and the four Shield Maidens.

"The first thing we have to discuss is Ian," Erika said. "He's a civilian and is not to be told anything or involved in any way. Zhanna, you will hold to the story that you and I were sent here for translation work. Understood?"

"I understand," Zhanna replied.

Hodge interrupted. "Before we make too many plans. Sheila received a call from Ryker today. It seems the MI-6 showed up at the Gypsy camp in Spain. He was forced to flee with Henry Wiltshire."

"Where are they?" Erika asked.

"He called Sheila from Marseille and told her they would take a train to Paris."

Erika frowned. Now not only did they have Ian to vie with, but also Ryker and Wiltshire. But the others would have to deal with them. Her time had come.

Erika looked at Kathryn. "Kathryn. You're taking my place as Shield Maiden leader for the remainder of this mission. You know what you have to do tonight. I will disappear before any of you rise from bed tomorrow morning. After that, the fate of myself and my daughter is in your hands."

[later that evening]

The former Gestapo Kriminalkommissar, Kathryn Fischer, had sat on the fountain ledge in the plaza outside the Hotel Ritz for nearly two hours when she finally saw Paula Burke walk out the front door. Kathryn didn't have to follow her far. Burke ducked into a bistro one block from the square.

The American woman took a seat at the bar. Unlike in the United States, where it was uncommon for single women to belly up to the bar, it was quite ordinary in Paris. Kathryn followed her in and sat down, leaving one seat between them.

Kathryn ordered a Green Fairy, the infamous Absinthe drink well known in Paris for producing odd thoughts and hallucinations.

Paula Burke looked over. "I've heard of that drink but have been told to avoid it."

Kathryn, who spoke English with a German accent, laughed. "You must be an Amerikaner."

Paula grinned and Kathryn slid over on the seat beside her. "My name is Sue. What brings you to Paris?"

"I'm Paula Burke. Nice to meet you." The women shook hands. "I'm a professor of French studies at Princeton University in the United States and I'm here serving as a translator for General George Marshall, our Secretary of State."

Of course, Kathryn already knew this information, supplied by Al Hodge.

"Princeton? Isn't that where Albert Einstein now works?" Kathryn asked to make conversation.

"Why, yes, it is. I have met Professor Einstein numerous times."

"Does he miss his homeland?" Kathryn asked.

"Germany? I don't know. I have never discussed that with him nor heard him comment on the matter."

The woman was truly an amateur, revealing too much information. Kathryn knew it would be an easy night. Before the evening was over, Kathryn would talk the naïve professor into letting her buy her a Green Fairy. When the drink arrived, Kathryn easily distracted the American professor as she produced a tiny vile from a pocket and added a small amount of an additional liquid to Paula Burke's Green Fairy.

Chapter 43

Hall of Mirrors

Paris
Next day—Tuesday, 09 November 1948

When the CIA team awoke, Erika Lehmann was gone from the Hotel Napoleon just as she had promised. Al Hodge, Kay Carr, and the remaining Shield Maidens knew they wouldn't see her again until November 11th. Hodge was still the mission coordinator, as he had always been, but Kathryn Fischer was now in charge of the Shield Maidens when they were in the field.

[later that morning]
General George C. Marshall sipped black coffee in his office in the Hotel Ritz. General Marshall, who during the war was appointed by FDR as the U.S. Army Chief of Staff and credited by Winston Churchill as being the "architect of victory" now served under President Harry Truman as Secretary of State. His appointment as Chief of Staff during the war placed him in command over such bright stars as Eisenhower and Patton, both of whom had to answer to him. Last spring, he had submitted what he named the European Recovery Program but was more commonly called by the press the Marshall Plan—a three part plan to rebuild a devastated Europe, stem the expansion of Soviet influence beyond Eastern Europe, and lay the ground work for what would be called the North Atlantic Treaty Organization. His contentious proposal was being met by heated opposition from the Soviet block and even some U.S. congressmen at home because of its estimated 13-billion-dollar price tag to just get it off the ground. Many more billions would be needed as time passed. Marshall had walked a tightrope since spring and had spent much time stumping the plan to lawmakers at home as well as in Europe selling the idea to a few hesitant heads of state of western European countries that would benefit under the plan's umbrella. Certain leaders of these countries thought the Marshall

Plan meant the takeover of Europe by the Americans and opposed the part of the plan that would rebuild a devastated Germany; the country that has inflected so much suffering across Europe.

The buzzer on Marshall's desk sounded for the fourth time this morning.

"Yes, major," Marshall said into the intercom.

"We have a fourth applicant for your French translator opening waiting in the office, General."

Marshall sighed. "Send him in." His interpreter, Miss Burke, had taken ill and Marshall needed a replacement quickly.

"It's a woman this time, General."

"Then send her in, dammit."

A young blonde woman walked in. George Marshall motioned to a seat and the woman sat down.

"Thank you for seeing me, General. My name is Erika Faust."

Marshall hated wasting time so he cut to the chase. "Tell me your background as it applies to this job."

"I work as a translator for the Department of State. I showed my identification to your aide and he recorded it. I'm fluent in French and it would be my honor to serve."

Marshall handed her several papers written in French. "Translate, please."

Erika looked at the papers and smiled. "These are children's nursery rhymes. The first is The Three Little Pigs. Do you really want me to read you a bedtime story?"

Marshall looked at her, then smiled. She was bold and he liked that.

"Why do you want this job?" he asked.

"As I said, to serve the United States. I met your wife at a reception in Washington last year. I admire her as I do you."

"You know my wife?"

"I met her briefly at a cocktail party. I doubt she remembers me."

George Marshall gazed at her for a long moment. "Your job won't be an easy one. You'll have to be at my beck and call around the clock. Also, as a State Department interpreter you already know that anything sensitive you hear during the course of your work is top secret. You'll go to prison for a long time if you were to divulge anything out of hand."

"I expect nothing less, sir."

"Call me General or Mr. Secretary. I will call you Miss Faust."

"It's Mrs. Faust, General. My husband passed away just over two years ago."

"I'm sorry to hear that."

Erika left out the part that her husband, Kai, was a German SS officer during the war.

"I'll have my adjutant book you a room here at the Ritz. Check-in this afternoon. There is an affair at the Palace of Versailles tonight hosted by the French prime minister. I'll need you there. Consider this a trial run with no promises of permanent employment. You'll need formal attire which you can get at the boutique here in the hotel. I'll have one of my aides accompany you so everything will be put on the expense account. Someone will come to fetch you in your room at 1800 hours. Be ready."

"I'll be ready, General."

[that evening]

It had been a whirlwind day for Erika. First, there was the stress of not knowing if she'd even get an interview with Marshall. During that interview, she added the little lie about meeting his wife last year in Washington. She knew people like the Marshalls attend so many cocktail parties, formal dinners, and charity affairs where they briefly meet many people. No one can remember everyone, especially from a brief greeting at a minor affair a year gone by.

Then there was the hustle to find a gown and get her hair done this afternoon. Luckily, she was able to accomplish everything without leaving the Ritz. Marshall's aide even procured her some jewelry on loan from a jewelry shop in the hotel.

She was ready when a young Army captain knocked on her door at five minutes to six.

"Mrs. Erika Faust?" he inquired.

"Yes."

"I'm Captain McBrayer. I'm your escort for tonight."

"Come in captain. I'm ready. I just have to get my wrap."

"Where are you from, captain?" Erika asked as she walked over to get the wrap she had laid over the arm of the sofa.

"La Mesa, California, ma'am."

"I've been to Los Angeles. Is that around there?

"La Mesa is just outside San Diego, ma'am."

"Captain, since you're my escort, 'ma'am' will sound quite awkward. Call me Erika. What's your first name?"

"Wayne, ma'am . . . I mean Erika."

Normally, Versailles was at least an hour's drive from downtown Paris, but the seven-car motorcade led by French gendarmes on motorcycles didn't have to obey stop lights or stop signs so it arrived at the Palace at ten minutes before the event was scheduled to start at seven. All the black Cadillacs had heavily tinted windows. Erika and Captain McBrayer rode in the fifth car. George Marshall and his wife were in one of the cars ahead. No one knew which one for security reasons. The designer of the Marshall plan had received death threats from French communists.

The Palace had been the main residence of French royals since its construction in the 17th century. The last monarch of France, King Louis XVI and his wife, Marie Antionette, had lived here for much of the king's reign.

Tonight's soirée was to be held in the grand Hall of Mirrors.

A uniformed Frenchman opened their car door and Erika and Captain McBrayer stepped out. She took the captain's arm as they proceeded up the red carpet into the Palace. Erika wore a shimmering gold gown that complimented her bright blonde hair tied up high on her head and held in place with a diamond-studded hair comb on loan from the Ritz. Captain McBrayer wore his formal military uniform.

"Erika," said McBrayer. "My orders are that when we see General Marshall, you will approach him and remain at his side during the evening. The general doesn't speak French."

"I understand," she replied. "That's why I'm here, Wayne. I'm ready."

Even though they had arrived a few minutes early, the soirée already seemed in full gear. Waiters weaved their way through a maze of tuxedoed or uniformed men of power and their elegantly decked out wives. Waitresses followed the waiters with trays of assorted canapes. Erika had been inside the Hall of Mirrors before but the long corridor of mirrors, priceless paintings, exquisite sculptures, and massive chandeliers was a place that took one's breath away each time one entered, regardless of the number of visits. Notwithstanding the room's beauty, Erika couldn't help sensing a pang of hard feelings. In this room, the Treaty of Versailles was signed in 1919, a spiteful accord framed by the victors of WWI aimed at punishing her country. The treaty, demanding ridiculous sums of reparations, sent Germany's economy spiraling out of control. Germans were out of work and starving, crime was rampant. The end result played into the hands of extreme German nationalists like Adolf Hitler who promised the German people he would smash the Versailles accord and put the people back to work. He delivered on those campaign promises. In the end, the only thing the Treaty of Versailles accomplished was a twenty-year truce between what many historians view as the same war.

George Marshall and his wife actually entered the Hall after Erika. Again, perhaps for security reasons. When Erika saw him she nudged the captain and he escorted her over. Marshall saw them coming.

"Good evening Captain McBrayer," Marshall said. The Secretary of State was in a black tuxedo.

"Good evening, General."

Marshall looked at Erika and turned to his wife. "Katherine, you have met Captain McBrayer. With him is my French interpreter for the evening. Unfortunately, Miss Burke took ill. This is Mrs. Faust. She works for the State Department."

Mrs. Marshall extended her hand and Erika shook it.

The 5-star general continued. "Mrs. Faust tells me the two of you met briefly at some function last year in Washington."

"It was at the Mayflower Hotel, Mrs. Marshall," Erika inserted quickly, knowing many highbrow balls, cocktail parties, and charity events attended by the elite were held at Washington's finest hotel. Surely, Erika thought, the wife of the Secretary of State would have attended some of those soirées in the past year.

Like anyone in her position, Katherine Marshall knew diplomacy. One never admitted he or she did not remember someone, even when they didn't. "Of course, how have you been, Mrs. Faust."

◊ ◊ ◊

About thirty minutes later, Captain McBrayer had been dismissed for the time being. His only other duties this night would be to coordinate the guarding of the American vehicles outside, then escort Erika back to the Ritz when the functioned ended. Katherine Marshall stood at the far end of the Hall talking to the French Prime Minister's wife and several other wives of high-ranking men in the French government. The Prime Minister, Henri Queuille, stood with a flute of Champagne talking to George Marshall. Queuille spoke some English but was not fluent, so, not trusting Marshall's interpreter, he had his own alongside—a man in a French army officer's uniform. Alongside Marshall stood the only woman of the foursome, Erika.

Queuille said in English, "I must say, Monsieur Secretary, your interpreter tonight is quite lovely."

Marshall did not care much for Queuille. "You wished to speak privately, Mr. Prime Minister. What can I do for you?" Queuille was a radical leftist and had given Marshall more trouble about his Marshall Plan than any other European head of state. The bold American general's patience had grown thin.

Erika translated into French for Queuille. The French officer nodded to the Prime Minister that the translation was accurate.

In French, Queuille said, "You and I must meet in my office in Paris tomorrow. Will ten o'clock in the morning fit with your schedule?"

After Erika translated, Marshall asked, "May I ask, why?"

"Puis-je demander pourquoi?" Erika said to Queuille on the general's behalf.

Queuille responded with, "J'ai reçu des informations sure une menace pour votre vie."

Erika turned to Marshall. "He says his government has received another threat on your life, Mr. Secretary. Shall I tell him you will meet him at his office tomorrow morning?"

Marshall grunted, "Very well."

Erika turned to Queuille. "Le general dit qu'il sera ὰ votre bureau ὰ dix heures."

The French Prime Minister nodded then abruptly, and rudely, walked away.

"Shithead," Marshall mumbled, but loud enough for Erika to hear. "Pardon my French, Mrs. Faust."

"Actually, General Marshall, in French, shithead would be *Connard."*

Marshall laughed. "You have spunk, Mrs. Faust. Let's find my wife and get a drink." He offered his arm and she took it. Erika Lehmann, a dedicated Nazi spy during the war, walked through the Hall of Mirrors on the arm of the Secretary of State of the United States, her wartime enemy.

[same evening]

Ian Minton refused Zhanna's offer to move into the Hotel Napoleon because he couldn't afford it and he wasn't going to let Zhanna, or his cousin Erika pay, so he still billeted in the rundown hotel he checked into his first day in Paris.

Ian did, however, manage to get two tickets to a cabaret show on the Left Bank where Edith Piaf was performing. Anxious for a night out in Paris with Zhanna, the boxer arrived much too early at her hotel door, but when she answered the knock, she was ready.

[later]

It was after midnight when the motorcade finally returned to the Ritz. As instructed, McBrayer dropped her off at her hotel room door.

"Come in, Captain," Erika said at the door. "Have a cup of coffee."

The Army officer stepped in, Erika closed the door and said, "Make yourself comfortable."

She let her hair down and gave him a sparkling smile, "Is there something other than coffee I can offer you, Wayne?"

Chapter 44

Admiration

Paris
Next day—Wednesday, 10 November 1948

Early this morning, Al Hodge called the Shield Maidens and Kay Carr together. Yesterday, Hodge sent Ryker to Lyon with Henry Wiltshire simply to get them out of the picture and help uncomplicate to some extent an already overly complicated scheme in Paris.

"Katherine, you took care of Marshall's French translator, right?"

"Yes, she'll have nausea and diarrhea for a couple of days but she'll be fine after that. By the time she recovers the mission will be over."

"Okay, we know Erika replaced her. Her Department of State translator I.D.s went through the check process and it was recorded that she was hired. Let's again go over the plan for tomorrow. Yesterday morning, I sent the death threat against Marshall to the French government, alluding it was from a communist, but of course he's not the target. Zhanna, do you think you'll have trouble identifying the real target?"

"No. Erika will contact me tonight as planned."

Hodge still had no idea that Sheila Reid had given him false orders from Leroy Carr. For Hodge, the mission was a 'go.'

[a bit later that morning]

The meeting with Henri Queuille proved anti-climactic. Last night in the Hall of Mirrors, the French Prime Minister summoned George Marshall to his office in the Élysée Palace to supposedly warn him of another death threat, but Queuille got that information out of the way quickly and spent most of the meeting once again criticizing Marshall's European Recovery Program when it came to rebuilding Germany.

Marshall was blunt, something that was in his nature. "Prime Minister, we have to learn from history. The Romans taught us that once an enemy is vanquished, a wise country will turn the conquered into friends. We didn't do that after the Great War and we see what that got us—another, even more catastrophic war. No one can blame the French for seeking revenge but leaving West Germany a wasteland will lead to nothing productive for your country or western Europe. This plan must go forward."

Erika translated.

Marshall stood, not waiting for a reply. "The United States of America is counting on your support. Thank you for your time, Prime Minister. I'll see you tomorrow night at the Armistice Day celebration."

And that was the end of the meeting.

The limousine ride back to the Ritz gave Erika an opportunity to express her concern to Marshall about the death threat.

Marshall almost seemed offended. "I had to coordinate plans during the war when I knew any plan would send many young Americans to their deaths. After that, am I expected to be afraid for my own life?"

Erika looked at him and said sincerely. "You're a great man, General."

"Poppycock. I'm a lucky man, nothing more, Mrs. Faust."

"Do you think the French Prime Minister will support your plan?"

"He'll have no choice in the end; the third point of my plan, NATO, will protect France and other countries from being overrun by the Soviets. The French people need that protection. So do France's allies in western Europe."

"I agree that taking revenge on the Germans will lead to nothing positive."

"By opposing the rebuilding of West Germany he's playing right into the hands of the Soviets even though he'd never admit it, even to himself. His days in office are numbered. I don't see him surviving the next election. De Gaulle will eventually take over."

It was an especially candid moment with his translator, proving how much he had grown to trust her in such a short time. But then, that was what Erika Lehmann was expert at. One only had to ask Henry Wiltshire.

◊ ◊ ◊

[that evening]

Leroy Carr knew Sheila Reid would give Al Hodge phony orders. She was a Shield Maiden after all. Unbeknownst to Sheila, the other Shield Maidens, and even Al, was Carr's condition to his agreement with Erika that he have final say on approving Zhanna's target. It was the only phone call from Erika that he allowed.

Erika told him the target and he gave her the go ahead. Before hanging up, Carr added, "Zhanna's shot can't be off. Remember our agreement, Erika."

"Yes, Leroy, I understand."

Carr hung up.

[same evening—Paris]

At the agreed upon time, Zhanna Rogova stood outside a telephone booth three blocks from the Hotel Napoleon. The phone rang. Zhanna answered.

Erika described her target.

"Very well," said Zhanna.

"Any questions?" Erika asked.

"No. I'll shoot him for your daughter. I have to go now. I have a taxi waiting here at the curb. I'm meeting Ian at a cabaret and you have already made me late." Zhanna hung up.

At the other end, Erika placed the receiver down and shook her head. *My cousin doesn't know what he's gotten himself into, but Zhanna is right, it's not my business.* Anyway, she had her own plans for the evening with Captain McBrayer.

Chapter 45

A Day of Celebration

Paris
Next day—Thursday, 11 November 1948
Armistice Day

Today was Armistice Day, the day World War I ended in 1918 and celebrations abound all around Paris, an indeed all over France, Western Europe, and the United States.

In Paris, the hub of the celebrations took place on the Champs-Élysées at the Tomb of the Unknown under the Arc de Triomphe. All day long, Parisians crowded the boulevard to watch parades, wave flags, and express their joy. The wine flowed. Many came early and waited all morning to garner a good spot to watch the afternoon festivities that wouldn't end until after the parades and short speeches by several French dignitaries and Frenchmen considered war heroes to the nation from both of the 20th century world wars. George Marshall was also on the slate for a few words as the representative from the United States, but his translator would be a Frenchman so Erika was not needed on the podium. Nevertheless, Marshall had ordered her to be nearby in case she was needed before or after his short speech, and the general ordered Captain McBrayer to make sure she was on hand. Marshall had informed her and McBrayer of this yesterday. After spending the past two nights in Erika's hotel room, the young captain from La Mesa considered it a very pleasant assignment.

After the parades and speeches, the celebration would culminate with a grand fireworks display launched from near the Eiffel Tower a short distance away.

Zhanna's shot wouldn't take place until during the fireworks display. The famous boulevard would be well lit, so a visual should not present a problem. Zhanna had made nighttime shots during the war under much less light. Of course, tonight there would be a legion of gendarmes on the Champs-Élysées there to keep order and protect the various dignitaries. The exploding fireworks would, or at least hopefully would, cover the crack of the Mosin-Nagant and give Zhanna a window of escape.

Now to the assignments of the Fischer sisters. The French Sûreté would have spotters with binoculars and two-way radios on the roof tops around the Arc. Kathryn and Stephanie's job was to neutralize any of them set up on the roof of the building Zhanna had chosen.

It was mid-afternoon when the women made their final scouting trip, weaving their way through the throng of celebrators who watched the first of the parades. Zhanna identified the place she wanted Kay to stand with her flag, then they walked toward the Arc to look over the small, empty grandstand that had been setup for the luminaries to sit that night, and the stage where the speakers would deliver their words into a microphone from a podium. Many members of the press were already crowded up to the stage vying for a spot where they might get an opportunity to ask a question of one of the dignitaries.

When the women were satisfied that they had seen everything they wanted to see, they returned to the Napoleon to make final preparations.

They had seen no clue of Erika, but then they knew they wouldn't until tonight. Everyone was underground and there could be no communication this day. Leroy Carr was unavailable in D.C. Sheila Reid had gone dark in London. Al Hodge stayed hunkered down in Paris, and Ryker had Henry Wiltshire in Lyon. Erika, Kathryn, Stephanie, and Zhanna were on their own. Carr had made plans to separate Kay in case the plot failed or was discovered. But for Erika and the other three Shield Maidens, they would be disavowed and suffer the full consequences if anything went awry. Hodge had made this abundantly clear.

[same time—Lyon, France]

Henry Wiltshire tried to eat his bean soup with his left hand. He was right-handed so this went slowly and awkwardly. On his right arm was a cast. Two nights ago, Henry made the mistake of trying to escape from the grungy hotel room while Ryker slept. Henry found out the hard way that it took only the slightest sound to awaken the creature. Ryker broke his arm for two purposes, Henry guessed. The first rationale was to please himself because Ryker enjoyed it, and the second was to teach him a lesson. The only reason he had a cast was because Ryker was expert at breaking bones and knew how to set them.

[an hour later—Hotel Napoleon in Paris]

When Zhanna returned to the hotel, Ian was sitting in the lobby. When he saw her, he stood.

"Ian, what are you doing here?" a surprised Zhanna asked.

"I came to see you, of course. I found a nice French café for our dinner tonight. I think you'll like it."

"Sit down, Ian." They both sat. "I cannot go out with you tonight."

"Oh, why?"

"I promised my girlfriends. We're going to watch the fireworks display."

"Let me go with you."

"I can't, Ian. You see, it's girl's night out. But we can do something tomorrow." Zhanna added in her silent thoughts, *If I'm still alive.*

"I understand," Ian said. "It's a good thing to have friends you enjoy being around. But we have a date for tomorrow, right?"

"Of course."

After Ian left, Zhanna went to her room to disassemble, clean, and oil her Mosin-Nagant 91/30. The Russian sniper/assassin was a stickler about cleaning her guns and did it often, even if they hadn't been fired between cleanings. She also had a personal little quirk to apply a small drop of oil to the cartridges, ensuring the empty shell casings would not bind when being ejected from the barrel.

She also called down to the desk for the latest weather forecast. Falling rain during this long-distance shot at such a precise target was her main concern. The forecast was clouds but a minimal chance for rain, at least until the wee hours of the night. Zhanna hoped they were right.

Chapter 46

A Red Gatsby Hat

Paris
Same day, that evening—Thursday, 11 November 1948
Armistice Day

The sun slowly sank behind the horizon like a freighter that had been torpedoed by a U-boat.

A number of Frenchmen who had been celebrating all day on the Champs-Élysées lay passed out on the curb or in the blocked off boulevard after enjoying too much wine. A few ladies were also among the group of prone Parisians. Like Army medics clearing a battlefield of wounded, work crews circulated with stretchers to remove those who had been too friendly with the bottle, taking them to tents. Apparently, this was not uncommon during the Armistice Day festivities in Paris.

As dusk started to relax itself on Paris, a uniformed Captain McBrayer offered Erika his arm and led her through the gauntlet of exuberant partiers until they finally reached a point near the stage by the Arc de Triomphe. He was fulfilling his orders from General Marshall to have her nearby in case he needed her after his speech. But that speech wouldn't take place for a while. First at the podium would be Henri Queuille and a half-dozen other French VIPs including Charles de Gaulle.

Erika wore a red Gatsby hat with a long peacock feather. The 1920s-style ladies hat fit in nicely with the era that sprung up just after the end of the Great War.

[30 minutes later]
A stubborn hint of civil daylight remained even though it knew its life neared its end as the speeches began.

It was time for the Fischer sisters to begin the mission. They had to neutralize any French scouts who would be working on the roof of the building Zhanna had chosen, and it had to be done before Zhanna arrived with her rifle.

The Russian sniper had decided to take the shot from the rooftop of the La Balzac Cinema on the Champs-Élysées. She had discreetly paced it off yesterday. Her shot from the roof top of the cinema to the grandstand area would be just at 1200 feet, a few hundred feet shorter than the distance she had been practicing. Yet, it was always advantageous if the target proved to be a bit closer than farther away; even though, being closer to the target raised the danger level for her as far as escaping. It was still a long shot—a surgical shot four American football fields away—but the slightly shorter range would be beneficial in case the rains came sooner than expected.

Kathryn and Stephanie spent the late afternoon and early evening in the La Balzac Cinema watching a French film entitled *Amour, delices et orgues,* a romantic comedy starring the French film stars Giselle Pascal and Jean Desailly. The theater was nearly deserted as everyone was outside on the boulevard enjoying the festivities. The film's dialogue was in French, and with no subtitles the sisters had no idea of what was being said on screen, but, obviously, that had nothing to do with the reason they were there.

◊ ◊ ◊

When the movie ended, the 19-year-old usher turned on the lights and walked into the theater. The three French couples he had seated were rising from their seats. The two women who had spoken English to him with German accents were not there. He shrugged it off. They must have gotten bored and left through a stage exit into the alley. He had worked here as an usher during the occupation and it seemed typically German. "Good riddance, Bosch," he mumbled.

◊ ◊ ◊

Kathryn and Stephanie ascended the fire escape ladder to the roof of the cinema making it a point to be quiet. It was now dark with the only significant light coming from street lamps below. When they reached the top, they gazed over the edge. On the roof in the very dim ambient light from the street they saw two men in French Sûreté uniforms on the opposite edge of the roof with their backs to them. The men peered through binoculars.

◊ ◊ ◊

The reason Erika had originally chosen the Hotel Napoleon was because of its location just four blocks from the Arc. Zhanna was ready. Her Mosin-Nagant was disassembled to the point it could be carried in a large shoulder bag that would not draw attention. The scope and ammunition were also neatly tucked away. Many women carried similar bags with food and water for their families on this day since many had arrived early in the morning and would spend the entire day with their loved ones at the celebration. Zhanna walked to the La Balzac Cinema only two blocks away.

◊ ◊ ◊

The two agents of the Sûreté stationed on the roof of the cinema heard footsteps behind them and quickly swiveled.

"What are you doing up here?" one of them demanded.

"I'm sorry," Kathryn said, "we didn't mean to startle you. The streets are so crowded; my sister and I thought this might be a good place to watch the fireworks."

"I'm sorry, Mademoiselles. You must leave immediately."

"We apologize, officers. This was clearly a mistake on our part."

◊ ◊ ◊

When Zhanna reached the roof of the cinema, she saw Kathryn kneeling behind the building's three-foot ledge that bordered the flat, tarred roof. Stephanie had already left to join Kay. Two unconscious police officers had been dragged to the far side.

"How long will they be out?" Zhanna asked as she knelt down beside Kathryn.

"At least three or four hours."

The Fischer sisters had cold-cocked the men with the butts of their handguns, then Kathryn had given each an injection of Nembutal.

"Have you spotted Erika?"

"Not yet," Kathryn replied.

Zhanna opened her bag and started assembling her rifle. It wouldn't be the first time she had to do so in the dark and it took her only a couple of minutes. Sighting the scope would be the only work, but it wasn't time for that yet. She didn't attach it to the rifle right away, instead using it like a telescope to help Kathryn look for the red Gatsby hat with the peacock feather amongst the shoulder-to-shoulder throng somewhere near the grandstand.

The speeches began.

[Washington, D.C.]

It was mid-afternoon on the East Coast and Leroy Carr sat in his office trying to work but finding it difficult. He spent more time glancing at the wall clock than he did looking over the paperwork on his desk. It would now be well into the evening in Paris.

[Paris]

The speeches last an hour all told. This gave Zhanna plenty of time to load the Mosin-Nagant, attach the scope and sight it. Kay had been located, but so far Erika had not been spotted. The women knew Erika was to get as close to the grandstand as possible so that's where Kathryn aimed the binoculars.

The fireworks were scheduled to start in five minutes when Kathryn said. "I see her."

"Where?"

"About ten feet from the front of the east corner of the grandstand."

Zhanna looked through her scope and found the red hat and zoomed in. It was Erika alright, on the arm of the American Army captain. Zhanna zoomed out and found Kay who had been holding up the American flag since the last speech ended. Stephanie stood beside her. There were many flags, mostly French but also some British, American, Belgian, and other allies during the First War, but they were being enthusiastically waved about which did Zhanna no good as far as judging wind speed. Kay, as instructed, held hers steady. Zhanna was still gazing through her scope at the movement of Kay's flag when the first boom of the fireworks display sounded. She judged the speed of the breeze and then refocused toward the grandstand.

◊ ◊ ◊

Zhanna Rogova hated fireworks. At least she hated the sound. The cacophony of the booming and popping aerials reminded her of the many times during the war she had been forced to burrow into the mud or snow like a mole to escape barrages by German artillery or rolling armor. But then, she was used to taking shots under the thunder of the guns. The rain was holding off. That was her main consideration.

◊ ◊ ◊

Erika still held Wayne McBrayer's arm as they looked to the heavens over the Arc de Triomphe where gold, red, green, blue and white rockets shattered and spiderwebbed the night sky. The breeze sent the acerbic odor of gunpowder, a smell all too familiar to Erika Lehmann, toward the crowd.

◊ ◊ ◊

Zhanna checked Kay's flag at the halfway point one last time, then refocused on her target four football fields away. She knew it best not to wait too long after the final check as the wind was a fickle flirt that could change its mind quickly. She had her scope adjusted for the light breeze and had her target in her crosshairs.

Zhanna Rogova calmly squeezed the trigger.

Chapter 47

Tackling the Quarterback

Paris
Same night—Thursday, 11 November 1948
Armistice Day

The fireworks rockets continued to scorch and blister the night sky. Erika held Wayne McBrayer's left arm tighter, keeping him still. She knew the shot had to come soon. Knowing the powerful 7.62x54mm round would pass through a body, she had positioned them where no one standing in front of them would be struck. It wasn't easy to do in such a crowd, but Erika knew exactly where the shot would come from and the trajectory.

Another aerial exploded loudly overhead just as McBrayer staggered and dropped to the ground. Zhanna's shot had been precise, entering his back just to the right of his right shoulder blade.

At first there was little reaction from the crowd as the rifle crack was muted by the loud booms overhead. It wasn't until Erika screamed for help that those around them took notice. "Someone's shooting at us!" Erika yelled.

This caused a panic and instead of helping, people started running for cover. Erika covered McBrayer's body with her own to protect him.

On the stage, George Marshall heard Erika's pleas for help and started her way. He was grabbed by his aides who tried to hustle him away, but he cursed at them and shook them off. Suddenly a second shot splintered the plywood podium near him. Marshall's aides, now thinking the general was under fire, ignored his orders, tackled him and covered him with their bodies. Henri Queuille and most of the other dignitaries were already off the stage and running for their limousines.

Marshall, laying at the bottom of a pile of men like a quarterback after a sneak at the goal line, bellowed, "Get off me, goddammit."

"I'm sorry, sir. We can't do that," a major yelled back.

"Then at least some of you go help the captain and my translator or I'll court martial all your asses!"

Two men got up, jumped off the stage, and went to help Erika and McBrayer.

A third shot ripped a hole in the United States flag displayed on the stage—the only flag that was hit among the flags of several countries.

◊ ◊ ◊

After the third shot, Zhanna said, "Time to go. Because of the two unconscious Sûreté men, they will know the shots came from here. We'll leave the rifle and spent casings. I'll wipe the rifle for my fingerprints. You wipe the shell casings." Zhanna ejected the two remaining live rounds so Kathryn could also wipe them.

All this took less than a minute then the two Shield Maidens were on their way down the fire ladder as the fireworks continued to thump the sky as a light drizzle began to fall.

Part 5

"There is not, there was not, and there never will be any romance about the spy trade. The silent war of the spy is mean, cold and bitter. It is the dirtiest side of war."

—Erich Gimpel, Abwehr spy captured in America during WW II, released in 1955.

Chapter 48

Watching the Clock

Paris
Same night—Armistice Day

Because of standard protocol insisted on by Harry Truman, an Army doctor with a medical bag was never far from George Marshall's side when he travelled overseas. The same practice applied to any cabinet member when travelling outside the States.

After McBrayer was moved to a safe point of cover behind the grandstand, Marshall's doctor stemmed the bleeding. Marshall, instead of waiting for an ambulance to meander its way to the grandstand through a panicked crowd, ordered his driver to speed Captain McBrayer to the nearest hospital in his staff car. Once it was determined that Erika was unharmed, Marshall had his men load her into the backseat of a second sedan with him.

"The medic told me Captain McBrayer's injury is not life threatening, Mrs. Faust," Marshall said as their sedan followed the staff car to the hospital. Blood covered her hands and soaked several places on her blouse.

Erika, the actress, said nothing and shook uncontrollably.

"Calm yourself, Mrs. Faust. The captain will be fine, and I saw what you did. You were very brave shielding him with your body."

[Washington, D.C.]

Leroy Carr wasn't going to leave his office until he heard from Al Hodge. Finally, just after seven o'clock Washington time he got the call.

"Leroy, Caesar has crossed the Rubicon," Hodge said from Paris.

Carr sighed in relief and hung up without replying. This told him Zhanna had made the three shots she was ordered to take and no one was killed per his orders to Erika. Also, no one had been captured—yet.

He pressed the buzzer on his desk and told his aide, "Get me Sheila Reid in London—quickly."

Fifteen minutes later, Sheila was on the phone.

"Sheila, I know you went against my orders to call off the mission, but instead of a court martial I'll give you one chance to redeem yourself. Contact Al and have him get my wife, Zhanna, and the Fischer sisters out of France before dawn. I don't care where they go, just get them across the border and then we'll make plans to get them back to the States. I want you to stay in London until Ryker brings Henry Wiltshire back there and releases him, then contact me for further orders."

"I did it because Erika has earned a chance to be with her daughter, Leroy. We all stand behind that, even Kay and Al."

Carr ignored her comment. "Any questions about your orders this time? They are specific and there will be no juggling on your part."

"What about Erika," Sheila asked

"She's temporarily on Marshall's staff. If she disappears it will look suspicious. She is to stay there for now and keep playing her part, but I want everyone except her and Al out of France before dawn. And tell Stephanie Fischer she's still responsible for keeping my wife safe. Don't fail me on this, Sheila."

Carr hung up.

When Sheila heard the phone go dead, she smiled. This was the first reprimand she had ever received from Leroy Carr, but he couldn't hide his intentions from her. He needed plausible deniability if this were to work out in the end. She picked up the phone and asked the Savoy switchboard operator to connect her to the Hotel Napoleon in Paris. She would follow Carr's orders to the letter this time, because she now knew that all along he had the welfare of Erika and her child at heart.

Chapter 49

Maiden Name

Germany
Next day—Friday, 12 November 1948

Kathryn Fischer was the one who picked up the phone in Paris when Sheila called. After Sheila told them their orders from Carr, they left immediately and made it out of France by hotwiring a French Renault they picked out from numerous cars parked on the curb around the block from the hotel. All four women, Kay Carr, Zhanna, Kathryn, and Stephanie arrived in Stuttgart, Germany, after a six-hour drive, crossing the border just as the clouds in the east turned orange. They abandoned the stolen car at the train depot and waited an hour to board an early morning train to Munich, just 2½-hours away. By ten o'clock in the morning they arrived in the city where the Nazi Party was founded.

[Paris]

Erika spent the night at the hospital. Wayne McBrayer's surgery went well. His right arm would be in a sling for two or three weeks but he was conscious and in good spirits when she left.

"I'm just glad you weren't hit, Erika," he had said.

George Marshall had instructed her to call his adjutant when she was ready to leave the hospital. The car delivered her to Marshall's office. The Secretary of State stood when the adjutant led her into the room.

"That will be all, Captain Gambrel. Thank you."

The man closed the door behind him.

"Please have a seat, Mrs. Faust."

They both sat.

"So, how is Captain McBrayer? My doctor tells me he'll be fine."

"He's in good spirits, General, and impatient to be released from the hospital."

"Who wouldn't be?" Marshall joked. "Mrs. Faust, I think by now you know I'm a man who gets to the point. Your dossier claims that, besides French, you speak fluent German and Russian, and Dutch. Is that true?"

"I speak some Dutch but not fluently. The other languages you mentioned, yes, I am fluent."

"Qualified and trustworthy German and Russian translators are in dire need," Marshall pointed out. "I'll cut to the chase, Mrs. Faust. I'd like you to join my staff. What do you say?"

"I'm honored, General, but I don't think you would want me."

"Not want you? Why?"

"I have criminal charges pending against me in the United States."

"What are you taking about?"

"My married name is Erika Faust. My maiden name is Erika Lehmann. You'll want to run that name through channels."

"Very well, I'll do that, but why don't you tell me right now what I'll find."

"I'm German and served as an agent of the Abwehr during the war. I conducted espionage against the United States and I have a murder charge hanging over my head in Cincinnati."

Marshall stared at her for a long moment, thinking. "And now, for whatever reason, you're being protected from prosecution by someone in our government, similar to the German rocket scientists, in exchange for something you can offer our country. Am I getting warm?"

"Yes, sir."

"Tell me about the murder charge."

"I killed a man who was beating and raping two innocent and helpless women. It had nothing to do with my mission."

[that evening]

Erika was back in her hotel room thinking how much her fate now lay in George Marshall's hands. She could only pray she had handled today's conversation correctly.

A knock sounded at her door. When she opened, Ian Minton stood in the hallway.

"Hello, cousin," he said. "I've called a few times today with no answer. Is Zhanna here? We have a date tonight."

Erika paused for a brief moment. "Come in, Ian."

They sat across from each other in the suite that had yesterday been home to Erika, Zhanna, and Kathryn. Now it was just Erika.

"Ian, as you know, Zhanna is a Russian interpreter and she was called away early this morning by the U.S. State Department to return to the Helsinki conference."

"I thought that thing in Helsinki was over."

"So did Zhanna, but apparently not. It was a spur of the moment thing, Ian. She didn't know about it until a driver knocked on the door to take her to the airport. I'm sorry. I would have called you, but I didn't know you had a date with her tonight."

"When will she be back?"

"I don't know," Erika said. "When it's over, I'm assuming Zhanna will be ordered to return to the States."

"America?"

"Yes. That would be my guess."

Ian sat thinking for a moment. "Can you get a message to her, Erika?"

"I can try, but I might not see her again until we're all back in America."

"Is there a pencil and paper handy?" he asked.

Erika handed him some hotel stationary.

When he finished writing the message, Erika sealed it in a hotel envelope. She had no desire to read it. It was none of her business.

Before he left, the two cousins hugged. Erika had few family members left, and she hoped to see him again someday.

At the door, Erika said, "Ian, go home to London. Zhanna won't be returning here. I'll get your note to her when I can. Take care of yourself and check in on my grandparents as often as you can. Goodbye."

[still later this evening]

Erika and Al Hodge sat together on the walkway outside a café on the Avenue Victor Hugo. Coffee had been served.

Hodge said, "Sheila confirms that Ryker did his job and delivered your old buddy, Henry Wiltshire, to London where he was released."

"That's good. Looking back now, putting poor Henry through that was needless. I captured him before Leroy suggested a different plan."

"I know you're anxious to hear the latest on Armistice Day," Hodge said, "so here's what I know right now. Because of the death threat I sent to the French government two days ago with communist propaganda against the Marshall plan included, the French government is considering it an attack by French communists. It's supported in their minds by all of Zhanna's shots last night being directed at Americans or the Stars & Stripes. I've heard nothing come out of Marshall's office. You talked to him today, what do you think?"

"Knowing he would find out about my history, I told him the truth." Erika didn't mention Marshall's initial job offer. Not because she felt any need to keep something from Hodge, but because she now felt it was a moot point after she fessed up to her history.

"That's good," Hodge replied.

"Yes, but he made no mention of a pardon."

"Keep hopes high, Erika. It looks like Marshall is impressed with you."

Erika looked at Hodge. She had given this man a world of problems over the past four years. She placed her hand across the table on his.

"Thank you for supporting me, Al. How are Kay and the Maidens doing?"

"They're in West Germany—Munich. We'll extract them as soon as we can."

"Munich?"

"Yeah, why?"

Erika knew the trouble the German Fischer sisters could get themselves into in Munich. Add to that, Zhanna Rogova was with them.

"Nothing. Just asking," she said. "I don't know about you, but I'm starving. Let's order something to eat."

Chapter 50

Upstairs in the Festhalle

Paris
Next day—Saturday, 13 November 1948

George Marshall was scheduled to fly back to Washington on Monday. For now, he sat reading the Department of Justice dossier on Erika Lehmann, the woman he knew as Mrs. Faust. More than a few of the entries of her past surprised, and even stunned the hardened military man.

He had told his adjutant to bring Mrs. Faust to his office that afternoon. After reading the entire dossier, he called the adjutant into his office and canceled the meeting.

[that afternoon—Munich]
Kathryn and Stephanie took Kay and Zhanna to the Augustiner brewery for lunch. That was just the start. Next up was the Hofbräuhaus.

[Washington, D.C.]
Leroy Carr had been summoned to the office of Admiral Roscoe Hillenkoetter, Director of the CIA.

"I just got off the phone with George Marshall, Leroy. What the hell is going on in Paris?"

"I'm not sure I understand, Roscoe."

"Erika surfaced in Paris working for George Marshall. How can that happen?" As far as Hillenkoetter knew, Erika had not been seen since she and Zhanna Rogova disappeared from the Mayflower Hotel in September.

"I'll put Al on it right away," Carr said.

"Where *is* Al? I haven't seen him in a while."

"I sent him to London. I thought Erika might show up where her daughter lives." At least this was true. "But Al reported in yesterday and

Erika is not in London (Al *had* reported in, and yes, Erika was not in London). I'll make sure he checks out Paris." Carr so far had been deceptive but had not told any bold-faced lies.

"Well, get to the bottom of it. Marshall wants to talk to you about Erika. Here's his number in Paris, he's awaiting your call."

Carr returned to his office and dialed Marshall through the CIA switchboard operator. Marshall's aide was on the phone within ten minutes.

"My name is Leroy Carr in Washington. The Secretary requested I telephone him."

Carr and Kay had once attended a reception where Marshall and his wife were present, but the two never spoke and had never met.

George Marshall had total access to not only Department of State and Department of War records, but also to the Department of Justice and the CIA. Even the curmudgeonly and politically powerful J. Edgar Hoover dare not withhold information from George C. Marshall. By the time Carr's call got through to Marshall, the general had learned a lot about both Carr and Erika Lehmann.

"Hello," Marshall said into the receiver.

"Mr. Secretary, this is Leroy Carr in Washington. I was instructed by Admiral Hillenkoetter to contact you."

"Yes, thank you for calling, Mr. Carr. I'm sure you're very busy. First, let me thank you for your outstanding work with the OSS during the war."

"Thank you, sir."

"We've had some excitement here in Paris the past couple of days. Your employee, listed in your records as Erika Lehmann, has been a major reason."

"Erika?"

"She does work for you at the CIA, is that correct?"

"That is true, Mr. Secretary."

"Tell me about her activities against us during the war."

Marshall had not put him in a position where he was forced to lie, which was a relief for Carr. Here on out, honesty was the best policy.

"Erika had only one mission against us. In 1943, she infiltrated a Naval shipyard that built LSTs in Evansville, Indiana. She stole some top-secret information and a vial of tellurium. The tellurium was recovered but she escaped."

"She said something about a murder charge hanging over her."

"After she escaped from Evansville, she laid low in Cincinnati for a short while. She walked in on two women being beaten and assaulted in a rundown apartment building she was living in. There were three perpetrators, two men and one woman. She seriously injured the woman attacker and one of the men but was forced to kill the other man. She saved the two innocent women's lives."

"How did she kill him?"

"Handgun."

"Why did she come to my office and apply for the job as a translator, Mr. Carr? It couldn't have been a happy accident."

"We received a threat against Charles de Gaulle that was supposed to take place on the stage at the Armistice Day celebration (Carr stopped short of mentioning the threat had come from Erika). I wanted someone close to you. Someone unsuspected, like a woman, who could handle herself."

"Strange coincidence," said Marshall, "that my translator, Miss Burke, suddenly came up ill at the last moment. Your people must have slipped her a helluva a Mickie."

"I'm sure she's fine by now, Mr. Secretary."

"Mr. Carr, I'll have more to say about all this. I should have been informed ahead of time about de Gaulle. I leave Monday for the States and will be back in Washington Tuesday morning. Be at Andrews to meet my plane. One of my aides will contact you with my scheduled arrival time. Mrs. Faust will be on the plane with me. Come aboard and we'll talk on the plane. You can take charge of her at that time."

Marshall had given no indication about a pardon for Erika.

[that night—Munich]

Zhanna and Kay had never been to Munich's world-famous beer hall, and Kathryn and Stephanie hadn't been back since the early years of the war.

It was Saturday night at the Hofbräuhaus which meant crowded tables, loud oompah bands, boisterous beer drinkers, and Bier Fräuleins in dirndls carrying amazing numbers of full liter Maß mugs to tables. Kay noticed that one waitress carried twelve Maß—six in each hand. Stephanie mentioned that, years ago, she had watched one sturdy Bier Fräulein carry twenty-four. It was during the Oktoberfest Bier Fräulein competitions.

They sat upstairs in the Festhalle, each with a Maß of golden beer in front of them.

"The beer is cold," Kay said after her first sip. "I thought the German's drank warm beer."

"Not anymore," Kathryn said. "The Führer changed all that at the '36 Olympics. He ordered the beer cooled for the Americans. Germans decided they liked it and it's been chilled ever since."

Kay had noticed many times that the Fischer sisters still referred to Hitler as the Führer. She had also heard Erika still use that moniker of respect. Kay knew all three women were shocked and abhorred when the truth about the horrors of the concentration camps came to light at the end of the war, yet to them he was still the *Leader.* It was a bit disconcerting, but she kept her tongue. Maybe when this was over she would ask them why.

Kathryn pointed out the stage at the end of the Festhalle and said, "Kay and Zhanna, the Führer gave many speeches from there over the years, going back to the early 1920s, the earliest days of the struggle."

Kay looked at the Fischer sisters, both of whom looked at the stage with what seemed to suggest a certain amount of longing.

Zhanna said, "I wish I would have been here for one of his speeches. I could have shot the bastard."

Stephanie turned to the Russian and said sarcastically, "It would have served you better to shoot that pig Stalin. He killed millions of his own people even before the war."

Kay added quickly, "Can we get some of those big pretzels? I'll buy."

"Fuck the pretzels and the Germans who made them," Zhanna said.

Kay knew what could happen if this escalated. She had to do something. "Ladies, listen to me carefully. Let's not forget why we all banded together. It was to help Erika. Let's not ruin it. I want this rancor to end now, and it *will* end if you want my husband's continued protection."

"Fuck your husband and the whore he rode in on," Zhanna replied. She had mixed up *horse* with *whore* in the American expression.

The Fischer sisters started laughing. Kay judged that a good sign and instantly added more comedy, "If Leroy is riding a whore, it's the last ride he'll take. As his wife I can guarantee you that!"

Kay's threat to withdraw her husband's protection had failed to diffuse the volatile situation but her quick-witted joke helped. Then, they were taken by surprise when Zhanna Rogova apologized to them all.

"I'm sorry for what I said. I met a man in London. A good man I'll never see again and my patience with life is drained."

No one had ever heard Zhanna Rogova, the orphan no one wanted and the killer of hundreds of men during the war, lay bare her soul. A soul with scars more gruesome than her hideous neck scar—scars that could not be concealed by a scarf.

Chapter 51

Ivan Solokova

London
Next day—Sunday, 14 November 1948

Axel Ryker sat in Sheila Reid's hotel room at the Savoy.

"I assume Henry Wiltshire returned to London unharmed," Sheila said. "Those were your orders."

"He is unharmed except for a broken arm," Ryker said matter of factly.

"What happened to his arm?"

"He tried to escape in Lyon. I decided to break his arm as an incentive that he not attempt another escape."

"Your orders were to bring him back unharmed, Ryker."

"Would you prefer he escaped? Don't tell me how to do my job, Amerikanerin."

Sheila frowned at him. "I'll let Leroy Carr deal with you when you get back to the States. Now listen. Last night I received new instructions from Leroy. Instead of returning immediately to Washington, Leroy wants you to remain here in London with me for now."

"Why?" Ryker growled.

"It doesn't matter why. Those are your orders from your boss. I was told to get you a room here at the Savoy. I've done that and you're under the name of Ivan Solokova. Room 427, here's your key." Sheila tossed it at him. "I was also instructed to tell you that you are not to leave the hotel unless I'm with you. You are to lie low. Use room service for your meals. We can't take the chance of you being spotted by MI-6 in the lobby or at the hotel restaurant. MI-6 keeps close tabs on this hotel. I'm your supervisor until you return to Washington, that comes from Mr. Carr."

"A woman being my overseer would never have happened in the Reich."

"You're no longer in the Gestapo, Ryker. Learn to live with it. You can go to your room now."

[same day—Paris]

Erika was in her room at the Napoleon when a U.S. Army major knocked on her door.

"Mrs. Faust?" he asked.

"Yes, Major Chandler." She had scanned his name tag over his right breast.

"I'm on General Marshall's staff. He has sent me here to escort you to the American embassy where you'll spend the night. Please pack your things. Tomorrow you'll leave for Washington on the General's airplane."

[near that same time in Paris]

"Al," Carr said from D.C.

"Yes, Leroy," Hodge answered in Paris.

"I want you to go to Munich and bring Kay and the Maidens back to Washington."

"Is there a problem?"

"None that I know of now, but Kay is with them and I don't trust the Maidens to stay out of trouble."

"I can't blame you for that when it comes to those crazy dames," Hodge replied. 'I'll leave as soon as I can. What's going on with Marshall?"

"It's not looking good."

"Holy Mary. What are you going to do, Leroy?"

"I don't know. Just get Kay home. She'll be too stubborn to leave without the other women. Ryker and Sheila are still in London. Take them with you to Munich."

"Okay," Hodge said. "I'll fly Sheila and Ryker to Paris tomorrow then we'll fly to Munich. We should be there tomorrow night. Where are the women staying in Munich?"

"The Platzl Hotel."

Chapter 52

Al Steps Out with the Shield Maidens

Paris
Next day—Monday, 15 November 1948

Sheila Reid and Axel Ryker arrived in Paris at eleven o'clock this morning. Al Hodge was waiting with another plane and by noon they were flying over the Eiffel Tower on their way to Munich, only a 2½-hour flight.

George Marshall had hoped to fly out of Paris when the cock crowed but some last-minute business in Paris delayed his departure. Finally, around two that afternoon, he, his staff, and Erika Lehmann boarded Marshall's U.S. Air Force DC-3. Marshall's staff was a large one and nearly all of the 32 seats were filled. Marshall and his top aides sat in the front. Erika was seated in the rear aisle, next to the bathroom with one of the few empty seats beside her. Wayne McBrayer was not among Marshall's entourage. The doctors wouldn't clear him to fly back to the States for at least another week.

[that evening—Munich]

The Fischer sisters and Kay Carr were back at the Hofbräuhaus but now Al Hodge and Axel Ryker were with them along with the other Shield Maiden, Sheila Reid.

They couldn't fly out until tomorrow and Hodge had always wanted to see the famous beer hall. He agreed to the dinner only if everyone promised there would be no trouble. They promised, of course.

The Hofbräuhaus took up nearly the entire block of the Platzl and the Bräuhausstraße and had many rooms, large and small. After dinner, the CIA group found themselves in a room on the second floor where arm wrestling contests were in full swing. Ryker entered the contest, and the Shield Maidens and Kay raked in the Reichsmarks betting on him. After a while, even Hodge, who had already drunk two Maß, started laying down money.

One burly man, well-known at the beer hall for his strength, sat down across from Ryker and boasted to the onlookers, "This ugly arschloch has won his last match."

Trying to intimidate Axel Ryker by calling him asshole was a poor strategy. Instead of powering the braggart's hand to the table, Ryker simply crushed three of the man's fingers after they locked hands. That proved to be the end of competitors willing to take a seat across from Ryker, and the arm wrestling ended for the night.

Sheila served as bookkeeper. The CIA group had won 70 Reichsmarks.

"This will buy a lot of beer," Sheila grinned.

"I think it's time to return to our hotel," Hodge said. "We start a long flight tomorrow."

"Are you nuts?" Stephanie said. "We're not going back to the hotel with 70 free Reichsmarks, and you're staying with us, Al."

"I'm not going to stay here and get shitfaced, and neither are you crazy broads."

Stephanie took his arm. "We'll see about that."

Hodge tried to pull away, but Kathryn took his other arm, flirted with him, and handed the middle-aged widower another Maß.

Chapter 53

Overslept

Munich, Germany
Next day—Tuesday, 16 November 1948

Al Hodge asked the hotel desk for a seven a.m. wake-up call. The ringing phone didn't wake him. Instead he sat up on the edge of his bed over four hours later at 11:15 a.m. with a roaring headache. He then went about calling Kay, Ryker, and the Shield Maidens in their rooms. The flight out would be later than planned, but they could still be in the air by mid-afternoon.

[same time]
After refueling and a lengthy maintenance check in Ireland late last night, George Marshall's DC-3 was now nearly hallway across the Atlantic Ocean. Erika, still in the seat next to the restroom, sat ignored by everyone on the plane, looking out the window at the ocean 13,000 feet below and thinking of Ada.

[30 minutes later—Munich]
Al Hodge was on the phone with Washington.

"Leroy, Rogova and the Fischer sisters have disappeared."

"What! Why?"

"I screwed up, Leroy," Hodge confessed. "I let them get me drunk last night."

"What the hell, Al?"

"I know. I blew it."

"Where's Kay?"

"She's safe and here right now, so are Sheila and Ryker."

"Let me talk to Kay."

"Okay, the Maidens left a message with her. She'll read it to you." Hodge handed the phone to Kay.

"Hello, darling," she said into the receiver.

"Are you alright, Kay?"

"I'm fine. Here's the message Al told you about. I'll read it verbatim. *'Leroy, you will never find us and we won't return to Washington until Erika receives her pardon. We'll call Sheila at her home each night until she tells us this will or will not happen. If it's not to be, we'll disappear forever. When we call Sheila, we'll talk for less than forty seconds so don't waste your time trying to trace the call.'* That's all it says, Leroy."

"Okay," Carr said. "I love you. Please put Al back on."

She handed the phone back to Hodge.

"Forget about trying to find the Maidens in Germany, Al. It will never happen with the Fischer sisters in their native land. Bring Kay, Sheila, and Ryker back to Washington as soon as possible."

"My Electra is on the tarmac here in Munich and had the maintenance check yesterday. It's ready to fly. We'll leave tonight, Leroy."

Chapter 54

Carr and Marshall Pow Wow

Washington, D.C.
Next day—Wednesday, 17 November 1948

A light fountain of tender rain fell on the Washington area in the early morning hours.

After a second refueling stop in Newfoundland, George Marshall's DC-3 landed on a wet runway at Andrews Air Force base in the mid-afternoon.

Leroy Carr had been requested by George Marshall to be on hand when his plane arrived. A request from George Marshall was nearly equivalent to a request from Harry Truman so Carr was standing on the tarmac under a black umbrella as the plane taxied toward its place assigned by the control tower.

The ground crew rolled the steps to the front fuselage door and people began disembarking. Some wore military uniforms, others business suits.

Carr waited. When it seemed the appropriate time, he ascended the metal stairs.

Still onboard was only George Marshall, one aide, and Erika.

"I assume you are Leroy Carr," Marshall said.

"Yes, Mr. Secretary. I'm Carr."

"Marshall motioned to the seat next to him. "Take a seat, Mr. Carr."

"Thank you." Carr sat down beside Marshall.

Marshall directed his aide to bring Erika forward. As the aisle had only two seats side-by-side, the aide placed Erika in a seat just behind them.

Marshall minced no words, as was his habit. "I will ask you only once, Mr. Carr. Is the story of Mrs. Faust's killing of the man in Cincinnati accurate? She saved two innocent women?"

"Yes, it is absolutely the truth Mr. Secretary."

"I have your word on that?"

"Yes, sir. What happened is documented from interviews of the victims on file with the Cincinnati police. The Justice department chose to ignore the reports because of Erika's enemy agent status during wartime."

"Then what is it you want from me?" Marshall asked.

Carr said, "Erika has served the United States faithfully for over three years, Mr. Secretary. Any American citizen who saved those women would have been declared a hero. She deserves a pardon so she can apply for U.S. citizenship and have a life with her daughter."

Marshall turned around in his seat. "You have a daughter, Mrs. Faust?"

With real tears welling in her eyes, Erika said, "Yes."

Marshall sat back in his seat and took a moment.

"Mrs. Faust, please get out of your seat and stand next to us," Marshall said.

Erika did so.

"Mrs. Faust, you are an extraordinary woman. You saved two women in Cincinnati and protected Captain McBrayer with your body in Paris. It seems you're in the habit of saving people. I meet with the president tomorrow to brief him about the political situation in France. I will mention your pardon. It will be the president's decision, of course."

"Of course, General," Erika replied. "And thank you so much. You don't know what hearing this means to me."

"It's certainly not a done deal, Mrs. Faust. This president is frugal with pardons."

Erika Lehmann, the tough leader of the Shield Maiden, said nothing and quickly returned to her seat and wept silently, overcome that her quest to be with her daughter might now have a chance. None of those tears were for Wayne McBrayer, whom she seduced then had Zhanna shoot.

Chapter 55

Give 'em Hell Harry

The White House
Next day—Thursday, 18 November 1948

Instead of sitting at his desk, Harry Truman preferred looking out the windows of the Oval Office onto the South Lawn while he was being briefed. This meant his back was to George Marshall as Marshall went over the French and German situations. Yet, this was no sign of disrespect as he held George Marshall in high regard. After all, Truman had picked him for his Secretary of State. The only major disagreement the two men had ever had was over Israel. Truman recognized Israel as a sovereign state last spring over Marshall's objections. The general thought doing so would play into the hands of the Russians, allowing them a foothold in the Arab lands with major access to the vast oil reserves of the Middle East, possibly even shutting down sales to the West.

Today's meeting had started over an hour ago. Truman didn't like large conferences, although sometimes they were unavoidable. Today, however, it was just him, Marshall, and Truman's trusted military aide, Harry H. Vaughn, in the room. Vaughn listened, took notes, and kept quiet.

"Sounds like France would be better off without Queuille, George."

"Depends on who would replace him, Mr. President."

"Anything new in Germany?" Truman asked.

"My trip to Berlin was just overnight. Our airlift is working, much to the Soviets' dismay."

"Good news," Truman said, then came away from the window and sat down behind his desk.

"Thanks, George. Is there anything else?"

"That's all for the briefing, Mr. President. There is another matter I'd like to bring before you. In Paris, my French interpreter fell ill and had to be replaced quickly."

"I'm sorry to hear that. Is she okay?"

"She's fine. The issue concerns the woman that replaced her, a CIA agent."

"A CIA agent?"

"She had identification that she worked for the State Department but I found out later that was a cover."

Marshall opened his briefcase and withdrew a large, thick envelope and placed it on Truman's desk.

"Her married name is Faust, but she's a widow. In the records, she's Erika Lehmann. In the envelope is everything from the CIA and the Department of Justice."

"Why does the Justice Department have information on a CIA agent?"

"She has a murder charge hanging over her. An incident that happened in Cincinnati during the war, but I'm convinced she was forced to kill the man to protect two innocent women."

"During the war," Truman said. "So she worked for the OSS?"

"No, sir. She worked for the German Abwehr."

Truman stared at Marshall. "Was she a member of the Nazi Party?"

"Yes, but she came over to our side toward the end of the war and has served the United States faithfully and well since that time. All the information is in the envelope. Mr. President."

"I'm guessing the CIA has been protecting her from the Justice Department."

"That's correct, sir. I'm asking you to consider a pardon, Mr. President. A sniper, who we suspect to be a communist, wounded a captain on my staff at the Armistice Day celebration in Paris. Unfortunately, the sniper has not yet been apprehended, but Mrs. Faust—Erika Lehmann—showed great courage by throwing herself on the captain to protect him in case of another shot."

He continued. "Besides French, this woman is a soldier at heart and speaks fluent German and Russian, Mr. President. You know how valuable someone like that can be to the United States. If you decide to grant the pardon, I'll put her on my staff. She can be of great service to our country."

"You want her on your staff? What does the CIA have to say about you stealing her away?"

"I haven't told them."

The President of the United States chuckled.

Truman sat thinking for a moment, then picked up the envelope and handed it to Vaughn. "We'll look at the information, George. I'll try to accommodate you unless we find something that would, for political or legal reasons, prohibit granting a pardon to a former Nazi. Gaining the White House only because a beloved four-term president died already puts the new guy behind the eight ball. Then, as you know, in the election earlier this month everyone expected me to lose to Dewey. Even some of my own staff had no confidence in me winning. Some of them started putting out feelers for another job in September and October. I'm not in a strong position with the American people right now. I won less than 50% of the popular vote and there is a large gang of congressmen, senators, and press out there hoping I'll prove them right and make a mess of things."

"I understand, Mr. President. The decision is in your hands."

Chapter 56

Frankfurt

Washington, D.C.
Next day—Friday, 19 November 1948

Kay, Al, and Sheila Reid arrived back in Washington two days ago. Ryker flew with them on the airplane but had now been sent back to Fort Dix, New Jersey. The Fischer sisters and Zhanna were still AWOL. In Erika's absence, Kathryn sort of melted into the job of Maiden leader by default. Her sister Stephanie was new to the group and didn't feel it was her place, and Zhanna wasn't interested in the job. Kathryn called Sheila each night. Sheila told her the good news about George Marshall's promise to talk to the president about Erika, but there were no guarantees and no word yet. They had left Munich and were currently holed up in a flea bag hotel in the red-light district of Frankfurt. Moving around to large cities was good protocol when one went dark.

[that evening]

After arriving back in Washington on George Marshall's airplane, Erika had stayed in the Carr's Annapolis home in the spare bedroom. Tomorrow, Leroy Carr would move Erika to the Mayflower Hotel. It was at the Mayflower that Erika usually stayed when Carr brought her to Washington from Camp Peary in Virginia where she served as a CIA instructor when she wasn't on a mission.

Since she would be leaving their home tomorrow, the Carr's took her to dinner tonight at Jocko's Pub, one of the Carr's favorite places in Annapolis. It wasn't fancy, but a place with good Irish and American food and a friendly pub atmosphere.

Drinks had been ordered and a pint of Guinness sat on the table in front of each of them.

"Leroy," Erika said. "I want to thank you again for going to bat for me with General Marshall. You'll never know how much I appreciate what you did. And thank you Kay for supporting me."

Kay said, "You don't have to thank me. All mothers deserve a chance to bring up their daughters."

They all knew it was Leroy who had taken the greatest risk by giving Erika the go ahead to have Zhanna wound Captain McBrayer. If that ever came to light it would mean Carr's ruin. But that was obvious, especially to Leroy Carr, and didn't need comment so it wasn't mentioned.

"Any idea when a decision about my pardon might come through?" Erika asked.

"No idea, Erika," Leroy answered. "Hopefully it will be sooner rather than later. Let's order. I know how much you like to eat."

[in Frankfurt, Germany]

The Fischer sisters and Zhanna decided to go out for a drink and ended up in a bar they thought benign but was in reality a place for prostitutes to solicit customers.

Before they even had a chance to order a drink, a man walked up to their table.

"How much for all three of you?" he said. "I have friends with me."

The three women glared at him. Zhanna's German was good enough to understand what he said but not good enough to relay her reply. She told Kathryn in English, "Tell him if he doesn't want to die with his severed ball in his mouth he would be wise to walk away right now."

Kathryn was glad to translate.

Something in the eyes of the women convinced the man to walk away without comment. Stephanie stopped a waitress and the armed women ordered their drinks.

"Where will you go, Zhanna, if Erika doesn't get her pardon?" Stephanie asked.

"I don't know. Unlike you two, South America is not an option for me. Certain countries there welcome ex-Nazis, Russians not so much. And I can't return to the convent in Honduras. That's the first place the Americans will look. Maybe I'll go to Cairo or Istanbul. I've never been to Cairo but I know some old comrades are there. I've been to Istanbul and know my way around that area. How long are we going to wait for an answer?"

"As long as it takes," Kathryn said. "That's why we asked Sheila to return with Mr. Carr. Sheila won't lie to us. If she tells us yes or no about Erika's pardon, we know it's the truth. Zhanna, please don't leave before we have an answer."

The Russian assassin lit a cigarette.

The weekend would pass with still no answer from Sheila.

Chapter 57

Carr is Summoned

Washington
Three days later—Monday, 22 November 1948

Admiral Roscoe Hillenkoetter, the director of the CIA, had been summoned to the Oval Office. The CIA's second in command, Deputy Director Leroy Carr was also ordered in because nearly all of the records in the CIA dossier concerning Erika Lehmann came from Carr's office.

"Thank you for coming, gentlemen," Truman said. He was sitting behind his desk this time and the curtains were drawn. George Marshall was not there. Only another Harry, the ever-present Harry H. Vaughn, Truman's close friend and trusted advisor was also included.

"Can we get you a cup of coffee?" Truman asked.

Both Hillenkoetter and Carr thanked the president but added that they were fine.

"We've studied the files on your Erika Lehmann and I have a few questions," Truman said. "First, what is your opinion of Secretary Marshall's request for a pardon?"

"Mr. President," said Hillenkoetter, "the Secretary knows the CIA supports a pardon."

"Is the dossier complete?" Truman asked. "Has anything been redacted?"

"Deputy Director Carr is in charge of Agent Lehmann and her files," Hillenkoetter replied. "With your permission, Mr. President, I'll defer that question to him."

Truman looked at Carr.

"No, sir," Carr answered truthfully. "Nothing is missing."

"And it's true, Mr. Carr, that this Erika Lehmann's father was a long-time friend of Hitler?"

"Yes, Mr. President."

"Tell me about this group mentioned in your files and referred to as (Truman looked down at a paper) the Shield Maidens. It seems they all have colorful pasts."

Carr went on to explain the backgrounds of Erika's partners. Army major Sheila Reid; Kathryn Fischer's history as a Gestapo officer; Stephanie, like Erika, a former Abwehr spy; and Zhanna Rogova, the Soviet sniper and assassin. At the end, he added, "Mr. President, like the German V-1 and V-2 rockets scientists, these women are protected by a policy approved by you."

"I know what I have and haven't approved, Mr. Carr."

"Sir, I point that out only to emphasize the CIA is doing nothing underhanded by employing them."

Truman addressed Hillenkoetter. "Roscoe, here's what will happen. I will grant the pardon. Then I'm transferring the Lehmann woman to Secretary Marshall's staff at his request. After that, Mr. Vaughn and his staff are to meet with these other women. Not here at the White House. Mr. Vaughn will decide on the place. After those interviews and Mr. Vaughn's reports, I'll decide on their futures with the United States government. I'm especially concerned with this 'Zee-ana Ruguva.'" Truman had a tough time pronouncing the Russian name. "From what I've read, her tractor doesn't seem to be pulling a full cart of hay, as we say in Missouri.

"Thank you, gentlemen. That will be all. Again, I appreciate you coming."

◊ ◊ ◊

The meeting at the White House had taken place this morning. It was now afternoon and Al Hodge sat in Leroy Carr's E Street office.

Carr had already briefed Hodge about the meeting with Harry Truman.

"So, we're going to lose Lehmann?" Hodge probed.

"Looks that way, Al."

"Look at it this way, Leroy. At least she gets her pardon. After that she can apply for citizenship and get her daughter. With Marshall, she can continue to serve our country. In the end, that's the main thing, right?"

"Yes, but we're losing our most productive agent and I'm worried about retaining the other Maidens, especially Zhanna. The Fischer sisters haven't committed any crimes here in the States, but, like Erika, Zhanna has."

"You can't worry about that, Leroy. The CIA will continue to get stronger as time passes, with or without them. You put your ass on the line to get Lehmann her pardon and it worked."

"I'll tell Sheila to confirm to the others that Erika will get her pardon, but I'm going to be honest and have her tell the others that they will have to undergo evaluation by the Executive Branch."

"Don't do it, Leroy. If they don't walk in, Lehmann will lose her pardon according to the conditions you told me."

"They will walk in, Al. They'll do it for Erika and her daughter."

[that evening in Washington]

Sheila received her nightly phone call from Kathryn Fischer and filled her in on Erika's pardon.

"That's wonderful news, Sheila," Kathryn said. *"We'll get a flight out for Washington tomorrow."*

"Kathryn, tell Stephanie and Zhanna that all three of you will have to go through an evaluation process by someone on the White House staff."

"Why? Because we disappeared?"

"I don't know why, but all three of you returning to Washington is a condition of Erika's pardon."

A pause came from Frankfurt. *"We'll be there, Sheila—for Erika."*

Chapter 58

The News

Washington, D.C.
Next day—Tuesday, 23 November 1948

Leroy Carr had waited to tell Erika about her pardon until Sheila had received contact from Kathryn and he was ensured all three of the Maidens would return to Washington. The bright blonde daughter of Karl Lehmann and Louise Minton Lehmann now sat in his office as she had done so many times in the past. Carr couldn't help but think that soon she wouldn't be sitting in that chair anymore.

Al Hodge stood by the window, facing them.

"I have the news you've been waiting to hear, Erika. The president will grant your pardon."

Erika was about ready to jump out of her chair as if the seat were spring loaded until Carr added quickly, "With a couple of conditions."

As quickly as the joy had come, it just as quickly deserted her. "What conditions?"

"Zhanna and the Fischer sisters have to undergo evaluation by aides to the president to determine their futures with our government. The president saw some things in the women's files that bothered him, especially concerning Zhanna.

"Another thing that concerns him is your team has no qualms about going dark without authorization. There are other things."

"Why didn't you doctor the files, Leroy?"

Hodge jumped in. "Lehmann, we're not going to withhold information from the President of the United States. The whole reason we do this is to support our country and it's our sworn duty to withhold nothing from the president."

"Al's right," Carr added. "With lesser government officials who have no official reason to know specific top-secret material, we can redact certain information if we feel it's in the national interest, but not with the president."

"What will happen to them?" Erika asked.

"With Kathryn and Stephanie, my guess is nothing," Carr answered. "I doubt their situation will change. But, like you, Zhanna committed felonies here in the States before she flipped over to us."

"Get her a parson like you did me, Leroy."

"Unlike you, Zhanna has more than one killing on the books here in the States and none of them were done to save an innocent victim. There's no way she would ever receive a pardon."

"What can happen to her?"

"I don't know, Erika, but you have my word I'll do everything I can to protect her, as I did you. And what happens to them won't affect your pardon. The only condition is that they walk in."

"You said 'conditions.' What are the others?"

"Only one more," Carr responded. "As soon as the pardon is granted, you'll leave us and go to work on General Marshall's staff. We'll miss you, Erika."

Erika looked at Carr and then at Hodge. She couldn't be upset with either of these men. Both had willingly put their careers on the line for her, even the cantankerous Al Hodge.

"I don't have any problem with leaving the CIA, Leroy. If I am to make a life with Ada, a job with less risk is a Godsend. But I will miss both of you."

She stood up, walked over to Hodge, and kissed him on the check. Then she did the same to Leroy Carr.

"Is that all for now, Leroy?"

"That's all. According to Sheila, the other Maidens should be on their way back to the States as we speak. Since the only condition is that they walk in, as soon as they arrive I expect your pardon to be processed. It only takes a stroke of the pen from the president. There isn't much red tape involved. Hopefully, by the end of the week you'll be free of all charges from the war years and can then apply for citizenship." Carr smiled. "Start studying your *Guide to United States Citizenship Handbook."*

"I've been studying it for a long time, Leroy. I think I can quote it word for word."

"And this isn't goodbye, Erika. You're still in the CIA until your pardon comes through and Marshall officially hires you. I'll have Sheila stay in touch with you daily, and sometime this week we'll all go out to dinner. You like a good steak. Kay and I know a place."

◊ ◊ ◊

As soon as Erika returned to the Mayflower Hotel, she called Ada in London just to talk. She wouldn't mention the possibility that soon they might be together. The woman whose father had been an early supporter of the Nazi cause, and whom Adolf Hitler had referred to as "little thing" when she was a youngster had been disappointed before, by both her Fatherland and the United States.

Chapter 59

MI-6 Holds a Wild Card

Washington, D.C.
Next day—Wednesday, 24 November 1948

The Fischer sisters and Zhanna had taken a commercial flight from Frankfurt to London, then boarded another commercial flight to Washington. The four-engine Pan-Am Boeing 307 Stratoliner sat down at the public Washington National Airport at a few minutes before noon.

As everyone disembarked down the ladder, passengers wondered at the sizeable contingent of Army military policemen waiting on the tarmac in covered Jeeps and sedans. Even more puzzling to the onlookers was why the MPs took three of the women passengers into their supervision but handcuffed only one.

[London]

Henry Wiltshire had been returned to London with a broken arm twelve days ago. After several interviews with Wiltshire, Sir James Ashworth knew that a CIA operative, Erika Lehmann, abducted Wiltshire, something he had suspected all along. Whether this was with or without Leroy Carr's complicity didn't matter. Sir James decided he wouldn't pursue the matter since Wiltshire was returned (although not unharmed per his agreement with Carr). He would file this under 'Carr and the CIA owe me one.'

In the clandestine world, it was always a positive thing to have someone in your debt, especially the American CIA.

Chapter 60

Middletown Tavern

Annapolis, Maryland
Two days later—Friday, 26 November 1948

Established in 1750, Annapolis' Middleton Tavern had served many a patron a drink or two over the past two centuries, including George Washington, Thomas Jefferson, Benjamin Franklin (a loyal customer when in the area) and many members of the Continental Congress. In present day, it was widely known not only for its history but also for serving delicious seafood and steaks.

Living near the Chesapeake Bay insured the Carr's of fine seafood anytime they wanted it. Yet, tonight was steak night and their guest was Erika. She ordered the porterhouse. Leroy and Kay decided on T-bones. Carr picked a bottle of Shiraz for the table.

The waiter popped the cork and poured everyone a half glass, then departed until it was time to return with the dinners.

"Good news, Erika," Carr said. "Kathryn and Stephanie have been cleared. Next week Kathryn will return to her job at the war college in Rhode Island, and Stephanie will return to Fort Huachuca in Arizona to complete her training that was interrupted. They'll be released from the brig tomorrow morning. I'll put them up at the Mayflower with you."

"That's better than good, that's great news, Leroy." Erika raised her glass and all three clinked them together. "What about Zhanna?"

"No news there yet."

"What's that mean?" Erika asked.

"She still has to undergo additional evaluation."

"So she'll continue to be locked up?"

"I'm afraid so, but I'm hoping all will be resolved by sometime next week. They want some Army shrink from Fort Benning to question her. He's supposed to be here Monday."

Carr tried to change the subject. "You must be very happy about your pardon. Unfortunately, it didn't come through today, but I expect the president to sign it over the weekend."

"I *am* happy, Leroy, but experience has taught me to never count my chickens before they hatch. That's a good American way of putting it. When I have the pardon in my hand, then you'll see me really happy."

"You'll get the pardon, Erika," Kay said. "If not, I'll disappear with you again."

Carr looked at his wife. Kay started laughing, but he couldn't tell if she was serious or just joking.

"When your pardon comes through," Carr said, "Kay and I want to have a celebration party for you at our home. Sheila, Kathryn, and Stephanie will be invited, of course.

As the waiter sat the plates of food on the table, Erika knew she had to do something to help Zhanna and she'd need Sheila Reid's and Axel Ryker's help as well as Stephanie and Kathryn's.

"If we have a celebration, Leroy, I'd also like Ryker to attend."

"Are you serious? You two have never gotten along."

"Yes, but he faithfully fulfills his orders and helped in a positive way on this past mission," Erika responded. Carr couldn't be more right; she hated Ryker, but she would have to put that aside to help Zhanna.

Chapter 61

Asking about Inka

Washington, D.C.
Next day—Saturday, 27 November 1948

As promised by Leroy Carr last night at the Middletown Tavern, Kathryn and Stephanie Fischer were released this morning from the stockade in Arlington. Both of the sisters were now staying together in a room at the Mayflower Hotel on Connecticut Avenue.

After long hugs with Erika, both sisters now sat in Erika's hotel room.

Erika started out by telling them Zhanna was at risk and filled them in on her situation. She then asked Stephanie a question. "Are you still in contact with Inka?"

"Not since I left on this latest mission," Stephanie replied. "Before that, I'd got a couple of letters from her when I was in Arizona."

"Is she still in Indianapolis with your Aunt Catherine?"

"Yes, she's in high school there."

Inka was a Czech prostitute whose real name was Zoe Schovajsa. Stephanie had smuggled her out from behind the Iron Curtain last summer. In Bratislava, where Stephanie had met her, Inka was sixteen-years-old at the time. She had recently turned seventeen.

"Steph, Zhanna is never going to pass the tests by the Army psychiatrist. I need you to call your aunt and tell her you'd like to show Washington to Inka. I'll pay for the plane ticket."

[that evening]

Erika reached Sheila Reid at her home.

"Sheila, I need to know the name of the Army shrink who will decide Zhanna's fate. Can you get that for me?"

"I already know it," Sheila replied. *"I'm in charge of securing his accommodations. It's Lieutenant Colonel Simon Bergwitz. He'll arrive in Washington sometime Monday. Why?"*

"We have to help Zhanna. Can you put him up at the Mayflower?"

"Not a problem," Sheila answered. *"What else can I do to help?"*

"I'll let you know, but just making sure Bergwitz is at the Mayflower will be a big help."

"He'll be there," Sheila said. *"I'll call you with his room number when I get it booked Monday."*

"Thanks, Sheila. And last night, Leroy told me of a party he and Kay would hold at their home when my pardon comes through. I requested Ryker be included."

"Ryker! Why would you want him?"

"I'll tell you later," Erika responded. "Just let me know when Ryker gets to town."

"I don't get it, but I'll let you know."

Part 6

They bid me take place among them in the halls of Valhalla! Where the brave may live forever.

—Viking invocation

Chapter 62

Special Stationary

Washington, D.C.
Two days later—Monday, 29 November 1948

This morning, an Army Convair CV-240 set down at Andrews Air Force base, having just arrived from Fort Benning, Georgia. Doctor (and lieutenant colonel) Simon Bergwitz stepped off the plane. Bergwitz was one of a select few Army psychiatrists called upon by the government from time to time for special cases. He knew nothing about his patient other than she was Russian, and he was scheduled to meet her tomorrow.

Bergwitz told his driver to take him to the Mayflower Hotel where his room had been reserved.

[two hours later]
A seventeen-year-old girl also arrived in the nation's capital, arriving on a commercial flight from Indianapolis and landing at Washington National Airport. When she saw Stephanie Fischer waiting for her, Inka rushed into Stephanie's arms.

[mid-afternoon]
A car with a CIA driver had picked up Erika at the Mayflower and delivered her to Leroy Carr's CIA office on E Street. When she arrived, not only was Carr in his office, but also Kay, Sheila, and Al Hodge.

"Sit down, Erika," Carr said. "Kay, Sheila, and Al wanted to be here when I gave you this."

Carr handed Erika an unsealed envelope. She pulled out the letter. Written on White House letterhead and signed by Harry S. Truman was her pardon for all crimes committed on United States soil. Erika was overcome and hugged the letter to her breast.

Kay and Sheila walked over and hugged her. Hodge didn't go that far, but even he smiled.

Chapter 63

Doghouse

Arlington, Virginia
Next day—Tuesday, 30 November 1948

Simon Bergwitz considered himself more of a doctor than a military man, so he wore a suit instead of his uniform when interviewing a patient. He thought his Lieutenant Colonel's uniform might create an uneasy feeling and he wanted his patients to feel unthreatened.

After arriving in Washington yesterday, he had spent last evening reading the dossier of his patient, a former Russian Red Army sniper named Zhanna Rogova who now in some unclear way participated in occasional assignments for the CIA. The dossier given him contained no specifics about her past missions.

But her past assignments were not his concern. His task was to evaluate her mental health so the powers-that-be in the State Department could decide about her continued involvement with the new spy agency.

This morning, an Army sergeant picked up Bergwitz at the Mayflower and took him across the Potomac River to an Army brig in Arlington just a few blocks from the National Cemetery.

One of the Army jailors led him to a small, drab, windowless conference room. Bergwitz didn't like it.

"Isn't there an office, or a room like a study with more comfortable seating where my patient might feel more at ease?"

The jailor, who had now dealt with Zhanna for a week, said, "With all due respect, sir, I doubt that's going to make a difference with your patient. She's bat shit crazy."

This angered Bergwitz. "Corporal, you're out of line. It's apparent I need to speak to your superiors about proper protocol and etiquette amongst the staff here."

"I apologize, sir."

"Just bring my patient to me," Bergwitz ordered.

"Yes, sir."

In about ten minutes, the corporal opened the door. Standing outside the door was a tall woman with jet hair wearing gray pants and a black and white striped shirt. Standard prisoner attire at this facility. Immediately noticeable was a horrid scar on her neck.

"Please come in," Bergwitz rose from his chair.

Without moving, she looked at Bergwitz then at the corporal. Before she stepped in, the woman grabbed the corporal's ear and twisted hard. He grimaced and pulled away.

Bergwitz, while looking down at paperwork, did not see what had just happened. When he looked up, he said, "Corporal, please close the door and wait outside."

When the woman stepped in, the doctor said, "Please have a seat."

She sat down.

"You must be Zhanna Rogova." He, of course, knew it was her from the photograph in her dossier. "I apologize for having to meet over a table. Apparently, there is not a more suitable place here in the stockade."

She looked around the room, ignoring him.

"I'm Doctor Bergwitz."

The woman finally looked at him. "I feel fine."

"I'm not that type of doctor. I'm just here to talk to you. What should I call you? Is Miss Rogova acceptable?"

Zhanna shrugged.

"Are you being treated satisfactorily here, Miss Rogova?"

"Fine. The food is good and several of the male guards watch me shower."

"They don't have matrons here?"

"Oh, yes. I get one of those to watch me when I use the toilet. The men prefer the showers."

"This should not be happening. I'll make the warden aware of this."

"I don't care if you do or you don't."

Bergwitz cleared his throat. "Miss Rogova, I'd like to know more about your childhood. The information in your dossier addressing that time in your life in the Soviet Union is limited. I did read that you were raised in a state-run orphanage. What can you tell me about those years?"

"It was an orphanage. What else do you want to know?"

"For instance, what was the interaction between the children and the staff?"

"They fed us and exercised us. We were disciplined if we broke a rule. What more could a child ask for?"

"What type of discipline?"

"Whippings in front of the other children or the doghouse," Zhanna answered.

"The doghouse?"

"They had a row of doghouses. A child was locked in one of those if he or she were caught breaking certain rules."

"For how long where the children kept there?

"It depended on which rule was broken. Some for only a few hours, others for longer. When I was eight, I spent two days in one for fighting with a boy. The worst part was I wasn't let out for the toilet so I soiled my clothes, and because I was balled up to fit in the doghouse I could barely walk when let out. But, like I said, they fed me. Many Russians walking the streets were starving in those days. I was lucky to get food. I have no complaints."

"I read nothing about your parents."

"I know nothing about them. I was told I was abandoned when I was one month old, left in an alley in Leningrad, so I guess I'm from there. That's where I went after I ran away from the orphanage when I was fourteen."

"Why did you leave?"

"I would have been allowed to stay there only two more years. Everyone was forced to leave when they turned sixteen. Many of the boys lied about their age to enter the military, many of the girls became prostitutes to survive."

"What did you do, Miss Rogova?"

"I walked the streets of Leningrad, stealing food and robbing people. I slept in a wrecked car in a junk yard until one night a hobo tried to steal my sleeping place."

"What happened?"

"I killed him, of course. I had a knife and I slit his throat."

"How did killing a human being make you feel?"

Zhanna looked at him quizzically. "It made me feel glad I didn't lose my sleeping place."

[that afternoon]

Sheila called Erika at the Mayflower.

"The Army shrink interviewed Zhanna this morning. I have no information about how it went. A second interview is scheduled for tomorrow and he's been instructed to submit his report on Thursday."

"That means we have to finalize plans tonight," Erika replied.

"Ryker arrived an hour ago," Sheila said. "He'll be in room 519."

"Thanks, Sheila."

Chapter 64

Free Champagne

Washington, D.C.
Next day—Wednesday, 01 December 1948

Zhanna was once again in the conference room with Dr. Simon Bergwitz. They had already talked for an hour. Of course, no prisoner was allowed a scarf, so her neck scar was again quite evident. Bergwitz had not mentioned it yesterday.

"Let's talk about your war years, Miss Rogova. In your dossier it states you were a sniper for the Red Army and toward the end of the war you were transferred to SMERSH."

"That's correct."

"When did you join the Russian army?"

"As soon as the Germans invaded us—June of 1941."

"What were your duties?"

"I was first assigned to help nurses care for the wounded behind the lines, but that was boring so I went AWOL and joined the men on the front. Things were going so badly, they apparently forgot about me. Many nurses and people in the field hospitals were killed by German shelling, some blown into so many pieces they couldn't be identified. They probably thought I was dead. Everything was chaos in those early days."

"Then you became a soldier and eventually a sniper?"

"That's right."

"Your scar?"

"That should be in the reports in front of you."

"It is, Mis Rogova, but I'd like to hear the story from you if you don't mind."

Zhanna shrugged. "I was captured and hanged by the German SS in a village during a battle outside the Korsun Pocket in 1944. The SS took great delight in hanging people slowly. They strung me up as the Red Army moved into the village. The Germans had to flee and I was cut down by comrades before I was dead. Here again I was lucky. Every one of my comrades captured with me was executed days earlier. The Germans kept me alive to rape me at their pleasure. They waited too long to hang me. This was their mistake and my fortune. I'm alive because they took their pleasure. I have led a charmed life."

Bergwitz swallowed hard. "And your time with SMERSH? What can you tell me about that?"

"I was an executioner and assassin. I earned many medals for my work," Zhanna said with pride.

Bergwitz didn't want to hear details.

"Miss Rogova, what do you think of bad people? Hitler for example?"

"I have no hope of Heaven—that's only for good people like a man I met in London. When I die I want to be buried with my rifle so when I get to Hell I can shoot Hitler, the son-of-a-bitch. If there's anyone else there you want me to shoot, I'll do it if I can have a cheese sandwich for my dinner tonight instead of the Wednesday night meatloaf."

[that evening]

Dr. Simon Bergwitz dined in the Mayflower Hotel restaurant then returned to his room, called his wife in Georgia, and started writing his report on Zhanna Rogova as a cold, December rain pelted his hotel room window.

He felt human sympathy for the Russian woman, but he couldn't let that influence his report. In his professional opinion, he was convinced this woman was delusional. A psychopath who had no more qualms about killing people than a butcher had about cutting up a dead chicken. He would make out his report for the State Department and turn it over to them tomorrow morning as instructed, recommending she not only have her ties with the United States government severed, but that she also be institutionalized.

A half hour later, as Bergwitz worked on his report, a knock came. Annoyed that he was being interrupted, he opened the door. In the corridor stood two hotel maids with a cart. One was a very young looking blonde, slight in build. The other a sturdy and athletic looking brunette.

"Hello, sir," the brunette said. "We have some champagne and fruit for you compliments of the hotel manager."

Bergwitz was surprised. This was unexpected, but he let them enter. Stephanie Fischer and Inka rolled the cart into his room.

The brunette opened the champagne and poured some in a crystal flute. "Sir, we've been instructed to ask your approval of the champagne before we leave."

"That's not necessary," Bergwitz said. "I'm sure it's fine. I'm working right now and will drink some later."

The brunette looked dejected. "If we don't follow instructions, we might lose our jobs."

Bergwitz sighed. "Very well." He took a sip.

◊ ◊ ◊

Simon Bergwitz awoke in his bed at five o'clock in the morning. Lying on his stomach, he suffered a raging headache and nausea. *What had happened?* He tried to collect his thoughts. The last thing he remembered was the two hotel maids from last night and taking a sip of champagne. Feeling like he might retch, he turned over on his back intending to go into the bathroom. When he rolled over, he saw in the darkness the silhouette of what looked like a large man standing beside his bed. Bergwitz shouted in surprise. He must be dreaming.

The shadowy specter turned on the lamp sitting on the small table next to his bed. Even much worse than the specter was now a massive man wearing a porkpie hat over a scarred face and a caveman mien.

"What? What? Who . . . who are you?" Bergwitz stuttered.

"Sit up, Jew," the hellish figure uttered.

Bergwitz tried to roll out of the other side of the bed but a massive hand grabbed his neck and jerked him back.

"I deliver a gift," the man snarled, then added a slur. "Bagel dogs will take anything that's free."

Axel Ryker pulled an envelope out of his inside jacket pocket and threw it on Bergwitz's lap.

The doctor ignored the envelope. "Who are you? I'm calling hotel security!" Bergwitz reached for the phone on the lamp table. Ryker broke the phone cord as easily as if were an over-cooked strand of spaghetti.

"Open the envelope, Jew."

Bergwitz's hands shook like a bartender mixing a martini. From the envelope he extracted three photographs. He looked in horror. The pictures showed him in bed with a naked girl. It was the young blonde maid from last night.

(Stephanie had a Leica micro-camera and she had taken the pictures. She and Erika developed them in Erika's room.)

"That girl you're in bed with is seventeen years old," the savage man hissed. "Here's what will happen, Jew. You will write a glowing report on the woman you have been interviewing—Rogova. In your report you will state that you find no indications of any mental troubles and give clearance for her to be released. If you don't, those photographs will go to not only your superiors and colleagues, but your wife, as well. You can keep those photos; we have plenty of copies."

"This isn't true! This girl is a maid here at the hotel. She and another woman brought a cart to my room last night! Nothing happened!"

"You'll find that there is no cart in your sitting room and that neither of those women work here. If Rogova isn't released by tomorrow, the photographs go out." Ryker then said loudly, "Enter."

Inka, the experienced Czech prostitute now turned Indianapolis high school student, walked into the bedroom.

"There she is!" Bergwitz exclaimed. "Ask her? She'll tell you nothing happened!"

"I enjoyed our night, Simon," Inka said. "I will be proud to tell everyone how manly you are."

Ryker ended it with, "Make your report this morning, swine."

Heinrich Himmler's favorite henchman, and the Czech prostitute Stephanie Fischer had saved in Bratislava, walked out and left Bergwitz to himself.

Chapter 65

Gathering at the Carr's

Washington, D.C.
Next day—Thursday, 02 December 1948

Al Hodge sat in Leroy Carr's office. It was mid-afternoon.

"Zhanna was released from the stockade in Arlington two hours ago," Carr told his longtime sidekick.

"Wow! That was quick. I'm glad she's out but with the negative reports we've gotten from the jailors the past week, I'm surprised she passed that Army shrink's evaluation. She is crazy. We all know that."

"Apparently, Lieutenant Colonel Bergwitz doesn't think so," Carr responded.

"Have you talked to Bergwitz?"

"No, he left town as soon as he handed over his report to the State Department. He couldn't get out of town soon enough—said he had some pressing business back at Fort Benning."

"So, you haven't read the report?"

"Not yet, but I was told it clears Zhanna for further duty. Marshall wants to see it first. His office will forward it on to the White House then Roscoe and I will get a copy."

"When is Erika leaving us," Hodge asked.

"She's to report to Marshall's office next Wednesday. Monday she'll be processed out of the CIA, then Tuesday processed into the Secretary of State's organization."

"I never thought we'd lose Lehmann until her luck ran out and she got killed. She's always been a royal pain but I'm glad she got her pardon. She earned it the hard way."

"I agree."

"Where is Rogova now, at the Mayflower with the rest of them?"

"Yeah. Sheila booked her a room when we found out she was cleared and released."

"Where do we go from here, Leroy? Lehmann's out, and Sheila's bum shoulder will eliminate her for most missions. As far as the Shield

Maidens, that leaves Rogova and the Fischer sisters. Are we going to keep them together?"

"I don't know, Al. Without Erika around to keep Zhanna in check, that's a concern. Kathryn is serving her country well at the Naval War College. Stephanie hasn't even finished her initial training at Fort Huachuca, let alone at the Farm. Now that the CIA has been around for over a year, we're getting more talented field agent applicants—male and female. Perhaps it's time to move on. Congress is tightening oversights, and people with shady pasts are becoming harder and harder for us to justify putting in the field. A couple of congressmen are even complaining about the Nazi rocket scientists in Texas at Fort Bliss.

"But decisions on the Shield Maidens and Ryker are for a future day. If the Maidens are no more, I'll make sure Stephanie gets a job when she's completed training. She can probably replace Erika as a trainer at the Farm or join her sister as an instructor at the war college. Zhanna can return to the convent in Honduras if she wishes. I don't know what the heck we'll do with Ryker."

Carr continued. "Kay is throwing a party for everyone as a celebration of Erika's pardon. It's at our home Saturday night. All the Maidens will be there, and Ryker."

"Ryker? At a party? In your home?"

"Kay insisted he be included."

"I always said Kay is a brave woman. I'll be there with bells on, Leroy. I've got to see this. And I'll come armed."

Both men chuckled.

[that evening]

The Shield Maidens gathered.

All five: Erika, Kathryn, Stephanie, Zhanna, and Sheila. Inka had to return to school on Monday, but she wanted to be with Stephanie for a few days, so she was also present. She would fly back to Indianapolis on Sunday.

They agreed to meet privately in Erika's room at the Mayflower to celebrate Zhanna's release. Staying just amongst themselves would eliminate any chance of them getting in trouble at some public place.

They all knew none of them could afford that happening right now, especially Erika.

Room service delivered champagne (vodka for Zhanna) several times over the course of the evening. Erika told the waiter to charge the alcohol to Leroy Carr's permanent account. Sheila, Carr's executive assistant, signed for it.

"Leroy's going to love this," Sheila grinned.

The other women laughed.

"Zhanna, this is from Ian." Erika handed her the note he had written her in Paris. Erika had not opened it.

Zhanna refused to take it.

"What's wrong?" Erika asked. The other women watched but said nothing.

"I'll never see him again. What would be the point of reading it?"

"Just take it. I promised him I would deliver it to you. If you don't want to read it you can throw it away. Either way, I kept my promise to my cousin."

Zhanna took the envelope, folded it, and put it in a pocket of her slacks. Later that night, she went into the bathroom and opened the envelope.

Dearest Zhanna,

I hope this reaches you soon, my love. Erika told me you were called away suddenly to Helsinki. I hope you can return to London soon, or perhaps I could come to you. I know I'm not the smartest man and I'll never be rich. But I will protect you Zhanna and treat you as you deserve to be treated. What I'm trying to say is I hope you'll consider making your life with me.

Love, Ian

Afraid Erika or one of the other women might come across the note, Zhanna tore it up and flushed it down the toilet.

Chapter 66

"He's so Sweet."

Annapolis, Maryland
Two days later—Saturday, 04 December 1948

It was not fashionable for CIA agents to be late. In their work lives, being on time could mean the difference between life and death. Everyone was at the Carr's home at the time Kay had chosen—7:00 p.m. All of the Shield Maidens were there, Al Hodge, and Axel Ryker. Stephanie was the last to arrive; although, still on time. Beside her was a teenage girl.

"I hope you don't mind, Kay," Stephanie said at the door. "A friend of mine is in town. This is Inka."

The always gracious Kay Carr welcomed the young girl. "I'm so pleased to meet you, Inka. I'm Kay. You are most welcome. Come in, both of you."

Knowing how some of the Shield Maidens liked to eat, Kay had the caterer bring nearly twice the amount of food recommended for the number of guests. One extra guest would not matter.

When Stephanie entered with Inka, Leroy stood talking to Al on the far side of the living room at a makeshift bar—Leroy with a gin and tonic; Al with his customary bourbon on the rocks.

Al looked at Leroy. "You didn't tell me Zoe Schovajsa was in D.C."

"That's because I didn't know it."

It took Hodge only a minute to say, "Are you thinking what I'm thinking, Leroy?"

Both men now wondered about Simon Bergwitz's unexpected report on Zhanna. The scenario of what might have happened with Bergwitz was textbook clandestine practice for blackmail of a male mark.

"Best to leave it alone, Al. It's over."

Hodge nodded.

Kay brought the young girl over to her husband. "Leroy, we have another guest. This is Inka. Inka, this my husband, Leroy, and Al."

Kay had never met Inka and didn't know her husband and Al knew her from a previous mission when Stephanie rescued her from a life of prostitution on the streets of Bratislava.

Leroy and Al again looked at each other. Zoe Schovajsa was using the name she used as a street prostitute in Czechoslovakia. This told them either Erika or Stephanie had ordered her to do this to prevent her real identity from becoming known.

After both men greeted the young girl and Kay took her away, Hodge said, "I agree, Leroy. It's best to leave it alone. The smoke is finally beginning to settle and digging into this will just throw a monkey wrench . . . make that a gorilla wrench, into the works."

Across the room, Erika had been watching. When Leroy caught her eye, he raised his glass. Erika turned away so he wouldn't see her grin. She had to give him credit. It was hard to fool Leroy Carr.

◊ ◊ ◊

Surprises abounded this evening. One of which was that Kay Carr apparently hit it off with Axel Ryker, a man who had never been invited to a social gathering in his lifetime that didn't have something to do with a mission. He couldn't understand why Kay had invited him. Much like Zhanna, human kindness was something Ryker had little experience with, either giving or receiving, and he was unsure how he should act. But he had thanked Kay for inviting him, and at one point, she took his arm and led him to the kitchen where the food was set up. Erika and Kathryn were in the kitchen replenishing their plates at the time. Apparently, Ryker had said something, probably unintentionally, that made Kay laugh.

Kay, unaware of Ryker's background, said to Erika and Kathryn, "He's so sweet."

Erika nearly spat out her drink but just choked on it instead; Kathryn dropped her plate on the counter.

◊ ◊ ◊

The biggest surprise of the evening was reserved for Zhanna, courtesy of Erika. The party was still going strong at ten o'clock when the doorbell rang. The hostess answered the door. Kay saw a large, tough looking man standing on the doorstep.

"Hello, madam," the man said. "Erika invited me. I've come here from London. My flight was tardy and I just arrived an hour ago. The taxi ride to get here from the airport took an hour. My name is Ian Minton. I hope I'm not imposing. Erika told me yesterday morning that a lady named Zhanna Rogova would be here. I flew out as soon as I could."

"Welcome," Kay said as she opened the door wider. Ian stepped inside. He had had no opportunity to check into a hotel and carried a suitcase in his left hand. Kay told him, "We'll put your bag in the closet."

Erika had told Ian that she would gladly pay for his flight, but he refused. Instead, he quickly pawned practically everything he owned of any value (at a considerable loss) to buy his plane ticket and something for Zhanna.

When Zhanna saw Ian enter, she turned away.

Erika went up to her. "Zhanna, Ian is here."

"I know that. Go away, Erika."

"What are you talking about? Go up to him. He came all this way just to see you."

"Leave me alone," Zhanna insisted. "Why did you do this?"

When Ian spotted Zhanna, he politely excused himself from Kay and walked quickly.

A half-hour later, Zhanna and Ian went outside. Erika Lehmann looked out a window and saw Zhanna smoking and holding hands with Ian as they stood talking on the curb. Erika knew if she was noticed watching through the window, Zhanna would be embarrassed. She closed the curtain and returned to the party.

Outside, Ian turned Zhanna toward him, took the cigarette from her hand and dropped it in the gutter. The tough boxer got down on one knee and pulled a small jewelry box out of his pocket.

Chapter 67

Advice from a Friend

Washington, D.C.
Two days later—Monday, 06 December 1948

A cold hand from the Atlantic came knocking on Washington's door on the day Erika Lehmann was processed out of the CIA. Exiting from the spy agency took all day with lengthy debriefings, exit interviews with several people, and paperwork which included affidavits Erika had to sign swearing she would reveal nothing about the agency or her past missions under penalty of lengthy imprisonment.

She was finally finished at 4:30 p.m. Before she left the E Street Complex, she stopped by Leroy Carr's office to say goodbye to him and Sheila. Al Hodge was not there.

"Best of luck, Erika," Carr said after she hugged him.

"Thank you, Leroy. I know the chances you took for me and I'll never forget."

Erika noticed a tear in Sheila's eye when they hugged.

She had signed up with the German Abwehr in 1938. When she walked out of the building on E Street into the cold, windy late afternoon, it was the first time in ten years she was not a spy.

Tomorrow, she would go through another long day of interviews and paperwork with General Marshall's people to begin the next chapter in her life. Yesterday, she had called her grandparents in London and asked them to bring Ada to the United States later this month so they could all spend Christmas together. Her grandparents were well off financially and didn't need her money.

She wouldn't take her test for citizenship until January, but she was now, at last, a woman free of the menace of criminal charges engulfing her like some toxic fog.

◊ ◊ ◊

[that evening]

Ian was leaving to return home tomorrow and Erika wanted to see her cousin. They agreed to meet for dinner at a Chinese restaurant called Hunan City on 8th Street NW in Washington's Chinatown. It was near Ian's hotel. Erika had offered to put him up at the Mayflower with her own money but, of course, her stubborn cousin refused.

When Erika arrived, Ian already had a table and a beer. When she got to the table he started to rise.

"Don't get up," she said. "We're family."

"I'm glad you got to see Zhanna, Ian. I know she was glad to see you. Too bad you have to leave tomorrow."

"I don't have to leave, but it's for the best."

"What do you mean?"

"Nothing. Let's order. What do you recommend? I don't know much about Chinese food."

Erika picked up the menu, and in a moment said, "I'll have the Chicken Lo Mein and a bowl of Won Ton soup."

Ian said, "I'll have the same."

When the waiter appeared, they placed their orders. Erika also ordered a beer.

After the waiter walked away, Erika said, "What's wrong, Ian?" She could tell his mood was dismal.

"I'd rather not talk about it, Erika."

"Is it something with Zhanna?"

The Englishman took a long drink of his beer. "I proposed to her at your party the other night and she said no."

Erika gazed at him, stunned. "You proposed to Zhanna?"

"Yes, why do you look shocked?"

Erika shook off the surprise. "I'm sorry. I guess it's because you two have known each other for such a short time. Do you two really know each other?"

"I've known her long enough to know what I want, but she doesn't feel the same so that's that, as they say. I can't blame her. Here I am a bricklayer with a pug boxer's face, and rough around the edges, while she's beautiful, refined, gentle, and used to an exciting life of travel for her work as a translator for powerful men. I can't expect a woman like that to settle for a man like me."

After hearing his description of Zhanna Rogova, principally the 'gentle' part, it was now Erika's turn to take a long drink.

[later that night]

Suddenly, Erika walked into Kathryn and Stephanie's room. "Have you seen Zhanna?"

"She said she was going down to the bar for a drink," Kathryn replied. "Why?"

"I need to talk to her. I'll see you later." The Shield Maidens had agreed to meet for one last drink together later tonight before they went their separate ways starting tomorrow.

Erika took the lift back to the lobby, went to the hotel bar, and spotted Zhanna sitting at a corner table by herself. She wasn't wearing her omnipresent neck scarf, revealing the damaged skin.

When Erika got to her table, Zhanna said, "Walk away, German. I want to be left alone." Even though the Russian could consume an enormous amount of alcohol, it was apparent she had downed enough vodka to supply some effect.

Erika ignored her orders and sat down. "Don't tell me to leave, Zhanna. You know I can kick your ass if you don't have your rifle with you, and I don't see it under the table."

"What do you want?" Zhanna downed another shot of vodka.

"I had an interesting conversation with my cousin earlier this evening. I'm sure you remember my cousin, the man who asked you to marry him."

Zhanna glared at her. Erika ignored it.

"What do you want to do, Zhanna? Return to the convent in Central America and live out your days as a lonely old woman when you have a good man who loves you and you love him?"

"I don't love him."

"Don't bull shit me, Zhanna. It pisses me off. You won't allow yourself to admit it because you think you don't deserve a good man."

"You're placing yourself in my personal business again, Erika."

"That's right. I am because I love you. We're sisters. Ian is flying back to London tomorrow. If you have any sense, before he leaves you'll go to him and tell him about yourself. You can't tell him about your current work with the CIA, but you can tell him about the war years."

"He won't want me when he finds out all the things I did during the war."

"Let him decide that. By the way, why aren't you wearing your scarf?"

"I didn't want any men bothering me. When they see my scar, they are repulsed and leave me alone."

"Did Ian see you without a scarf before he proposed?"

"Yes."

"I don't need to say any more. I'll see you in an hour when we all meet down here to say goodbye."

Erika left the table.

◊ ◊ ◊

Gathered at a table in the same Mayflower Hotel lounge later that evening were Erika, Kathryn, Stephanie, Zhanna, and Sheila. Inka had left Sunday morning on a three-hour flight to return to her adoptive family in Indianapolis (Stephanie and Kathryn's aunt and her husband). Zoe Schovajsa had a math test to take at her high school on Monday.

This was a private time for the Shield Maidens, who had been through so much together.

Drinks had been delivered.

"Apparently Inka has gotten more comfortable on airplanes," Stephanie commented. "Remember her flight to Berlin, her first time in an airplane? She panicked. I thought I was going to have to knock her out."

The others laughed.

"You left the CIA today. Is that right, Erika?" Kathryn asked.

"Yes. It took the full day. I arrived at E Street at seven o'clock this morning and didn't leave until after four, but's it's done. Tomorrow I go through what I assume will be the same long process in reverse at the State Department. What about you, Stephanie?"

"I leave for the Army base in Arizona tomorrow. Leroy told me when I complete the training cycles at Fort Huachuca and then at the CIA Farm at Camp Peary he would find me a job."

Kathryn told everyone, "I leave tomorrow for my old job in Providence. Sheila, what are your plans?"

"I'll remain at E Street with Leroy, at least for now. I don't know how long I'll stay. My husband and I have talked about starting a family. He has a good job, and I can retire with military disability because of my injuries suffered in the line of duty. If I become pregnant, I'll retire. At least that's what Ricky and I have talked about."

"Zhanna, what are your plans?" Sheila asked.

"I'll return to Honduras. The nuns feed me well and I enjoy working the vegetable gardens. I'll continue to work for the CIA when called upon."

Chapter 68

Processing In

Washington, D.C.
Next day—Tuesday, 07 December 1948

Around Washington, and indeed around the country, remembrances of the Japanese attack on Pearl Harbor that took place on this day seven years ago were arranged. In fact, departing flights were running behind schedule at Washington's National Airport. A sizable number of charter airplanes took up runway space, arriving with Pearl Harbor survivors on board, coming to Washington from across the nation by invitation of the president.

Because of the clogged runways, Ian Minton arrived to find a long line at the ticket counters of people wanting to purchase tickets to fly out of the nation's capital to destinations both domestic and abroad.

While standing in the deep line behind a couple with a small child, Ian felt a hand take his arm. It was Zhanna.

"Zhanna, I'm surprised. I didn't think you'd be here to say goodbye."

"I haven't come to say goodbye, Ian. If you don't mind losing your place in line, may we talk?"

[that afternoon]
Stephanie and Kathryn Fischer were gone. Sheila had found Stephanie a seat on an Air Force C-47 cargo plane headed to Detroit to pick up a load of replacement Jeep transmissions to be delivered to Camp Carson, Colorado. From there she would board a smaller plane to Tucson where someone from Fort Huachuca would pick her up and drive her to the base.

This morning, Kathryn boarded a train for the ten-hour trip to Rhode Island. The Fischer sisters had said goodbye over an early breakfast in the hotel restaurant.

Erika had a big day ahead. Much like the previous day when she was processed out of the CIA, today was also spent in numerous interviews at the Department of State building on C Street NW. Following the interviews and polygraph tests, she was fingerprinted and photographed numerous times. A physical exam by an Army doctor from Walter Reed was conducted. Erika's scars from knife and gunshot wounds were photographed and recorded during the examination. Many papers were read and signed, including, like the CIA, vows of confidentially which if broken came with severe penalties.

She never saw George Marshall. The gauntlet ended at five o'clock in the afternoon (she had reported at eight this morning).

The last person she saw that day was one of Marshall's aides, a friendly man in a business suit. "I'm Mr. Hawkins. I'll call you after your interviews and polygraph tests are evaluated and your background check is completed."

"When might that be, Mr. Hawkins?" Erika asked.

"Hard to say. It might be a couple of days. It might be a week or longer."

"I'm no longer with the CIA so they won't be covering my stay at the Mayflower."

"We'll take care of that until Secretary Marshall makes a final decision after a review of your interviews and polygraphs. If he decides to hire you, we'll find you an apartment, which you will pay for out of your salary."

"Very well, thank you," Erika said.

"You're welcome. Good luck."

[that evening]

Erika and Zhanna were now the only Shield Maidens left at the Mayflower. Zhanna was not in the hotel room when Erika finally returned after today's marathon at the State Department. She took a quick shower and was just walking out of the bathroom in a towel when Zhanna walked in.

"Zhanna, after I get dressed I'm going to find some dinner. Do you want to go with me?"

"I can't tonight. Ian is taking me out."

Erika looked at her. "Ian told me he was leaving this morning to return to London."

"He changed his mind. People have the right to do that."

It was then that Erika noticed the ring with a small, humble diamond on Zhanna's left-hand ring finger.

Zhanna saw her looking at the ring. "As you suggested, I told Ian everything about my war years including being raped by the SS and my duties as an assassin with SMERSH. He still wants me." Tears welled in Zhanna's eyes and she quickly turned away. Erika went back in the bathroom and closed the door so as not to embarrass her. No one had ever seen Zhanna Rogova cry.

Chapter 69

Cugino's

Washington, D.C.
Next day—Wednesday, 08 December 1948

Zhanna never returned to the hotel after her dinner date with Ian last night. It was well after dawn when she walked through the door looking tired and disheveled. Erika had already returned from breakfast.

"Hello, Zhanna. How was your date?" Erika asked with a straight face.

"Very good, a nice dinner."

Erika suppressed a grin, wishing to not give Zhanna a hint of what she knew the engaged couple had spent their time doing throughout the course of the night.

Zhanna added, "Tonight, Ian would like to take us both to dinner if you're available. Have you heard from your State Department?"

"Not yet," Erika answered.

"Then you are free for dinner?"

"Yes."

"Good. I will let Ian know later. I need sleep. I go to bed."

[that evening]

Knowing Zhanna liked Italian food, Ian Minton had chosen an Italian restaurant named Cugino's on 19th Street NW, not far from George Washington University. Zhanna didn't enjoy spaghetti, which she associated with worms infesting corpses, a sight she had seen too often during the war. But she liked other Italian food, and tonight she was content (at least to the extent her troubled soul would allow).

The Wednesday night special was lasagna and that's what everyone ordered. They sat in a booth. Zhanna and Ian huddled close on one side; Erika sat across from them.

"Congratulations to both of you on your engagement," Erika said as she cut into her lasagna. "What are your plans?"

"Zhanna and I have talked briefly about that," Ian replied. "I've asked her to return to London with me and she agreed. I can always get work there as a bricklayer. That job is in high demand right now. There is much rebuilding that still needs to be done because of the Blitz and I can earn extra money boxing."

"That sounds wonderful," Erika said. "I know you'll be very happy."

Zhanna said, "I told Ian I will continue my work as a Russian translator with the United States government for a while until we get on our feet."

This told Erika that Zhanna planned on continuing her work for Leroy Carr because they would need the money.

"Have you set a date for your wedding?" Erika asked. "I hope I'm invited."

"We've thought about sometime this spring or summer. Maybe in Cheltenham where most of my family lives. Of course you'll be invited, Erika. You're family."

Chapter 70

$152 a Month

Washington, D.C.
Five days later—Monday, 13 December 1948

Erika had gone through the process required by the Department of State a week ago. Finally, on Monday, she received an early morning phone call.

"Mrs. Faust?"

"Yes."

"This is Mr. Hawkins. The Secretary would like to see you in his office in one hour. A car will be dispatched to fetch you. Please be waiting on the curb in front of your hotel in thirty minutes."

When Erika arrived at the State Department building, the driver parked and took her to Marshall's office on the fourth floor where she sat in an anteroom for forty-five minutes.

Finally, Mr. Hawkins appeared and took her to Marshall.

"Ah, Mrs. Faust. It's nice to see you again," Marshall said.

"General, I want to thank you for proposing my pardon to the president."

"You might wait a few months to decide how thankful you are, Mrs. Faust. Some people say I can be a hard taskmaster. Let's not waste any time. Your State Department identification will be under your married name. This might save you, and me, some uncomfortable questions. Some people you might come across when fulfilling your duties might have heard the name 'Erika Lehmann.' Your records with the CIA will be expunged. Admiral Hillenkoetter has agreed to that. There's no more Erika Lehmann as far as being linked to the United States government is concerned."

"I understand, General. My daughter's surname is Faust and is the name I'd like to use for myself for her sake. Other children can be cruel and bully a child who doesn't have the same last name as the father, accusing her of being illegitimate."

Marshall listened but didn't comment.

"You'll work fulltime, Mrs. Faust. That means here in Washington and when I go overseas. Even here in Washington there are times I meet with German, French, or Russian officials, whether at official meetings or at embassy cocktail parties and events. Also, if someone in the State Department needs a translator, I might assign you to work with that person, either here or aboard. When not by someone's side serving as an interpreter, you'll spend time translating documents here in this building for an organization I established last year at the State Department. It's called the Bureau of Intelligence and Research or more often referred to as the INR. When you're not on assignment overseas as a translator, you'll work for the INR as one of our analysts of German affairs. You'll stay busy, I can promise you that."

"Yes, sir."

"Any questions or reservations?" Marshall asked.

"No, General."

"Very well. You're hired, Mrs. Faust. Mr. Hawkins will take you to his office, get you on the payroll, and give you your identification."

"General, may I ask if there are any planned trips outside Washington around Christmas?"

"No, not outside Washington until after the New Year. I know your daughter is coming here for Christmas. Nothing will interfere with her visit."

Erika was surprised he knew about Ada's trip, but then he was the Secretary of State with all the resources of the United States at his disposal.

Marshall ended the meeting with, "You can go with Mr. Hawkins now. Welcome aboard." Marshall stood and extended his hand. She shook it. "I expect your loyalty, Erika."

"You will have it, General, and thank you again."

The wily Marshall suspected the woman he had just hired was behind Captain McBrayer's shooting. During the war, he himself had devised Machiavellian plots to accomplish a purpose. A ruthless female soldier with her training who spoke four languages, including Russian, was someone the United States could use in the present political climate and he wanted her close. Besides working as a translator, her expertise on Germany and Germans added to her linguistic skills would increase her value as an INR analyst for NATO, which Marshall expected to be up and running by spring.

In Hawkins' office, Erika had to again sign several more forms before she was given her State Department picture I.D. under the name of Erika Marie Faust. Marie, her grandmother's first name, was her real middle name.

"We have some apartments available in large complexes built after the war for returning G.I.s and their families," Hawkins told her. "I'll have an aide secure you one of these apartments. They aren't fancy but are clean and modern. There are two of these housing units in Washington, one in Arlington, and two in Alexandria. I don't know which one you'll be assigned to until the aide gets back to me. All have a bathroom with a toilet, sink, and a bathtub. You won't have to share a common bathroom and shower in the hallway. They also have a kitchen with modern appliances: a gas stove, kitchen sink, and an electric refrigerator instead of an icebox. They were built for families, so they have two-bedrooms. It might take a few days to get one reserved for you. You'll stay at the Mayflower until that happens. You have to pay rent for your apartment—$45 a month. That includes utilities. Full-time State Department interpreters are paid a monthly salary of $152. Any questions?"

"No, all that sounds fine."

"Needless to say, any travel with the Secretary or a member of his staff will not be at your expense."

"I understand, Mr. Hawkins. The salary is acceptable and appreciated." It was $12 more a month than she made with the Central Intelligence Agency. However, she had no living expenses with the CIA. As a trainer at the Farm, she billeted for free at Camp Peary and ate her meals in the mess hall when not on a field assignment. Now she would have to pay rent and buy groceries. With that considered, in reality she was taking a pay cut. Regardless, she would have been happy with any arrangement that allotted her the prospect of making a life with her daughter. She had her own money tucked safely away at the bank in Zürich, but she could not raise red flags by being extravagant. She'd have to live within her means from her new job to avoid raising eyebrows.

Hawkins ended with, "Check in with me daily while you're still at the Mayflower so I can apprise you on anything relevant." He rose from his chair, signaling the end of the meeting.

Erika stood. "Yes, Mr. Hawkins. And thank you."

When Erika walked out of the State Department building, the same car and driver waited to take her back to the Mayflower. In the back seat, she crossed herself and said a prayer of thanks. She was free and counting the days until her grandparents brought Ada to Washington for Christmas.

Chapter 71

A Question about Zhanna

Annapolis, Maryland
Two days later—Wednesday, 15 December 1948

Al Hodge had eaten dinner with the Carrs and they all were now in the living room with their coffee.

"Great dinner, Kay," Hodge said.

"Thanks, Al."

Hodge added, "I love your cooking."

"Needless to say," Leroy joked and pointed to the small paunch above his old friend's belt.

"Hey, that's muscle. I'm in good shape for a 40-year old guy."

"You're 49, Al," Leroy reminded him. "You'll be 50 next summer."

Kay smiled and changed the subject from Al Hodge's middle-age spread. "Boys, what's the latest on Erika and the other ladies?"

"Kathryn and Stephanie left Washington a few days ago," Leroy answered. "They're still with the CIA. Oh, I haven't given you two the news. Zhanna is engaged to Erika's cousin."

Hodge bellowed, "Rogova? Engaged? You're joking, Leroy!"

"Afraid not, Al."

"Holy Cow! The poor sap doesn't know what he's in for."

"Will you be losing Zhanna?" Kay asked.

"She doesn't have the option of leaving the CIA like Erika. Erika was pardoned of her crimes. Both Zhanna and Ryker committed crimes on United States soil that will never be pardoned. If they leave our protection, they both will have to pay the piper with the Department of Justice. And Ryker has more to worry about than United States justice catching up to him. He's wanted for war crimes by the European tribunals. You didn't know that, Kay."

"No, I didn't. He was so charming at Erika's party last week."

Hodge gawked at her with his mouth gapped open, looking like a dullard and wondering to himself, *What did she just say?*

"You will allow Zhanna to marry, won't you, Leroy?" Kay asked.

"I can't stop it—not with Zhanna Rogova. If I tried, she'd quit the CIA and run off with him. She knows how to stay hidden. It might take us years to find her if we ever did. We just lost one Russian speaking field agent; we can't afford to lose another right now. We have plenty of Russian-speaking analysts. We can recruit retired Ivy League college professors who taught Russian for those jobs and being accent free for them doesn't matter. They never leave their office. But it's extremely tough to find younger people who can be trained as field agents who speak that language fluently and foreign accent free like Zhanna."

"Then Zhanna won't be returning to the convent in Honduras, obviously," Kay noted.

"She has asked to move to London with her fiancé. I granted her request. In the end, it's better for the CIA. Living in London, we can get her to any hot spots in Europe where she might provide a service a lot faster than getting her there from Central America. I want to do several interviews with her to make sure she knows how important it is to keep knowledge of her work with the CIA from Ian, so she's not leaving for London until sometime in January. She has to be fully aware how important it is that her future husband continues to believe that she works strictly as a translator for American dignitaries."

"I hope her marriage works out for her," Kay said.

Hodge said, "I just hope Rogova's future husband doesn't end up waking up on fire in bed if he complains about that night's meatloaf."

Chapter 72

Valhalla Won

Washington, D.C.
Christmas Eve—Friday, 24 December 1948

The apartment building chosen for her by Mr. Hawkins turned out to be located in the Cleveland Park area of Washington. A lucky break for Erika. She was told the area schools were good, and it wasn't far from her new job. Dropping off and picking up her daughter from school would be an easy matter when Ada enrolled for the next semester after the Christmas break.

Erika moved in last week and immediately set about decorating for Christmas in anticipation of her daughter's arrival. She went all out: a Christmas tree with candles in the German tradition, figurines of Saint Nickolas on shelves and on windowsills, holly and mistletoe here and there, and plenty of presents for Ada.

Her grandparents arrived with her daughter yesterday. Ada stayed with Erika last night. Seeing their granddaughter's small flat, Louis and Marie Minton insisted on staying in a local hotel against Erika's objections.

"Ada can sleep with me, Grandpapa. That leaves the second bedroom for you and Grandmama."

But the Minton's were determined give Erika time alone with Ada so to the hotel they went.

For tonight, Erika spent most of the day preparing the traditional German Christmas evening meal of Weihnachtskarpfen—a fish dinner of carp—the Christmas Eve dinner she remembered fondly from the happy days with her late parents growing up in Oberschopfheim, a small village in Baden near the Rhine where she was born.

Erika had invited Sheila, but she and her husband had annual Christmas plans with his family. Leroy and Kay Carr would be with his family in Conowingo, Maryland. Al Hodge had left town two days ago to spend Christmas with his sister and her family in Ohio.

For Christmas Eve, it would be Ada and Erika's grandparents, and Zhanna and Ian who had delayed his plans to return to London until after the New Year when Zhanna could fly out with him.

Her grandparents arrived around five o'clock, Zhanna and Ian a half hour later. Ian brought with him a bottle of wine, Zhanna a bottle of Asbach brandy from the Rhine River wine region she knew Erika liked.

Everyone enjoyed dinner even though carp for a Christmas Eve dinner was alien to everyone at the table except Erika.

"I never knew carp could be so good," Ian said at one point. Not knowing his comment was awkward, he meant it as a compliment.

"Thanks, Ian," Erika said graciously.

Erika asked her grandparents, "Grandpapa and Grandmama, what are your plans? I hope you can stay in America for a while."

"We have to return to London next Tuesday, Erika," Louis Minton responded.

"Zhanna and Ian, how about your plans?"

Ian answered. "Zhanna has been cleared by her translation bosses to move to London after the New Year."

"I'll keep my job with them, Erika," Zhanna added.

The two women looked at each other. Erika knew Zhanna had little choice but to remain with the CIA, as was Erika's situation before she received her pardon.

"When do you take your citizenship test, Erika?" Zhanna asked.

"Next month, January 11th. General Marshall was able to speed things up for me. I have to accompany him overseas later that month and he wants me to be sworn in as a United States citizen before the trip."

"That's wonderful, my dear," Marie Minton said cheerfully. "What are your plans for Ada's care while you're away?"

"The trip will be only a few days. Sheila and her husband will take Ada to their home here in D.C. Before I leave next month, I'll take her to visit Sheila and Ricky at their home several times so she's acquainted. Ada will love Sheila."

In Germany, gifts were never opened before Christmas morning, so when people were ready to leave, she handed out presents to her grandparents and Zhanna and Ian. They had brought their presents to Erika and Ada when they arrived which were now safely tucked away under the tree, patiently awaiting tomorrow morning.

An hour after everyone left, Erika Lehmann changed into a bathrobe and sat down on the sofa. Her British grandparents were Anglican, so that is the church Ada had been attending in London. But she and her husband Kai were Catholic, as were many Bavarians. She and Kai had Ada baptized into the Catholic faith when the child was two weeks old. Erika would raise her as a Catholic and teach her German as a second language.

She gathered her daughter in her lap and they sat for a moment admiring the flicker of the candles on the tree and basking in the sharp smell of the pine. Erika began singing in German a Christmas lullaby to the seven-year-old Adelaide Faust who soon fell asleep in her mother's arms. It was a lullaby Erika remembered her German father singing to her all those years ago in Oberschopfheim when she was little and would fall asleep in his arms.

Outside, no snow fell on the nation's capital this Christmas Eve, but through her window, Erika gazed into the cold heavens at a fat, dusty moon defended by an army of ghostly clouds that stood sentinel over its beloved mother planet that God himself had bequeathed. She considered this an omen.

The daughter of Karl Lehmann and Louise Minton had finally won Valhalla. If not for herself, at least for her peacefully sleeping daughter.

The Erika Lehmann Spy Series

Book 1: ***Invitation to Valhalla***
Book 2: ***Blood of the Reich***
Book 3: ***Return to Valhalla***
Book 4: ***Fall from Valhalla***
Book 5: ***Operation Shield Maidens***
Book 6: ***Hope for Valhalla***
Book 7: ***Search for Valhalla***
Book 8: ***A New Valhalla***
Book 9: ***Shield Maidens Return***
Book 10: ***Valhalla Won***

Other books by Mike Whicker:

Proper Suda (a novel)
and
Flowers for Hitler: The Extraordinary Life of Ilse Dorsch
(a true life biography)

All books are available in print copy from Amazon.com, bn.com, and as e-books from Kindle.
Signed copies are available from the author for shipping.

Author welcomes reader comments
Email: mikewhicker1@gmail.com

Acknowledgements

Thanks to Erin Whicker in Jeffersonville, Indiana, for another fantastic job proofreading the rough manuscript.

I'm always in debt to my weapons specialist, Gary Klemens. Gary, an Alcohol Tobacco and Firearms administrator, hangs his hat near Cleveland, Ohio. Thank you, Gary, for your valuable help on numerous Erika novels. Your knowledge of weaponry never ceases to amaze me.

As always, an earnest thanks goes to my friend and attorney David Jones (an impressive historian in his own right) for supplying sound guidance and invaluable critiques of the manuscript.

— *Mike Whicker*

CPSIA information can be obtained
at www.ICGtesting.com
Printed in the USA
LVHW041919230323
742415LV00001B/22

9 780999 558232